THE BACKWARD
TIME TRAVELER

Parker Rimes

ISBN 978-0-6450964-0-8

Cover design by Jules Lewicki.
Cover photograph by David Charouz.

*"Only to the white man was nature a wilderness
and only to him was the land 'infested' with 'wild' animals and
'savage' people.
To us it was tame, Earth was bountiful and we were surrounded
with the blessings
of the Great Mystery."*
—Black Elk

CONTENTS

CHAPTER 1

Keera discovered the monk early in the evening.

"We need to talk." He sat easy on her couch, hands clasped over his belly. She waited in the living room doorway, inspecting him with interest.

"We talk all the time. What's so special about tonight?"

"There's a situation," Bardo said, shifting a little. "I thought a face-to-face might be appropriate."

"What kind?"

"It starts back a few years."

"Can you be more specific?"

"You know we hate to do that." He shrugged as if to apologize, as if he'd try harder in the future. As if.

"And I fit into this, how?"

"It's hard to explain. May I show you instead?"

"As in a vision?"

"No, as in a visit."

The astral. A trip to other dimensions that illuminated, dazzled, or confused, and often left her befuddled for days afterward.

"I have a class to lecture in the morning," she said. "I'd prefer a clear head. When you've taken me on these visits before, they've totally fuzzed me out the next day."

"You'll be clear as a moonbeam."

She sat on the sofa opposite him. Her spirit guide of the last few years looked as solid as any flesh. Once, she had tried touching him; her fingers found nothing. His robe was coarse and creased, his bowl-cut hair needed a trim. Did mirrors exist in Bardo's world? Food was still of interest: his roundness attested to that, fat stains on his robe proved it.

"What's this all about?" she asked now.

"There's a healing stone you should see." Bardo wasn't referring to a crystal; no such commonplace thing for him. A personal visit meant something else. And the delicate way he'd approached the matter suggested that she wouldn't like it.

"That's it? I get to see a stone?" Bardo shifted again. "There's more, of course. It's kind of a mission. Let me show you, and you'll understand."

"I knew it." She almost wagged a finger at him. "You often say a mission, a task, whatever you want to call these things, will be easy, and they're anything but."

"I never say easy, I say you could do them."

"You imply something cruisey, a barefoot walk on a freshly trimmed lawn, a light summer breeze my only obstacle."

"You pull together conclusions that aren't an accurate summation of my suggestions."

There was no getting around Bardo. He had the answer to all arguments, all objections. Why wouldn't he? He had to be a thousand years older than her, for a start. That was a lot of built-up wisdom right there. No argument.

"Look," he said. "You don't have to do this."

"Don't be silly, my curiosity is aroused. Just give me straight answers."

"I'll try, but every answer seems wrong if you don't ask the right question."

Keera gave up. She pulled two cushions from the lounge and dropped them on the floor. She slipped one under her knees and another behind her head.

"Are you ready?" Bardo asked as she wriggled into comfortable stillness.

"I'm not promising anything, you understand."

"Agreed."

She closed her eyes. "Take me away."

Separating from her body without help from Bardo could often be a protracted process. First, she had to reach the appropriate state of calm, wait for the vibrations that rippled through her signaling imminent separation, and finally, allow herself to float free.

Long ago she'd understood that leaving her body allowed her to penetrate the normal barriers of consciousness. She also became frustrated at the difficulty of it all. The endless nights of waiting to separate, the teasing vibrations that skipped along her spine, then stopped without her lifting free. The exasperating dreams that grew more and more vivid but never turning into full out-of-body experiences.

Then one night she drifted above her bed, her physical self below. The moment was both unnerving and exhilarating. With practice, and Bardo's help, she moved anywhere in the universe. He showed her other worlds, other times and, at certain incomprehensible moments, introduced her to levels of existence that she couldn't begin to grasp.

Tonight, the separation took seconds. Keera closed her eyes, and she lifted into rushing darkness, borne forward to an unknown destination. Dim light broke through, and tipis appeared; dozens of them alongside a creek; horses grazing.

It was night here, wherever they were, Bardo was a shadowy figure close by. A fire blazed at the edge of the camp; people gathered around wrapped in buffalo robes. Some sitting, some standing, all of them relaxed and chatting. Women squatted near their men; children ran loose and free, chasing each other. Like any family campsite in the country. Apart from the buckskins, the robes and the feathers that adorned most heads.

They drew away from the fire and glided through the rows of tipis glowing pale bronze from internal cooking fires. She glimpsed drawings on the tipi skins. Not modern, no pastiches of old images. This was no painted village for tourists, no neat paths for paying customers. No. Too shabby, too strewn with other, smaller fire sites, horse droppings, and buffalo hides drying on rawhide lines.

They were in the heart of an Oglala Sioux camp somewhere, sometime in the past. At least one hundred and fifty years prior. She wanted to smell the air, stroke the hides, sit with the people.

Bardo took her closer, passing through a cottonwood, the leaves streaking coldness and damp through her ethereal body. This, she'd never figured out: how she received physical sensations without a physical body.

They entered a tipi by ignoring the opening and penetrating the hide wall instead. Sensitized to atomic levels, she noted its roughness, the exterior moisture from the air clinging to it, and the greasy, smoky layer on the inside.

The tipi contained three adults focused on a boy lying on a pile of skins. He was about ten years old, and thin enough to show too many bones. His chest coated with a sheen of sweat; his legs pumped like hesitant pistons.

An old man, a healer, sang a song over him. He moved as if he was fifty years younger, shaking scratchy, shuffling sounds out of stone-filled gourds, his necklace of bear claws swaying in a rhythmic counterpoint.

The two others, sitting near the tipi wall, were the parents, she realized, their faces set hard against calamity. She drifted closer and partially merged with the father. He shivered, and she moved away.

The boy has an infected wound. This kills within forty-eight hours. Bardo filled her in. No sounds, just his thoughts penetrating her consciousness.

The healer removed a cloth-wrapped bundle from a deerskin pouch and unwrapped it with concentrated reverence. A ragged stone, the size of a man's fist, lay in his palm. Its crystalline structure contained orange flecks with blue striations, and the healer gripped it like the Holy Grail.

An energy emanated from it—powerful as a life force. The healer lowered the stone onto the boy's chest and began another song. His voice gathered new strength; pulsing vibrations filled the tipi. *Hey-a-a-hey! Hey-a-a-hey! Hey-a-a-hey!* A healing song. She recognized it from the time she recorded Oglala healers in South Dakota. A calling to the Great Spirit to help the body tap into the universal healing energy.

The stone rose and fell with the boy's labored panting, but within minutes, the oscillations slowed, his breathing came easier, and his legs stilled. His mother cried aloud, an exclamation of thanks. The healer placed a hand on the boy's forehead, straightened and nodded at the mother. She broke into a hesitant smile and glanced at her husband, who showed nothing of what roiled inside him. That was the way of these people; Keera had met enough of them to know.

She tried to move forward, to inspect the stone, but the blackness returned, and she floated in space. Light reappeared to show a roadside parking area overlooking a creek running through a small depression. A wooden board announced a historic site, and as she drifted closer, she understood exactly where she was.

Wounded Knee.

South Dakota.

Present day.

The location of the final, most brutal clash between the Sioux and the US government in 1890. The last serious attempt of the Sioux to resist the elimination of their way of life which had left them defeated and heading for extermination.

Keera scanned around for any living forms, any energy trace of the awful moment when the US Army's 7th Cavalry opened fire on several hundred men, women, and children, and slaughtered half of them. But nothing remained but a sign saying once there was something here—something terrible.

Bardo took her over grassy plains, over the few highways that linked to muddy tracks, past cabins, rusted vehicles, and other remnants of the industrial age. Fridges without doors, automobile parts, box mattresses, and foam squares dotted yards; the leftovers of items families had once bought, but could never again afford to fix or replace.

Outside a cabin, a man slept, or lay unconscious, under a blue tarpaulin. Was there no room inside, or had he passed out after too many beers, and someone, blessed with pity, had dragged a cover over him?

She'd been here before. Pine Ridge, the reservation home of the Oglala Sioux Tribe. The Oglala were one of the seven Lakota groups of the Teton Sioux. The descendants of Crazy Horse. No longer the free-ranging conquerors of the Great Plains, the Lakota now only existed as offcuts of their former selves. Herded into small enclaves, and dependent on a government that seemed puzzled that they hadn't yet died off. After all, a nomadic people had been forced to stop being nomadic. What did they have to live for?

A tug told her she was returning home, back to the physical world. Keera opened her eyes in her living room and waited for the rest of her senses to accept the familiar reality. To wake her nervous system and to remind her muscles she needed them again, she moved through a series of slow stretches.

What was that trip all about? Bardo knew her specialty was early Americana, and immersing her in a band of Oglala was as tantalizing as could be. But any plans Bardo had for her wouldn't include relaxed sightseeing.

In the kitchen/dining area, she flicked on the electric kettle. A battered chrome thing that flashed a brief spark at its base before the water began to heat. A left over from her student days, the kettle refused to die, and she refused to waste money on another until it did.

"Where were we?" she asked aloud.

"You were right," Bardo said behind her. "An Oglala camp, two hundred years ago, and today." He was occupying a kitchen chair.

"And you yanked me out so soon? We have so little information about those times. Few Europeans crossed the plains then, except for occasional trappers and hunters."

She added the boiling water to a teapot of chamomile leaves. "And you took me to Pine Ridge."

"Correct."

"To show me stuff I knew already? That those people do it tough?"

"Reminders have their place."

"Can you take me back to the camp?"

"You will get your chance."

"A proper trip this time?"

"A very proper trip. We want you to bring the stone back to the present."

"What?"

She stared at Bardo with growing comprehension. She'd been right: he was asking her to volunteer for a mission. "How? A solid can't travel through non-physical dimensions." She pulled a cup and saucer from a cupboard.

"You'll find a way."

13

"Why? The old healer only used it to focus on while he was healing. Impressive all the same."

"The stone amplified his power, but works on its own. The Oglala need it now. And for more than physical healing. They call it the *Wakan Tunkan*, the Sacred Stone."

He meant spiritual stuff, a cleansing of the soul thing; a general uplifting. "As you know, the Oglala of today exist as a poor version of what they once were," Bardo continued. "The presence of the Stone will revitalize them."

"Good health is vital, of course."

"The *Wakan Tunkan* will provide more than health. It'll bring them power. Once they were warriors, respected and feared, not fringe dwellers."

"The Stone will be a source of energy?"

"In a manner of speaking. It'll re-ignite their ancient spirit and assist them to right the wrongs done to them."

Bardo wasn't talking about a successful legal case here. It would take more than court judgments, more than presidential decrees, to turn back history. He had to be referring to a new movement. One to sweep aside centuries of ingrained attitudes.

"Governments respect power," Bardo said. "At the moment, people who live on reservations and government handouts, don't have any. You can help change this."

Okay, fine. Kind of. But why her? "Can't you guide somebody else? One of their people? The Stone must exist somewhere in the present day."

"We showed it for a reason. You've been chosen."

Bardo hadn't answered her question. She tried again. "But why me?"

"That's what I said, but I was told to follow orders."

An old joke, a reminder he regarded her as the less-than-the-ideal student, too independent minded for one thing. Too argumentative for another.

"Wouldn't an Oglala be more appropriate? I only observe these people and their lives; I'm not one of them."

"Detachment is an asset. An Oglala's belief in spirits and omens would hinder him."

Hell of a task, this. Find and bring back this Stone from two hundred years ago. Transport a physical item from the past, via a non-physical dimension, to the here and now. Couldn't be done.

"You'll find a way," Bardo said again.

"I haven't committed to anything yet. You're assuming stuff."

"We discussed the situation and decided you'd be the perfect choice."

"Know something? I'm not the right person for this. I'd love to explore the lifestyle close-up, of course. But I'm not an Indiana Jones type of academic, not a thrill-seeking explorer."

"You saw the reservation, and how the Oglala live. Should they continue like that, or are you willing to do a small thing to assist them?"

Bardo was working her guilt button. He wouldn't demand she do anything he asked—he was never pushy that way—but he'd keep talking until she saw no option but to follow his suggestion. "There's nothing small about what you are asking. I can bring harm to those people by being among them."

"You might if you're careless, because non-involvement is vital. You'll go back for one reason: to secure the *Wakan Tunkan* for the future."

There was no way out. A refusal, and she'd regret it all her life.

Bardo said, "By the way, you'll be working with another."

"What the hell? What kind of other—a medium?"

"Oh no." Bardo smiled sweetly. "Definitely not. A normal man, a little wayward, but he owns a good heart. We like him; you need him."

"What's the point? He'll be useless."

"The reason for his presence will become apparent in time. Call, he comes."

"Please tell me how."

"Announce what you have seen."

"Announce?" What was he thinking? "You understand what will happen to my career if I bounce around spouting out-of-body stories?"

"Bang the drum discreetly."

The chair grew emptier. Bardo had left her plane. Keera Miles, assistant professor at the Department of Anthropology, University of Chicago and natural born medium, ran her fingers through her hair in frustration.

One trip, one thorough trip to the Oglala camp was worth twenty years of research. She would have to stay in their midst, with access to first-hand knowledge of the way the people lived and thought. She'd observe customs close up, take part in ceremonies. Be one of them, at least for several days, maybe more.

How to do this wasn't clear. Never had she stayed out of her body for more than an hour. Of course, time moved differently on the next plane. Often after spending what seemed hours in a location, she found only minutes had passed when she returned to her body. But this mission wouldn't be a short one. Not unless Bardo helped a lot, and that wasn't his style. His way was to suggest a course of action and then step aside.

And this time he was insisting on a partner. A novice at best, and a stranger. Like her task wouldn't be tough enough, she had to carry this guy through the bewildering alleyways of the next dimension. For a reason that might become clear in the future. What if this guy kept hitting on her? How was she supposed to function and deal with that stuff at the same time? What if he was stupid, or worse, a cynic? Someone she had to explain everything to. Twice.

What a way to make a tricky mission more difficult—Bardo insisting that a complete stranger join her on the expedition of her life. Pain and gain in equal measure. She threw a look at the ceiling. "Thanks, Bardo, you've made my night."

You're welcome.

CHAPTER 2

Z ach found Feliks the loan shark in a Polish restaurant on North Milwaukee. The Pole sat alone. A short, dapper man, Feliks was draped in a dark suit with a soft cream shirt unbuttoned at the throat. On the table in front of him lay a bottle of vodka, a small bowl of caviar nestling in a larger bowl of ice, and a plate of sliced rye bread. Feliks held a glass in his hand and waved for him to sit.

A waitress placed a chilled glass on the table and shuffled away. Feliks poured. "*Nazdrowie*." He raised his glass to his lips. "Good health."

Zach threw the vodka down his throat. "I need a loan," he said, stating the obvious.

Feliks refilled both glasses. "Your car? It's needing mechanical attention, so soon?"

He was referring to a classic 1966 Rangoon Red Mustang GT 500. Drove like a dream and chewed money like a paper shredder. Some part of it wore out nearly every week. But after three years of ownership, it thrilled him still. "No, it's good. Maybe gearbox issues coming up, but not right now. I need money for investment."

Feliks was a popular man in this part of town. Especially with people who needed short-term funding. People who hoped to last the week without the sides of their stomach sticking together. People like that don't negotiate the cost of salvation. This left Feliks free to set his own rate. He was a fair man—he bled everybody. No favorites.

Feliks spooned caviar onto the bread. "How much you want?"

"Say, ten thousand?"

"The vig is three hundred dollars a week. That's a lot. Can you afford it?"

"Sure, but why don't you reduce it because I'm a good customer, and you're a socialist."

Feliks laughed, a machine gun crackle. "I am not socialist. If I was, I'd still be in Poland. I am natural capitalist born in the wrong place. That is why I moved to America."

Zach had written a few stories on the people in the Polish community. Feliks's name came up a few times. Within six months of his arrival the wiry little Pole had created a loan sharking business from scratch, and six months after that no rival existed. The reason wasn't hard to define. Feliks worked with a total absence of fear, and a mindset developed in a country where the rules for survival changed every day. This endowed him with a sharpness the homegrown rivals couldn't match, and his employment of ax-wielding enforcers put a solid floor under his risk taking.

Feliks pulled a Marlboro out of its packet and fired up a lighter, a slim gold item matching the chain at his throat. "For ten, I should ask for collateral. I think your car is all you have."

"Nobody gets the car," Zach said. "I'm good for the money; you know that."

"This is not the way to do business. I have been reading Harvard Business books. I have to grow my business. Avoid big risks." Feliks blew smoke.

"You're an unlicensed moneylender; you're already taking risks."

Feliks blew more smoke. "Today I am simple moneylender, tomorrow I am new Rockefeller. I am learning much. I know that repeat business is the best business, which is why I treat you nice. Also, customer service is important, which is why you get money tomorrow. Vig is three hundred dollars."

"That is way too much." The interest rate of a hundred and fifty percent per annum was more than too much—it was crippling.

"My rates have to reflect the risk. All books say that. I'll lend you money, no problem. Same vig as before. I operate on strict capitalist principle. If you want a handout, go to church. Ask Father Wladyslaw if he has ten large for you." He drained his glass and pointed at Zach's, untouched and waiting. Zach shook his head.

"Good customers deserve discount rates. Your business books teach you that?"

"I have not read that far yet. The vig stands. But I give you clean notes. Straight from quality bank." He eyed Zach with curiosity. "What investment interests you? The stock market? You have information not available to ordinary persons?"

Zach did have valuable information. About a horse in Epsom, England. "I'm telling you, Zach, the bet of the year," his college roommate Lyndon had told him over the phone. Lyndon worked for a British merchant bank, but his love of the turf superseded everything. "We're into this beauty that won twelve to one on its first outing. Lost a few more races at tighter odds and when they went back to tens, it won again. The guys in on this trousered thousands. I had a lazy grand on it myself."

"What's the price for the next race?" he heard himself ask.

"At least eights. Send me your fun money before Wednesday and I'll do the rest. I'll get top odds, and you'll love me for ever and ever." Zach had thought about this for a least a half hour. One grand would give back eight. Ten would return eighty. Of course it wouldn't happen, not if his past record of sports betting was a guide. But still, it might. Just this once he would get lucky. It was worth a shot.

But the stake required outside financing and the only source available sat in front of him. He said, "My information is so confidential that if I disclosed it I'd be found snoozing with the salmon the next day." The little Pole made enough money without his help.

"I understand," Feliks said sourly. "The secrets of the universe are not for everybody. How long will you require this investment money?"

"Just the one week; this is a short-term involvement."

"Very well, because you are good customer with steady job I will not ask for collateral. Still three hundred a week."

The interest rate was astonishing, ten times what credit cards raked off. But he'd maxed out his cards and the bank was no longer his friend. Feliks' money would do for now; one week's vig was a small price to pay to get eighty thousand dollars. "Okay. Three hundred a week it is."

"Come back tomorrow. Your first instalment is due on Thursday."

"Thursday? Are you kidding? I get the money tomorrow, and you want the first week's vig the next day?" What crazy shit was this?

"Efficiency is an important part of my operation. For me, it's best you pay on Thursdays."

"So, if I pay back the loan by the next Thursday, I don't get charged again?"

"After the first Thursday, you have entered next period of the loan. Of course you must pay again. This is business transaction."

"But that means I get charged twice in the same week."

"I have learned," Feliks said, "that the calendar of capitalism has its own logic. Do you still wish to borrow?"

The fucker was double dipping him. Six hundred bucks to borrow ten grand for a few days. Six hundred bucks to pay back after collecting eighty thousand plus his original ten back. Irritating, infuriating even. But shit … "Yeah," he said. "I'll be back tomorrow."

Outside, a bag lady halted as he stepped onto the sidewalk, and measured him up with rheumy eyes. Probably wondering if he was sufficiently lubricated to fling a couple of bucks her way. He was. Zach dug into his jeans and plucked out a bill. A twenty. Damn. He fished around his pockets for smaller denominations but didn't find any. What the hell. He'd be collecting ten large tomorrow, he could spare it.

The woman accepted the proffered note carefully and held it up to the light. "You think it's a forgery?" he asked. "You lose nothing even if it is." The bill must have passed the test; she stuffed it somewhere in her outsized overcoat.

"May Jesus smile upon you today," she mumbled and shuffled away. Smiling would be good; laughing, not so much.

◆ ◆ ◆

Keera opened her door to Kenton Maxworthy from the Chicago Post. "Hello," he said, "I'm—"

"Yes, I know." She offered her hand.

Maxworthy was late forties, stocky, wore a ponytail and a black zipped hoodie over greasy skinny-leg jeans and black hi-tops. His whole dog-eared life on public display. His grin was way too smirky, and her heart sank. He wouldn't listen to her story—she got that right off. He was the kind who preferred talking about himself to listening to others. She led him down the hall into the living room and gestured to one of the sofas facing each other.

Maxworthy looked it over and whistled. "Nice place you have."

He ran a finger along the mother-of-pearl filigree bordering the coffee table. Maybe figuring out if it was real or a tacky Chinese copy.

"Fortune telling paying off well, is it?" he said, in a way he hoped it wasn't.

"I don't tell fortunes." She kept any edge out of her voice.

He sat down and leaned forward, arms on knees. "So what gives? Your press release was pretty short. This healing force. Does it come from crystals, a kind of universal energy flow that you can tap into? I know 'em all, been around for years. UFOs, alien implantations, channeling, crop circles, magnetic people, etcetera, etcetera. Is this something new or something old dressed up? Nice top."

His vision directed at the man's shirt she'd thrown on that morning. The chest area, mostly. Keera eyed him with distaste. This wasn't what she wanted. A new-age kind of guy yapping on about a whole lot of unrelated issues. A guy interested in her top. She should offer him a drink of something, but she didn't want him in her home a second longer than necessary. Maxworthy didn't notice she hadn't replied.

"You're a psychic, right?" he said. "You've got a message of some sort? I'm a bit psychic myself."

"Really?"

"Yep, I see us having a drink later in a real buzzy kind of place."

She should have fastened the upper button on the shirt. "What section of your paper are you from?" she asked, ignoring his prediction. The contact call had been brief, and she had paid little attention. She was too surprised how quickly she got a response. She hadn't checked with Bardo if Maxworthy was to be her helper, just assumed it. Now, she hoped like mad she was wrong.

"I'm freelance, actually. I dropped in to see what was up, and the editor gave me your press release. 'Deal with this,' she said. You have to laugh, don't you? These straights don't have a clue about the real world, do they? Always going blah blah about politics and things when the important stuff is right under their noses."

"What important stuff is that?"

"You know, the hidden side of life, what the mainstream media won't touch except to laugh at. The netherworlds."

The netherworlds. The guy was a walking fantasy novel. "But what section is this story going to be in?" she asked.

"Hard to say. Depends. I might farm it out to another publication if the editor doesn't want it. Nexus magazine is always looking for new stuff. So is Many Worlds. A few radio stations would go for this, too. Heaps of internet outlets."

Keera put her hands together to stop them seizing Maxworthy's collar and throwing him out. "I thought you were from the Chicago Post?"

"Yeah, well, it's like I said, I freelance. The regular guys wouldn't touch this sort of thing, but the eds know I don't mind it. I write the liner notes for bands' CDs too. Just a few local ones but I'm talking to big names for future publication. Anyway, enough about me. Tell me what you have, and I'll take notes, and then we can have a drink. Ever tried a saketini?"

She stood. "I don't think you're the right outlet for what I have."

Maxworthy stayed seated. "You sure? You won't find anyone better suited, you know. I can inject a serious note, not the college-level stuff most writers use. People take notice when they see my byline."

"Sorry." She moved to the front door and threw it open, Maxworthy behind her. "Sorry to have wasted your time."

"What's the problem, babe? You want a story or not?"

"I do, but it has to be handled correctly. Goodbye."

"I get it. You're a bit freaked by media attention. That's cool. Not a problem. I can show you how to deal with the media. What's on and off the record. I know this stuff."

She extended a hand. A mistake.

Maxworthy grabbed her fingers and circled his thumb over the back of her hand. "The drink offer is still good," he said, trying to make meaningful eye contact.

Keera slipped her hand out of his, backed into her hall and closed the door. She stalked into the living room.

"Holy God," she exploded. "Why did you send me that one?"

"Nobody sent him. You invited him." Bardo had reverted to his physical form again, and now occupied Maxworthy's place on the sofa.

"You knew he was useless, so why didn't you stop me?"

"You didn't ask. We don't volunteer information as a rule. We like to be asked."

"I thought I could do this much by myself."

"It's always worth trying." Keera lit two scented candles to banish any lingering trace of Maxworthy. "What's going on here? I never lean on anyone to accomplish a task. So what gives with this assistant you're forcing on me?"

"You'll achieve more with cooperation. This is one of the lessons of your life."

"Really? Other people hold me up."

"They don't hold you up much. They help you formulate your ideas better if you let them."

"Okay, okay, enough of the wisdom. What's the next step?"

"May I point out the obvious? You haven't completed this step yet."

"What's the use? They'll all be like that. I might as well do this on my own." She stood at the main window and glared at the street. "I just don't see it happening. Getting some novice to separate from his body and work with another one? God, even convincing him to try will be impossible."

"Your helper has no psychic ability, that's true. But he's confident in any situation."

"So is a large dog. Can we have a more rigorous selection procedure?"

"Let's stick to the plan, shall we?"

A new thought arose. "How will this assistant be able to cope with a full body entry? He's totally new to this sort of thing."

"His target body already hears voices. He won't resist a new one. Not even one that controls his limbs."

"Voices?"

"Mischievous entities. They do no harm. We'll banish them at the right time. Your partner will get all the help he needs."

Well, that was a start. But why did she need a man? Hadn't needed one before.

"In that society," Bardo said, "you'll need a man with you. You'll also require help afterward. It'll become clear in time."

"Is he going to make moves on me like this one?" Bardo said,

"He's a man."

Terrific. A novice, a cynic, and probably an ass grabber as well.

"He'll be an addition to your life. Not a burden."

"Well, he's sure taking his time turning up. I sent out five press releases and I only got one response. You saw the quality of that."

"You'll get a new response soon."

"Terrific. Another greasy applicant." Another one like Maxworthy and she'd pull out of the whole damn thing.

"Observe the quality of the man behind the speech. Make your decision. It is your task, nobody else's."

"When will this partner come?' she asked. "This vital part of the whole mission."

"He has issues to overcome first. He complicates his life. When he appears, you'll know him."

"How?"

"He'll refuse to help."

CHAPTER 3

Z ach pushed open the glass doors to Cityscape's editorial area. No one raised a hand in greeting; no one met his eye. He shook off his jacket, draped it over his chair. Nicola, the twenty-year-old intern, hammered a keyboard at the next desk.

"Hi," she said, her eyes still fixed on the screen.

He was in trouble. He lowered his head to her level. "I'm fine, thanks for asking. How was your evening?"

"Um, good. Can't stop. Edwina wants this right away." She bashed the keyboard some more. "Made me rewrite it because of two adverbs in one paragraph. Wants to see you, too. ASAP."

"Figured something was up. She in a good mood?"

"So not in a good mood with you, Zach." Nicola looked up at him, her sweet baby browns magnified by her glasses. "You'll get a telling off, I reckon."

"Getting used to them," he replied.

Edwina Moss was the latest editor-in-chief. Unhappily in her forties and with a figure cut trim by a rigorous diet of salads and stress, she knew how to be nasty. It didn't matter. Earlier today, about ten a.m. Chicago time, his sure thing in the UK had raced. Lyndon would call any minute with the cheerful news that his buddy Zach was eighty thousand richer. That kind of money made a man confident, able to wear any stormy editor with relaxed equanimity.

Edwina, on the phone in her glass-walled office, spotted him, and bent her fingers, beckoning like a traffic cop.

"Good luck," Nicola whispered.

Edwina waved him to a seat. "Tell me, Bones, when did you have the operation?"

"What operation?" She leaned forward. "The one where the doctors removed your brain and filled the space with porridge?"

Nicola had it right; it was going to be a big telling off. For what?

"What do you have against Alderman Dufresne?" Edwina asked.

Ah, the Dufresne interview. "He only looks after his own," he said. "The crime rate is down where his voters live—shall we say the tonier end of town? Where the policing gets more resources. The rest of us benefit little. He's very pally with big money and his major interest is positioning himself for the mayor's desk in a few years."

Edwina regarded him with unconcealed irritation. "For God's sake, Bones, did you just wake up after a twenty-year nap? Dufresne is no bleeding-heart liberal. He regards the business of politics to be business."

"The interview was as bland as I could make it. Hell, his PR people could have written it. What's all this about?"

"Caspar, you recall him? Caspar Weiss, the owner of this periodical? He called me last night."

"He's a pal of Dufresne's?"

"Oh yes. Dufresne called him because Harvey got to him during the evening to check something in your copy. And Dufresne was shrill with indignation. Caspar was not exactly subdued either when we spoke."

"What was Harvey doing? He's not the fact checker." Harvey was the chief copy editor and a sniveling weasel. "Just shaping the story," he'd say as he butchered a perfect piece. Their mutual antipathy exploded into heated verbal exchanges most weeks.

Edwina said, "He spotted a paragraph where you claimed Dufresne was keen to build a monument to the suffering of the gay community."

"Oh, that."

"Yes. Oh, that."

"Well, it's what he said all right but—"

"Impossible. The man is a certifiable homophobe. If the law allowed, he would line up all the gays in town and shoot them. Harvey, like all of us, knows this. He called Dufresne's office for confirmation. Dufresne denied it. Then he contacted Caspar and threatened to wreck all his future property development applications if this magazine printed anything that suggested he was tolerant of gays." Edwina took a drink of water from a cut glass. Didn't offer any to him. "To save me listening to the recording of the interview," she said, "could you please repeat for me word for word what you asked and what Dufresne said about gays?"

Zach cleared his throat. "I asked if he thought it was a good idea to erect a monument to acknowledge the suffering of gays in our community."

"And?"

"And he said, 'yeah, right,' which I took as an affirmative."

She stared at him as if he had crawled out of a stinking garbage can. "Oh my freaking aunt. I don't believe this. You're stone cold crazy. You put this paper in jeopardy just to satisfy some juvenile urge to stick it to somebody in a high place, and nearly cost me my job and Caspar's next deal." She swallowed more water like it should have been whiskey. "Can I explain our position to you? We run a simple city lifestyle magazine. Some celeb interviews, restaurant and movie reviews. We run shopping supplements. We like to be more serious sometimes, so we publish profiles of politicians and the occasional investigative piece you do so well.

You follow me so far?"

He nodded and wondered if it was worthwhile explaining that he had only left in the gay quote as a joke. Something to share with somebody around the water cooler. Never intended for publication, it would have been cut during the copy-editing process. Harvey would have known that. He'd deliberately made the joke backfire, the bastard.

"What we don't do is rock the boat," Edwina said. "Especially when it could cost money. Dufresne has many friends. Friends who advertise with us now but might not in the future. Get the picture?" He nodded again. "Caspar wants you out."

"Fine by me," Zach said. He should have switched to an internet news site ages ago. The print business had all the growth potential of silent movies.

"However, I talked him out of it."

"I understand. Top writers are hard to find."

She gave him her cobra smile. "I said I would have you covering shopping mall events. You know, appearances by minor television celebrities and singers who once lasted thirty seconds on a crappy TV talent show, special offers to mark ten years of a discount outlet. That sort of thing." She swallowed the last of the water in triumph.

"You do that; I resign." He couldn't let her humiliate him. The bitch smiled wider.

"You can't without repaying all your bonuses. It's a tight contract, and we won't hesitate to enforce it."

The fucking bonuses. He should have seen this coming. The Human Resources guys had called them bonuses, not pay raises, which they really were. He'd signed the new contract and forgotten it. It didn't seem important then. Now, these bonuses added up to almost half a year's salary. Which he didn't have. Until his bet came in. He could wait another afternoon. Edwina took his silence for surrender.

"I have a couple of interesting stories for you already." She slipped on reading glasses and peered at a press release sheet. "Here's a good one. Brackeneck Farms are installing a petting zoo in the Westlakes Mall for the school break. They'll have goats, sheep, and chickens so little children can experience a natural way of life in the safety of a shopping center." She raised her eyes. "This is a wonderful opportunity for some cute observations and maybe a human-interest angle. Let's say about two hundred and fifty words of warm prose?"

He stared into the floor. Edwina picked up and perused another sheet. "Jeepers, a top story screaming to be published. A psychic will reveal a new healing force in the world, but only to personal interviewers. No picture attached, Bones, but I suspect she's about sixty-five and colors her own hair. She'll want to charge you for the interview. If you pay, it comes out of your pocket. I won't okay it."

She handed the press releases to him. "Let me have those stories by tomorrow, will you? I'll have more by then, but I can't guarantee they'll be as exciting as these." Waved him to the door.

Zach was halfway back to his desk when his cell chirped into life. He checked the screen. London calling. Good news week started now. "So, buddy boy," he said, "how much are you transferring to my account?"

"Brace yourself, Zach," Lyndon said. "The dumb beast ran home in the middle of the field."

"Say again?" A cavity opened up inside him; all his hopes dived in. "Somebody made arrangements, got it boxed in, couldn't get a clear run. Most unexpected. Most suspicious."

"You. Are. Kidding."

"What can I say?" Lyndon getting all breezy like he didn't know Zach's ten Gs was more than play money. "The dark forces of the racing world win again. But we'll be back. The word is it peeved certain people to be left out of our little plan. Discussions are being held. Hold the front page, Zach, the silver lining grows every day. Gather your pennies together."

"Like how?" As if he could dig up another sizable stake to benefit from a second chance. "There's a discrepancy in our earning capacities, have you noticed? You gamble mega millions in pension funds to enrich your company and yourself while I battle the forces of evil and get paid in mouse droppings."

"You've nailed our respective situations perfectly. Look, I dropped a few large ones myself, if it makes you feel better. I'll call when the moment arrives."

"That's so comforting," he said, and hit the phone icon. An eventful day so far. He was ten thousand dollars poorer, not fired but humiliated, and the best was yet to come—the talk with Feliks.

He'd missed a payment.

CHAPTER 4

The next night Bardo guided Keera back to the Oglala camp. As they gazed at the tipis and horses and people invisible to them from the earth side, he pointed out a young woman bent over and shuffling. She stooped like a much older one battling a cruel wind, and walked with no obvious purpose.

A new widow Bardo explained. The trauma of her life has caused a shift in her perspective. Her name is Rain Bird.

Rain Bird. The woman whose body Keera was to take over. She knew about entering bodies—something she had experienced, but the other way round. Spirits slipping into her body so they could speak, pass messages. All that required was a tuning into their frequency. Simple if you were born to it—a matter of a few month's training to refine it. How this widow would react was an unknown.

How do I do this? Keera asked Bardo silently.

You embrace her. Start with the head and throat, the rest of the body will follow.

She moved closer and made initial contact. Rain Bird, Keera knew, would experience a rush of energy all over, a soft something gripping the throat and prickling as the two spirits merged. The woman stopped walking and shook her head as if to free it from bad thoughts. Keera tried to control the arms. Not possible. Rain Bird waved them like a windmill gone mad.

She's not letting me in, she's frightened.

She'll think about the experience all day. Tomorrow will be different.

The second night they found Rain Bird near the creek. She was alone and dipping a buffalo bladder into the water. Metal containers were still uncommon, and precious in this time and place.

Try merging. If she panics, talk to her.

Keera moved closer and attempted merging. Rain Bird dropped the bladder and stood with a cry. *"Aaaieeeh!"* Keera backed off.

Keera said, "Do not be frightened. I have come to help."

"Who are you?" Rain Bird asked. Her face frozen, her body stiff.

"A friend."

"No. You're a death spirit. I am ready." She sank to the ground and squatted with crossed legs and arms resting on her knees. "I am ready to die. I will sing my death song." She didn't pause to compose herself but launched into a keening wail. "I have lived my life, I am ready," she sang.

"Wait," Keera broke in, alarmed that she might die simply because she wished to.

"I am no death spirit." "You are evil spirit then. I will sing my song of protection."

"Not an evil spirit," she said. "I'm your friend." "I am Rain Bird, widow of a fine warrior. I am ready for any spirit." She closed her eyes and chanted a new song.

Tell her Eagle Chaser awaits her but not today.

"Eagle Chaser is waiting, but he says it is not yet your time to join him."

Rain Bird stopped chanting and opened her eyes. "When is my time? I have no strong heart for living these days."

"I don't know when you will end your days." Keera surprised

how quickly the woman accepted her presence. "We need to be together first. For a short time."

Rain Bird looked about her. 'Where are you? I see no bird, no ground animal. Nothing that would hold a talking spirit."

"I am close. I wish to share your body. Will you allow this?"

Rain Bird was no longer breathing heavily. Her curiosity had replaced fear. "Have you lost your body? Was it not fit for use when you passed into the land of many tipis?"

Keera had expected no questioning. "My other body is not fit for here, but your's is. I can help you during my stay."

The woman looked off into the distance. "My burden cannot be lifted. It is mine alone." She owned a fine sense of the dramatic; that much was clear. "Does my husband still want me?" This after a long pause.

"Yes." She didn't have to mentally construct an answer, words came from without. "He'll wait until you have completed your tasks and can join him."

Rain Bird nodded, cementing in the answer. "I have tasks? You'll help?"

"Yes. You must be still. Allow me to move in closer. Keep your mind quiet of thought."

"I'm ready." Rain Bird closed her eyes again, waiting.

Keera slid into the woman's body. Her blood pumped madly, the muscles tensing. Hurried thoughts tangled with her own. She sensed synapses sparking as messages hurtled up Rain Bird's spine to the brain, messages with news of a strange invasion. She tried to make this new body her own, telling herself it was so, that the strangeness was temporary, that it would pass. It worked. Rain Bird stayed quiet, accepting as Keera settled further into her body. It was much smaller than her own. The arms stopped six inches short of where she expected—a startling discovery.

Roughness. No layer of soft underclothes between the flesh and the deerskin garment. She hadn't expected to be so sensitized to another's body. When Bardo had made it clear that she was to take over another body, she had assumed she'd be taking up a new role. It was nothing like that—she was assuming new physical burdens.

Rain Bird's arms lay across her knees. Keera tried to move the right arm back to the buffalo bladder. It moved like a marionette's. Jerky, no fluidity, but she grasped the rim. She held it under the water to fill it, the other hand steadying it. To anyone watching it looked a simple scene, a woman refilling a container. To Keera, it was the first halting step on a new planet.

Where has Rain Bird's spirit gone? She asked Bardo.

She remains close. If you do anything that alarms her, she will try to take her body back. Be aware of this.

Keera rose to her feet and turned to the camp. A man stopped her, blocking her path. Stocky, with a bear claw necklace. A medicine bag also hanging from his neck. She recognized him. The healer she'd seen with the young boy.

"You stand unsteady," he said. "I watched you fill the bladder with confused movements. If there is bad medicine in this place you should stay away." He locked dark eyes on her, his face without soft lines, his mouth tight.

Say hello to Red Leaf.

"It was a momentary dizziness," she replied. "It has passed."

"Momentary it should be. You have no husband, and you cannot lie with another man until the mourning period is over. It is too soon for you to be with child, even if you were foolish enough to create the occasion."

She summoned up wide-eyed indignation. "I would never dishonor the memory of my husband."

He thrust his face closer. "Your voice is peculiar Does your throat scrape when you talk?"

"Only my heart aches. Can you hear the noise it makes?"

The healer regarded her in silence for a minute, and she wondered if he had any psychic ability. Could he sense a new spirit in Rain Bird? But, apparently satisfied, he walked away.

He's very aggressive, she said.

He remains the leader because he's suspicious, grasps situations quickly, and acts without fear.

And he has the Stone.

Correct. In his medicine bag. Unless he sleeps.

That's good to know. For a moment, I thought this was going to be a tough task.

Sarcasm does not become you. He won't relinquish the Stone easily. Remember this.

Keera withdrew from Rain Bird and waited for Bardo to take her home. The woman looked around, looked back at the bladder of water and then the creek with a puzzled expression. She can't remember filling it up Bardo said. That'll keep her quiet for a while.

When Keera returned the next time, Rain Bird accepted her presence immediately. She put down a basket of berries and waited for Keera's merging. The Oglala woman didn't talk to her, which was useful, and Keera didn't speak through her either as she wandered through the camp. Now she knew she sounded different there was no point in alerting Rain Bird's family in advance that something had changed in her. Having access to her body gave her access to her nervous system, it didn't bring automatic access to all of her conscious mind. She had to learn many of the woman's daily patterns and habits, so she didn't inadvertently act out of character.

"Are you in a dream state?" asked a voice behind her. She turned to see an older woman, waiting for an answer. "You have walked past your family's lodge twice now," she said.

"It's no dream," she replied. "I was lost in my thoughts of Eagle Chaser." Who was this woman?

"Remember to use your medicine bag to guide you through this time of mourning."

"I know that." But what else to say without revealing her ignorance of Rain Bird's life. Her first test as one of them and she was scrambling for answers.

The woman held out her hand for the basket she was carrying and Keera handed it over. When the woman ducked back inside the tipi, she followed.

Two people sat inside.

Meet the family.

The woman peered inside the basket.

Looks Back Woman. Your mother.

An old man sat near the internal fire, chewing on stringy meat and apparently lost in his thoughts.

Three Dogs, your father.

Two dogs, only two dogs, lay next to the father, both of them eyed her with interest, cocking their heads. She sat further from the fire than the men, and said nothing. A fourth member of the family wasn't making any eye contact at all. He stared into the fire as if he could see the entire universe there.

Your partner's target, Eagle Chaser's younger brother. His name is Slow Hand.

Slow Hand looked as lively as a burnt stick, and Keera wondered then what role he would play. And what kind of person he was?

Three Dogs looked up. "You didn't take Slow Hand with you today. Berry gathering is a tedious business on your own."

"Somedays, Father, I like to be alone with my thoughts. A widow has plenty to think about; her future is uncertain." Might as well keep to familiar subjects.

"Your voice. Sounds like you found bad medicine as well as berries."

The damn voice. A mix of hers and Rain Bird's. Nothing she could do about it. "Red Leaf noticed it, too," she said. "He decided it was nothing important."

"That eases my mind. If Red Leaf is unconcerned, then nobody should worry."

Easy for him to say. He didn't have to sneak into Red Leaf's tipi sooner rather than later and take the Sacred Stone, the *Wakan Tunkan*.

That Red Leaf would kill to keep.

CHAPTER 5

Nicola handed Zach a black coffee. "It was rough, eh?" she said. "I heard Edwina through the glass."

He didn't reply but drained the cup in two swallows. Glanced at his cell, saw voicemail waiting and dialed the access number to avoid more conversation. He shouldn't have.

"Hello, Zach, Feliks. We have to talk, as you know. Please call, now."

He killed the cell.

"You all right?" asked Nicola. "You want an aspirin?"

"I want a different life."

Edwina was beckoning to Nicola, and she rose. "I hope she's still not mad at anybody."

A picture of Feliks floated into mind. Asking why the payment was late. With Boggie standing alongside. Boggie the bone man. Zach had met Bogdan Popescu the last time he came for a quick cash injection. He was Feliks' enforcer, a large Romanian farm boy with meaty mallets for hands and a jaw hammered out by a blacksmith. A huge man who liked to splinter bones like a dog on a marrow hunt. The thought of a Boggie interaction would make anybody's skin contract.

He should have paid the first three hundred when he collected the money. But he'd sent all of it to Lyndon. All of it. Not even fifty left in his wallet till his pay hit his bank account next week. He'd fix up Feliks then. But not now, not today. He'd understand. Zach was a good customer, reliable and salaried. A few days wouldn't matter.

His phone rang. Mother. The one who refused to give him a middle moniker because it was "too bourgeois". She also plumped for Hegel as an ideal boy's name. Luckily his father clung to the rights to his first name and insisted that the boy get a sensible one.

"Zach? Why don't you come over for Sunday lunch? It'll be Japanese; I'm making my wasabi."

"Sounds great." Another afternoon discussing the sixties and trying out experimental ethnic dishes. He couldn't wait. "How's Dad?"

"Still coughing and wheezing. Emphysema, I reckon. But, it's got him off the weed."

"When's he going to a doctor?"

"When the health system of this country gets reformed."

"I'll have a talk with him on Sunday. He should consider a more sensible time frame."

"Good, and I'll tell you how the protest against genetically modified food went."

"Remember to keep calm, Mom. Don't whack any cops with your placard."

"Nah, I won't. They look so young now I hate to hurt them."

He remembered his mother explaining the principles of non-violent non-cooperation many years ago.

"It's an effective technique for social change," she had explained.

"So how come you got busted for hitting that cop?" he had asked.

"I told him he was being used by the forces of big business, and how he was one of us, and suffered like one of us, and he laughed at me like I was stupid or something, so I hit him."

Now he said, "Remember, it's supposed to be a non-violent protest. I don't want to see you on the six o'clock news being dragged into a wagon."

"Sure, sure." Mom changed the subject. "Will you bring that nice Linda over again? She was unreconstructed but seemed capable of grasping the correct line."

As far as he was concerned, Linda was constructed close to damn near perfect, but physical perfection is never the only factor a man needs to consider. "Um, she's no longer in my life."

His mother was silent for a beat, then asked, "Was she offended when I pointed out her slavish devotion to the dictates of the fashion industry perpetuated gender oppression? Because if she was, then—"

"No, Mom. It's just that we had only gone out a few times, and she started talking about moving in together. Kinda freaked me out."

His mother laughed. "Well, far out! Fearless reporter, the people's friend, Zach Bones terrified of sharing his remote control."

"I like living alone. One day I'll find someone who understands that."

"Zach, I'm not an idiot, and I know you will never settle down with one woman. You're an emotional gypsy, always roving, always looking for a good time. If I weren't your mother, I'd be tempted to call you sexist."

He sighed. "I don't see how I'm sexist. I don't regard women as second-rate; I don't expect them to perform menial duties, and I treat them like the other humans in every way. Except that I don't want a close relationship with them, just a fun one. I don't want to live with them, I don't want to choose furniture with them, and I don't want them suggesting we get a sensible car. Is this a problem?"

"You are dangerously close to treating women as sex objects

only." He could almost hear his mother's lips tightening.

"Not so. I'm not interested in their bodies if I can't engage the mind." Quite true, quite often.

"Hmm. I'll see you Sunday. We'll talk some more." The phone went dead. The week was turning out better by the minute. He tried to focus on the press releases. He didn't deserve this. Not the fabulous lifestyle section. Today a petting zoo and some ditzy psychic. Tomorrow a new line of Italian olive oil that probably came from Libya, or new ideas in pumpkin comestibles.

Nicola returned to her desk flushed with excitement. "Edwina said I could do an interview. You'll never guess who, it's so random."

He regarded her wearily. "I don't know, who?"

"Tracey Wojcik."

"Is that a singer that sounds the same as the others?"

Nicola sat down, eyes shining. "It's a girl who used to go to school with Harry Styles in England. He used to be in One Direction. She says he was just sooo nice at school, always singing and stuff. It's part of a series called School Friends They Left Behind. That's so like what I want to do."

"You'd be so like good at it, too." He read the top press release sheet. It didn't say much. The headline read: A new healing force discovered. A second line read: More information available to personal callers only. Under that, a phone number and a name. Keera.

"This should have been trashed," he muttered. "That vindictive bitch saved this just for me."

"You say something, Zach?" Nicola asked.

"Nothing you could print," he replied, punching the phone buttons again. A smoky hello answered his call.

"Hi. This is Zachary Bones from CityScape magazine. I have a press release here about a healing force." Made it sound like a normal thing.

"Oh yes, CityScape. When would you like to meet up?"

Fucking never. "Can I ask you a few questions now? We do most of our interviewing over the phone."

"It's not convenient." East Coast accent, cool, modulated voice. Not the eager, ditzy type he expected. Sounded his age.

"When will be convenient?" Things were looking good. If she couldn't make a time today or tomorrow, he'd ditch this piece of crap. Move on to the next hell.

"I'm free this afternoon."

"Fine, I'll call you after two."

"We need to meet. The subject is complex."

She was kidding, right? "Keera, may I call you Keera? You may have noticed that we're not National Geographic. We love local people; we help promote local ventures. A few lines are usually enough. But the three you provided are a bit slim by any standards. I assume you're selling some new healing. Is it soap, hot rocks or a fresh way of being at one with the universe? We can help. Of course, our advertising department will ask you to buy a page in exchange for our glowing copy. Do we really need to meet?"

"I am not selling anything." Her response flinty. "I have information that may prove interesting to the right person. I need to ascertain which person that is. If it's you, come over at two. If it's not, then say so. I have to leave right now."

"It's not how we do things," he said, his irritation rising to match hers. "I can't schedule so much time for a minor item. A phone interview is usually enough."

"It may be for some, but I need to know more about you if you're going to write this story." Who did she think she was? He wanted to close the conversation on this spiky bitch and ditch the job, but Edwina would take it as a rebellious gesture. Might dish out worse tasks. And staying out of the office was also a good idea. He bottled up his irritation. "Two p.m., you said?"

"That would suit me."

She gave him directions to a street in Old Town, and he ended the call. Made another one to the PR woman for the petting zoo to arrange a meet-up in an hour. First, the goats, then the ...

His phone chirped, but he ignored it. Might be Feliks.

"See you later," he said to Nicola as he walked away. Nobody looked up as he passed. The word was out he'd been humiliated, and around here, humiliation outranked leprosy on social distancing.

CHAPTER 6

Keera terminated the call with Zachary Bones and wondered how on earth reporters ever got stories if they acted like total dicks. This one was barely an improvement on the sleazy one, although brisk irritation was preferable to distasteful come-ons.

He needed her story; she picked that up right away. His initial reluctance to agree to her terms was understandable. But then he'd switched attitudes without warning, taking her details, promising to meet. Cynical or what? The meeting would be a waste.

A couple of hours later the reporter stood at her door relaxed and confident, reading her like she was reading him. Except she was better at it.

"Hi, Zach Bones," he said.

"Keera." She offered her hand. His was firm and warm, and the contact ignited a surge of images. A racehorse galloping amid others, a red car, a pile of money. Bardo giving her a glimpse into his mind. She couldn't make immediate sense of it; this Zach Bones sure carried weird stuff in his head.

Externally, he was in better shape. Good looking, Anglo-Saxon, with a touch of East European genes that blended higher cheekbones into the mix. Dark-haired, taller than her, he wore self-assurance like it was tailor-made. She picked up no sense of entitlement, either from his bearing or his position.

She led him to the living room. He took his time scanning the marble fireplace, the bookshelves that flanked it and the hand-crafted coffee table. Sunlight spilled in through the bay window, adding a soft glow.

"Nice place you have here," he remarked as he sat. "The psychics I've met run their show from, let's say, more compact premises." His aura was robust, pulsated with energy, his earlier edginess over the phone gone. She sat opposite him.

"It's my father's," she replied. Waited. He didn't need to know more until she saw how he handled the interview. Another image intruded. Two men outside her home, in an older car, waiting for him. They weren't friends of his; they'd followed him here. She put the image aside; she might say something to him when he was leaving. Just might.

He pulled the press release from his pocket and placed it on the coffee table. "It says you're announcing a new healing force in the world." He did a poor job of keeping the sneer out of his voice.

"It sounds quite formal when you put it like that, but yes."

"I should start at the beginning, I guess." He worked his phone screen and started the recorder. "What's your last name?"

She leaned over and switched the cell off. "I can't tell you that right away. I have to trust you first. The telling of my story complicates my daily life. I have a career to protect."

"Okay, then. We'll deal with that later." It surprised her he wasn't more confrontational about recording her. Over the phone, he'd been very insistent that she do things his way. Now, he was probably working slowly into the interview, getting to know her before tougher questions came.

"How did you get to become a psychic?" he asked.

"Who said I was psychic?" He picked up the press release.

"You're right, it doesn't say that here, but—" "I'm a psychic medium."

"Please explain, for the benefit of our readers." He was mocking her like a high school wise guy. She hadn't expected that, and she wanted to slap his head off."Mediums connect directly with the spirit world, psychics sense things. I have both abilities."

"You mean you talk to dead people?" Just like you think in cliches. He irritated her more each second. "If you like, if you want to think in headlines. Mediums communicate with those who have left their earthly body, yes. Their consciousness, their personality survives, Mr. Bones. The core of you, that bundle of information that makes you unique."

"This information bundle survives death, you say."

"Consciousness arrived in the universe with the Big Bang. Thirteen point five billion years before there were any humans. It doesn't need a physical entity to function. Your consciousness will remain in existence when your body has returned to dust."

He grinned at her. "You sound like a fire-breathing preacher on this topic."

"You asked me a question; I answered it. I don't lecture. If you need more information, consult a search engine, Mr. Bones." You might learn something useful instead of sitting here and making fun of me.

"Yes, well. Call me Zach. When did you decide to become a medium?"

"You don't decide. It's a calling. You can ignore it, but a medium makes many people happy, no bad thing."

"A hard point to argue."

He was smirking again. If he sprouted one more condescending remark, just one, she would throw him out. Leave him to the waiting men outside. "I often saw spirits as I grew older, and they talked to me."

"What did they say?" "They wanted to deliver messages to their loved ones on earth."

"You must have been popular." "I tried to ignore them. With over a hundred billion dead humans out there and many fewer mediums, it's easy to get swamped."

"Do you do sittings for regular clients?" he asked.

A new image arrived: herself sitting at a table staring at a crystal ball. What stupid stuff was he thinking now? Was there anybody out there who had sensible ideas about the afterlife?

"No," she said. "Sometimes if I can help a friend I will, but my interest is not in that area." It was time to cut to the main event. Find out if he could cope with the concept. "I have a post-graduate degree in Native American Studies from Berkeley. It's part of my life's work to study the lives of the first inhabitants of this continent."

"It must have been paradise, before white men and machines arrived, and fouled the place up. Terrific, unspoiled mountains and prairies and forests. Wild game everywhere, pure, clear water tumbling through the creeks and rivers."

The guy was surprisingly poetic. Best to straighten him out. "Compared to ours, their lives were quite brutal in fact. A simple life looks very appealing on paper, but the reality is more about fighting for a safe life in an unforgiving environment embedded with relentless enemies. I don't know how much time they had to sigh wistfully at gorgeous landscapes."

He ignored her, caught up in some internal vision of the past. "And then they were starved out of their lands by the wholesale slaughter of the buffalo. It's a sad history."

"A technique the US Army learned in the Civil War. Destroy the food chain and resistance collapses."

"And then, and then they get tricked out of the regions they agreed to settle on."

He grew more animated as he spoke. Something deep inside him must have reacted to this injustice, even from long ago. This was no fake sympathy, and he knew the basics of Indian history. All this would help him understand what they were to do and give him the right attitude when they entered the Oglala camp. If it was him who joined her.

"A tragedy and a blight on our nation." She held his gaze, waiting for more helpful images to surface. None did. "I used the term Native Americans because that's the academic way of referring to these nations, but they describe themselves as Lakota or Cherokee, just as a European would say he's French or German, rather than European."

Zach waved a hand as if brushing aside academic concerns. "I won't argue with that, but what have these societies got to do with this healing force?"

"If I tell you, I need your word you won't print what I reveal unless you believe me."

"Why do you care? I'll write up what you say, put an interesting spin on it, and the readers can make up their own minds."

God. He was no better than the last one. "I don't want an interesting spin on it. I need a committed writer to explain it. Not a collection of clichés masquerading as reportage." She paused to push her anger down. "What's with you lot, anyway? Can't you write a story as it's given?"

He replied, with a little heat himself. "I'm a journalist, I write your story the way I see it. If you require a stenographer, consult a search engine."

Very funny, Mr. Bones. And illuminating. He was prickly about his reputation, prided himself on his integrity. And this was encouraging news—he cared about his stories.

It meant he'd take pains to get them right. It had taken a week to realize why she needed an assistant, like Bardo had said. Someone had to announce the finding of the sacred stone. Someone with credibility, not a medium who didn't want her true identity revealed. Someone like this resentful, cynical guy. For God's sake.

He broke into her thoughts. "Why don't you just write a letter to the editor?"

"It won't get published. I'll sound like a crackpot. I'm surprised any reporters responded to what I issued."

"Your press release," he said, softer now. "It's the work of an amateur. Nobody serious will follow that up."

"You did."

"It's a long story, but I was sent here."

You sure were. Was he the one, or another damn test?

CHAPTER 7

Keera brought in a pot of tea from the kitchen. "I don't do coffee," she replied to his raised eyebrow. "Too stimulating. This is Earl Grey."

Zach grimaced at the flowery flavors, and it cheered her. I know you prefer coffee, I know you need coffee, but you've been too condescending for me to oblige.

"Look," she said. "Let me tell you what this is all about, off the record, and if you think I'm a crackpot we forget the whole thing."

"Let's do that."

"In my work, I access the astral plane—"

"Astral plane? Like where you float around without a body?"

She searched his face for evident disdain, but if he felt it he'd suppressed it.

"The planes are other levels of existence."

"But you can get into them now?"

He sounded curious, which was a start. "Only the first level, but it's enough."

"How?"

"It's easy and complicated at the same time." An evasive answer, but explaining astral travel techniques to a reporter would take

52

forever.

"Isn't it frightening? As in really-messing-with-your-mind frightening?"

"Many entities exist there, some are harmful. Don't try it without a guide—it's not Disneyland."

"What do you do when you're, um, on the astral plane?"

"I go to places and observe from the spirit side."

"Like a ghostly peeping Tom?"

He was smirking again. The shit. She had to stop this.

"Before I continue," she said, "can I explain something?"

"I'm all ears."

"I don't object to you being skeptical. It's a natural reaction when people face the inexplicable. What I do object to is ingrained cynicism. And you're full of it."

"I'm not." He sounded aggrieved.

"You are so full of it. You use your cynicism to protect yourself from having to think."

"That's not true."

His obvious indignation proved her point. He valued his integrity, became defensive when it was questioned.

"I'm here to write a story that interests our readers," he added.

"Maybe you started out with that idea, but right now you are belittling me before I've finished."

Zach raised his hands in peace. "I don't agree, but please continue."

He was acknowledging her point, another encouraging step. She took a moment to regather her thoughts, and came out with the big statement: "I can also travel back in time." She waited for the guffaws.

"You time travel?"

This time, only the faintest sarcasm underlined his response. He was making an effort.

"Time doesn't exist out there," she said, "it's a physical construct."

"Excuse me, but aren't you disagreeing with the finest scientific minds in the world?"

She shook her head. "If a handful of people can look into the future and make predictions that become verifiable, then time is not as we know it. In fact, thousands do this every day. Anyone looking into the future is bypassing time."

"Could I just go somewhere cool and hang out with Homer, or comfort Cleopatra?"

He was impossible. She wanted to kill the interview. Only Bardo's words stopped her. How will I know him? she had asked. He'll refuse you, Bardo had replied. This Zach would never believe her story. He'd never agree to be part of the mission. That made him the best candidate so far. She now disliked him even more. "Shall I continue?"

"Please."

"On one of my visits to the past I came to an Oglala camp in what is now South Dakota."

"Aren't they Sioux?"

"A branch of the Sioux, one of the seven Lakota groups living in North and South Dakota. During this visit I observed a healer, a medicine man if you like, carry out a ritual where he used a fist-sized stone to heal a feverish child."

"A medical marvel."

He was sneering again. If he's the one, I'm going to throttle him the first day. "My guide tells me this stone has healing powers not found on Earth. This—"

"Wait a minute, who is this guide?"

"Everybody has a spirit guide. "What's his name?"

"Bardo."

"What's mine called?"

"How would I know? That's for you to find out. If you open yourself up, you'll hear him advising you."

"I'll try turning the music off in my car sometime," he said. "What is this stone made of? Couldn't we use it today, to help sick kids?"

"Yes, but it appears to be the only one."

"Why is that?"

Time to give him the next fact he couldn't swallow. "Because it came from Mars."

He burst into laughter. "It's been a wonderful story, but I can't write this. It sounds, as you said, like the work of a crackpot." He didn't fiddle with his recorder or the press release, the normal preamble to leaving. He simply stared back and waited for her to continue.

"You're aware that small meteorites collide with Earth constantly?" she said.

"Sure, I've seen the movies. Civilizations wiped out, etcetera."

"That's the big ones, once in a million years. There are over twenty thousand smaller cataloged meteorites on earth, and about fifteen of them identified as coming from Mars. Their molecular composition is similar; their isotopes are not."

"This means what?"

"We don't know yet, but this one possessed energy, like a magnetic force but stronger. A healing energy. The Oglala call it the *Wankan Tunkan*, the Sacred Stone.

Zach scratched his head like he was arranging this information into sensible piles. "So you've seen a rock you believe comes from Mars and has healing properties. Interesting."

"Interesting? Do you realize what we have? A painless cure, a non-invasive medical technique, the Stone to be analyzed and copied, cloned, at least investigated, to help millions of suffering people." She didn't refer to the higher purpose of taking the stone; he'd only be more incredulous. No images came to guide her next request. She plunged forward anyway. "Would you like to get the Stone?"

He straightened. "What do you mean—get the Stone?"

She slid forward on the sofa. "We retrieve it."

"Are you crazy?"

His bewilderment was comic.

"You're saying we can go back in time and grab a rock?"

"I can't do this alone. I need a man I trust."

"What makes you think you can trust me? I don't believe a word you're saying."

"True, but I feel you're a truthful reporter. Think of it, Zach. The most amazing story you'll ever write: a sacred stone that cures."

"Hey, hold back a minute. Why don't we drive over to South Dakota somewhere and dig around an old camp site and pick up this Stone?"

"It can't be done like that."

"Why not?"

"Because it's not easily found now. It might lay under the soil anywhere from Montana to Texas."

"So that's the end. What a shame." This time, he gathered up his cell and her press release as if to leave.

"No it's not. There's only one way to get it." He waited. "We go back in time and take the Stone while it's available." He stood. "Look—" She stood with him. He was resisting, but he wasn't rushing away. "It's easy. We go back to the Oglala camp, grab the Stone, hide it somewhere. Once back in the present day, we drive to the same area we were before and collect it."

"Why can't you just bring it back on your next visit?"

"Because you can't transport material things through non-physical dimensions."

"Let me get this right. Somehow you take us both back into a circle of tipis, and nobody notices that we are different. The Oglala will be standing around in deerskins and feathers while I try to blend in with my jacket, cotton tee, jeans, and sneakers. Won't they notice?"

"No. You'll be like them."

"How so?"

"Your spirit will take over another man's body."

"What? Are you talking about channeling? I'm supposed to channel an Indian?"

"No Zach, he's going to channel you."

***

Was she for real? "This is so wacky," he said. "Is there a hidden camera somewhere, maybe lots of people laughing at me on YouTube tonight?" Keera put a hand on his shoulder. Soft, like it belonged there all night.

"I know this all sounds weird and unbelievably crazy, but it's possible."

"So you say, but your plan defies all logic. It's not possible. How long do we spend with the Oglala?" Why was he arguing a silly point with her? Why wasn't he walking out?

"A few days maybe, their time. No longer."

"What happens to us here?"

"You mean our bodies? Nothing. When we return, it'll be like waking after a strange dream."

"No, not logical, not possible." He turned toward the door.

She gripped his shoulder a little tighter. "Zach, there is no logic as you know it, not out there. It's a different world, with new rules. I understand it, and I'll look after you."

I'll look after you. Yeah, right. She'd mess with his mind big time and leave him a floundering wreck.

"It's easier than you think," she said.

"I don't want to point out the obvious but if time travel is so easy why don't we all do it?"

"It's easy, but not as easy as learning to ride a motorcycle. There are techniques to master, and I can show you how."

"Techniques? That's all it takes? No wormholes in space, no mysterious vortex, no portals?" She removed her hand; he wanted to put it back.

"You sound like a cautious person," she said, "which is not the first impression I had of you, so I'll explain the principles."

"There's a good idea." We'd have more fun doing this over a couple of drinks. She surveyed him, as if she had overheard his thoughts and dismissed them as unworthy of a response.

"Like I explained before, your consciousness does not require a body to survive."

"This is still news to me, and my consciousness."

"It's the truth. Once you put yourself in a hypnagogic state—"

"A what?"

"It's that state of consciousness you often experience when you wake from sleep. When you are fully alert but have no physical sensations. That's the starting point for your consciousness to leave your body."

"We have to sleep together first?"

This girl was full of surprises. She gazed back at him long enough to make him uncomfortable. "Is there more I need to know about this?" He asked.

"Yes. I was only waiting for the laughter to die down after your last hilarious interjection."

"Sorry, my irrepressible nature just burst through. Can't always control it."

"That's what 'irrepressible' means."

"Okay, okay." No way could he do this. And with such a prickly person.

"This whole thing is ..." "Crazy, right?"

"Crazy unbelievable."

"Do you want to save millions of lives?"

"Sure, but I have a credibility problem with your method. Besides, I'm supposed to be at my mother's on Sunday."

She acknowledged his fresh belittling with a slow blink, extended her hand. "I was hoping you had an open mind."

Zach gripped her hand, but she withdrew it after a perfunctory shake and walked him to the front door. Outside, on the steps, she looked up and down the street.

"By the way, two men were waiting for you here, but they've gone now."

What?

"I got that it was about a horse and money," she said, and his stomach contracted sharply for the second time that day.

"What did the men look like?"

"One was much bigger than the other."

"What else can you tell me?"

"Like I said, I don't do fortune telling."

He recognized a slap in the face when it stung. He walked to his car. Drove away. Two men, Keera had said. Feliks and Boggie. It had to be, but following him? Feliks would be nervous about the missed payment, but nervous enough to track his problem all over town? Maybe. But the throwaway remark. "It's about a horse," she'd said. That had floored him. No way she knew of the bet. No way she could have guessed. That simple statement gave her more credibility than all the crap about meteorites from Mars with healing powers.

She obviously knew more about him than she was telling, and she was showing him that she knew. This sounded, at first, like payback for him laughing at her during the interview. But it was more than that. It was bait. A little sliver of evidence that she had the powers she had claimed. Nobody knew about that damned horse except him and Lyndon. Not even Feliks had found out.

Did she read his mind? Did she get a convenient message from above? The racehorse wasn't a lucky guess. Not possible. She had zeroed in on the biggest problem of his life and refused to elaborate. She knew her words would eat away at him for days. Something to draw him back and talk again.

Hey, they were on the same page. Destined to be together. For a time at least. Her cobalt gaze had transfixed him from the start, and it wasn't due to any psychic powers. Her scent; he didn't recognize it, but it worked: he could barely stop his hands from caressing her. Her cotton blouse, although buttoned chastely to the collar, failed to disguise her figure. Even her bare feet poking out from torn jeans stirred him.

Until she'd questioned his motives. Gave him a school-teacher moment. What did she expect, for Chrissakes? Write up an awe-struck piece about a discovery that would change the world? A Sacred Stone? Jesus.

And what was she doing mixed up in this paranormal mumbo jumbo? She was moneyed. That living room was the same size of his parents' whole apartment. Her father didn't work for a minimum wage. She was a trust-fund baby, no doubt. It showed in the expensive rugs, the furnishings, the spacious rooms. Here was the puzzle. The rich don't hanker for the afterlife; they have too much fun in the present one. So what was she doing, sprouting all this astral travel gibberish? She was an enigma, and a stunning one.

He shouldn't have squashed her ideas. Should have kept his thoughts to himself, if it was possible in her presence. She was right to complain; he had acted like a schoolboy when he should have been more professional.

Something else. She didn't want him to write anything yet. Only to help her, and he'd turned her down without thinking. What was she asking? To time travel to the past? Well, that wasn't possible, but being taught the basic techniques and maybe other goofy stuff by Ms. Gorgeous a damn fine bad way to spend a night or two.

This could stretch to a long piece about learning to astral travel for the leisure section. It might take a few nights to get the right angle. Who knew where that could lead?

CHAPTER 8

When Keera returned to the living room, she found Bardo sitting on the sofa Zach had vacated.

"I guess he's the one then," she said, not entirely pleased with the idea.

"He likes you."

Him beaming like teacher encouraging his favorite pupil.

"He hid it well, so annoying."

"Not well enough. You sensed his desire to see you again."

She shrugged. "As if that's important right now."

"Nothing wrong with having colleagues with pleasing features."

She sat opposite him. "He's reluctant to get involved and is cynical as can be. Isn't that a drawback?"

"He's not reluctant to get involved with you."

"Aren't we supposed to be focusing on retrieving the stone?" Zach was physically attractive, that much she couldn't deny. Quick-witted, ready to laugh. A sparkling aura surrounded him. A seductive combination for her. Except for the immature attitude.

"He'll help. His reasons may not be pure, but his performance will be energetic. The man throws his heart into matters he cares about."

"He was no shrinking violet, but the cynicism was wearying."

"In his profession, cynicism is an asset; the easily awestruck would be useless on this mission. Don't worry, Mr. Bones will adapt to any situation."

"So, what happens now?" She was impatient to start. It had taken weeks to channel into Rain Bird's body and become familiar with it. This Zachary Bones might prove to be a slow learner.

"He was once a college athlete." Bardo cut into her thoughts. "And body aware, as they have to be. You found it difficult to manipulate strange limbs; it won't be for him. In his football days, he often acclimatized to injured body parts. He made do then, he'll make do again. His Oglala body will make no great demands; the man involved is no elite warrior."

"So I noticed. When do we start?"

"Your proposition fits in well with his current situation. It'll become more attractive to him with every passing moment."

Keera said, "The Stone. What do we do after we retrieve it? I can't just announce I found it somewhere."

Bardo drummed fingers on his knee. "You're such a bolter; you haven't even got hold of it yet. These matters have a habit of forging their own paths. You'll see the way forward at the right time. Your friend will help with that."

"He's not my friend."

"Your partner then."

"That sounds worse. You keep pushing me at him. Why?"

"Oh, no reason. You two are well matched, that's all. But ..."

"That's right, it's my call," she said. "Leave my private life to me. You're worse than a maiden aunt worrying that I'll turn out the same." He regarded her placidly, made her feel ungrateful. "It's not that I don't appreciate you helping me," she added, "but when you get too personal, I feel invaded. I have to have thoughts of my own."

Bardo nodded in agreement. "Indeed you do. It's just that—"

"Are you announcing a reason to mess with my privacy?"

He held his hands up in surrender. "I'll say no more on the subject."

"Thanks."

"Except to point out that a person's development moves in unexpected ways."

"Finished?"

"Yes. For now."

He settled back in the sofa and waited for her next question. She couldn't tell if she'd offended him by being snappy. She decided he wasn't. He was a patient father to his child. His monk's robe still displayed the remains of a snack, but how did he eat solids?

"I don't eat, I don't have to," he said, reading her mind.

"I hadn't asked the question," she said sharply. "Do you read my thoughts all the time?"

"They come tumbling out like spilled objects. I can't stop being helpful, collecting them, arranging them in order."

"Okay, let's leave it there for the moment. I'm still curious why there are food stains down your front."

"I was once here, on this planet, and I enjoyed the food. Now that I don't need any, I keep a reminder of how wonderful eating can be. I ate too often, but you can guess that from my waistline."

"When were you here?" she asked, caught by the thought that Bardo had once been a monkish glutton.

"Your medieval times, in England. We monks lived rather freely until the king destroyed the monasteries. That's when I passed over, too."

"Executed?"

"No, I fell down a well trying to hide from the soldiers."

This was a different Bardo than she had in mind. He didn't sound so spiritually raised when he was still bodied. "In England. But you have a Tibetan name?"

"I changed it later."

"Why?"

"Not telling." He leaned forward. "Enough about me. The channeling. Once you two have moved into those bodies, you'll have limited time to complete your task. In their terms, two sleeps. After that, I won't be able to control the other forces at work. The original owners will take them back. It's best to go in and out quickly."

"Two sleeps? That sounds like plenty."

"Don't bank on it."

◆ ◆ ◆

Before Zach returned to the CityScape offices, he stopped at Rocco's Roast House. The bench opposite was empty until Feliks slid onto it seconds after the coffee arrived.

Feliks fixed him with cold Slavic eyes. "You missed the first payment."

"Ah, I meant to call." The fucker had been following him.

"Of course you did, Zach. You have good manners. But you've caused me trouble."

"Trouble? What trouble? I'm a little late, that's all." He rushed his answer like he had rehearsed it all day.

Feliks bowed his head in mock agreement. "You're right, but an ordered society needs rules. You have incurred penalty. For causing trouble, there is extra charge of only two weeks' payment."

How stupid had he been? He'd given Feliks room to enlarge his profit, and the little shit hadn't hesitated. "A six-hundred-dollar penalty for missing a three-hundred-dollar payment? You kidding me?"

"There is another change also. Because you defaulted on payment you have to pay next week in advance."

"What the hell?"

A waiter approached the booth, lifted inquiring eyebrows at Feliks, who ignored him. The waiter hung there for a few seconds and left. Feliks leaned forward like he had something important to share. "I am reading about Total Quality Management. You've heard of this?"

"I don't read management books."

"This is simple idea, but good one. You organize everything so you don't have extra work. It saves money."

"So?"

"Late payments make extra work, and I charge you extra."

"No. Bullshit. You're putting me on. I'm behind only three hundred, and you want twelve hundred. I can't believe it."

Feliks pulled a packet of Marlboro from his jacket but didn't take out one. The no-smoking rules must apply when you leave your home turf. He said, "I am not putting anyone on. I am explaining situation."

"I'm not paying the extra."

"You owe me a week's vig plus double the same amount in penalty. Plus next week's vig. Payable right now, otherwise you have bigger trouble."

"Trouble? We're having a conversation, that's all."

"Wait until you converse with Boggie." Feliks jerked his head at the exit. Boggie sat near the door, wriggled fat fingers at him. "Nobody likes a conversation with Boggie."

Boggie wasn't Zach's first choice of conversational partner either. Being in good shape was no match for the sheer size of the Romanian. He wouldn't be able to touch any keyboards for months afterward.

"He likes to eat," Feliks said. "I assumed cabbage rolls and sausage would be his main diet. A cheap overhead for me." He shook his head in wonder. "Boggie, he has discovered hamburgers, hot-dogs, pizza. Even sushi he likes. Also shrimp, which is unusual for his people. He is not as cheap as I expected."

"What do your management books say about that?" "I find nothing about what your staff should be eating. The problem for me is that I should be seen in quality car. Not old like yours, but a new Mercedes. In America, it's important to make successful appearance. But Boggie eats in car. So, I keep old car. It smells of shrimp."

"Sounds like a simple management problem. Sit and discuss it with him and if he fails to improve his behavior, fire him."

"I can't, I can't. He is excellent worker. I have no bad debts this month. None. This is new for me. I never dreamed that the price of good cash flow would be smelly car. I am learning much in America."

"It's an interesting place."

"The loan is large," Feliks said, giving him the cold blue eyeball again. "Large money makes me nervous."

"Makes me even more nervous. Every day I don't repay your large money, it gets larger." The full horror of the situation was now scrawled across his universe. This was no contract between equals, either of whom could haggle terms and conditions. What Feliks wanted Feliks got. Today, a fine for lateness, next week, another penalty for early repayment. He knew a steady cash flow when it walked in the door. "Look, I had unexpected problems. I get paid next week, and you'll have your money."

Feliks tapped his forefinger on the table. "When you get paid is your problem. When I get paid is also your problem. I want money today. You have a nice car, you told me. Bring it. I am honest man. When I sell it, I give you what is left after I deduct my money. Of course I have to charge extra for the extra trouble. I am business man in America."

Zach thought of Feliks' hands on the Mustang. He pictured Boggie throwing shrimp shells onto the back seat. "Feliks, look." He tried to find the right words. "Next week–"

"Always I hear 'next week'. If I want to know the future, I go to fortune teller. Get money, and I see you here in one hour."

"I got an important interview to attend. Maybe tomorrow?"

Feliks snorted. "One hour, you bring the money, or we come to you."

"I can't, as I said. I have to go out."

"Zach, Zach. The longer you take to pay, the longer I have to let Boggie talk to you."

"Okay, okay. I'll go to the office and see who's got any cash. Back in an hour."

"Good," Feliks replied, and he signaled a waiter. Zach dropped some bills by his cup and scrambled out of the booth. A hard rain thrashed down as he left. God throwing nails at his people. Zach knew how He felt.

The editorial section was buzzing as the deadline grew closer. Not the best time to distract people with loan requests, but Zach had no choice. Maybe fifty in his pocket and maybe two hundred in his humble checking account, the credit cards maxed out. He started with the closest target.

"I'm so out," Nicola said. "These shoes I saw ..."

"Okay, I got it." Zach moved to the copy editors' area. Deserted except for Veda, the hottest babe in the room, and she knew it. "Say, Veda." He tried to sound casual. "Um, can you loan me a hundred till payday?"

She leaned back and stretched her arms up, watching him deliberately not watching her breasts lift. "Is this to fix up your ride, Zach?" she asked. "You know you've never taken me out in it."

"Must have slipped my mind." The things a man had to do to get a loan these days.

"Had a time in the back seat of one of those once." She transfixed him with moist eyes. "Sometimes wonder what it would be like again."

"I don't have any experience of that to share with you. The upholstery needs a lot of care. Gotta be careful with high heels, bra catches, that sort of thing. You know what I mean? Gotta watch the wear and tear."

"The wear and tear. I love a man who worries about wear and tear."

He cleared his throat. "Um, the money. What can you do?"

She slumped back in her seat. "Got a twenty I was saving for a good bottle of wine. You can have it."

"Thanks, Veda. I'll let you know." He hid his chagrin. "Where's Harvey, by the way?"

"Called in sick. Wish he'd do it more often. Such a bottleneck. Sits on the copy for ages and we can't leave until he's okayed it."

"Why don't you figure out the perfect murder then? I'll support your alibi."

Veda stabbed at the keyboard. "If murder cured all my problems, I'd be a one-woman crime wave."

Zach saw Edwina working her phone again. If she spotted him, she'd give another ratty assignment. He thought of trying the ad guys. Them that always flashed thick wads during happy hour. Might be good for a hundred each. Trouble was, they believed they made all the money for the magazine; editorial was the space to be filled in between the ads. A writer asking for a loan would trigger a fresh round of snickering arrogance. Forget it.

Thirty minutes left to hand over twelve hundred dollars to Feliks or hand over his car keys. Not the car, that was a given. But he didn't want Boggie working on his face either. His best chance was to stay away until he had the money. With actual folding stuff in his hand, the little money grubber might be in a better mood when they next met. All he needed was a hideout.

Edwina walked past his desk and dropped a press release on it. "Crazy Cath's, the discount appliance people, are having a special promotion. Can you talk to them and produce a hundred and fifty words for a small insert in the Living Well section? Monday by eight will be fine." She walked away then returned to add, "That's a.m., not p.m."

He dug into his jacket pocket and dumped his phone and Keera's press release on his desk. Regarded it for a full ten seconds. Picked his phone up again. "Keera? It's Zach Bones from City-Scape. I've been staring at your number. It said to call you. Let's try that astral thing, huh?"

"I must be slipping," she said. "I expected your call a half hour ago."

CHAPTER 9

Zach avoided the elevator and galloped down the firestairs two at a time. Five floors later, with his chest heaving, he opened the door to the car park and peered in. No Feliks, no Boggie. He started up and didn't relax until he eased into traffic. He thought of Keera and the entire weekend together, when anything could happen. The future sparkled like Saturday night lights.

When he reached her street, he found the same parking spot. Curious. Strolled up to her door and pushed the buzzer. It made no sound, but she opened up anyway. In dark green pants and a loose white tee. Bare feet again. Looked delicious.

"Glad you changed your mind," she said, stepping aside for him.

"There's a journalist creed: to boldly go where others don't."

A polite smile to acknowledge the joke and she led him to an inner room. A jug of water and glass sat on a table; two chairs flanked a wall, exercise mats, and cushions already on the floor. "We start here," she said. "Anything that causes our bodies to react, like a sudden or loud noise, will force our consciousness back to a familiar shelter. I've taken every precaution to reduce any disturbance. This is the quietest room in the house; you can't hear the street, the window is triple-glazed, the phone is disconnected, as is the door intercom."

Keera picked up the two chairs, placed them facing each other.

Her movements were brisk, businesslike; her face a study in concentration. "Sit down, please, and I'll explain what we are about to do."

Zach perched on a chair as she took the other. They were close enough to touch, and he edged his chair closer. She said nothing.

"Normally," she said, "transferring your consciousness to the next dimension requires a lot of practice, but with extra help we'll make it tonight. It starts with breathing."

"Been breathing as long as I can remember."

"Not in the right way. After a few minutes, you'll hear a humming or rumbling sound. As it grows louder, you'll think there's a jet taking off next to you."

"We shoot out of our bodies like rockets?"

Keera paused as if gathering strength for a monstrous task ahead. "Listen and you'll learn faster. Vibrations will run along your spine; they may even pulse up and down it in a regular rhythm. Stay with them, embrace them, they are the sign that your vibrational rate is being altered."

"My what?"

"You, we, all of us, live in a specific range of frequencies. These are determined by the atoms and molecules that drive us. Consciousness is not so hampered. But your physical body has to be retuned slightly so separation can occur."

"This makes no sense to me at all."

"It doesn't have to," she said. "You're going to separate whether or not you understand."

She sounded so sure. "I'm not convinced, but I'll try it."

"Of course you will, Zach. You're a person driven by curiosity." She smiled like she was encouraging him, but she was mocking him also. "Keep your eyes closed, so you don't jerk back into this world if you get startled. When the noise and vibrations stop, wait a few minutes and open your eyes. You should see your body and mine below you."

"Oh really? Doing what?"

Impatience flashed across her face. "Just being. The light in the room will be dim, gray. Don't worry about it. You may also find other people present. People you can't see now."

"Other people?" He raised an eyebrow. "Ghosts, you mean?"

"I mean those who have passed to the next level but remain attached to this house. I've seen a few here. This place is old; many have lived here before me." She half smiled at him. "You're afraid of ghosts, are you?"

He laughed. "Hell, no." But she unnerved him with her certainty.

"You'll manage; you're not a schoolboy."

"But these people you who lived here before and are now dead, won't they hate us? Like, we're in their space. Just theorizing here."

"You catch on quick. Some will, some won't."

"Where will you be? Aren't we doing this together?"

"I'll be around, but you might not see me. It won't matter. We'll come together again when we materialize in our new bodies."

"How will I know where to go?" He couldn't believe he was asking pointless questions. Time to get going and fail.

"Once you separate, you'll follow me automatically. You'll feel you're flying at a million miles per hour through darkness. You may see things in passing."

"Like what? Some Frankenstein thing?"

Keera gave him the long blink again. "No. Possible mischievous or confused entities. Ones who won't approach the white light, and prefer to stay in this in-between level."

"White light? The famous White Light? When people have near-death experiences, right?"

"It's a portal where people pass through to enter the next level.

Often those who've had a religious upbringing assume it's the Gates of Heaven and expect to find St. Peter waiting. If they carry guilt they can be nervous and stay away. Then they hang about on the physical level and bother the living. Children, too, often prefer a familiar environment, which is the home they lived in before they died. Any more questions?"

Hundreds, none about astral travel, all of them about her. "Are you kidding? First, how do I enter a body?"

"Don't worry, it'll happen, it's been arranged."

"Oh, right. That makes me feel better. How do I operate a body that's not mine?"

"With difficulty at first, but you'll get the hang of it. Enough for our needs."

"You're so convincing," he said. "This trip sounds like a complicated fancy dress party."

"To be honest, there are loose ends, but I'm hoping we can sort them out as we go." The answers were evasive; nothing would happen. But it was best to appear eager.

"How do I become an Indian?"

"Have you ever seen a Western movie? All the Indians are actors. That'll be you: an actor, for a short time. Got it?"

He fell silent. Anything else flippant he said at this point might antagonize her. He needed to be cooperative, friendly and visibly disappointed when nothing happened. Then he would shrug and say aw jeez, it didn't work and let's try tomorrow and, in the meantime, shall we send out for pizza and watch a movie?

Keera closed her eyes and sat still. Like she was getting instructions from the next level. Zach waited, and wondered what movies she liked.

Keera stood. "Take some clothes off."

What a mind reader she was. "So soon?" he said. "Don't we get to know each other first?" She stared at the ceiling. He slung his jacket over the chair and dropped his shoes under it. Knelt on the mat.

"On your back," she ordered, and placed a pillow behind his neck and another under his knees. A few more quips rose to his lips but died. No street noise entered the room; his breathing came in raspy takes. She took her place beside him.

"Do I hold your hand?" he asked.

"No. The physical contact will interfere with the vibrations."

"You expect me to get this right the first time? Wouldn't practice help? We can pretend we're possessing each other's bodies or something?"

"Zach?"

"Yes?"

"Do you want to do this or not?"

He lay still, half disbelieving that he was part of this dopey supernatural ritual, and half incredulous that he was in a darkened room lying next to this tasty creature. And doing nothing about it.

"Close your eyes," she said.

He kept them open, a couple of questions left. "You've done this tandem thing before, right?"

"Not in this context."

"What do you mean?"

"This isn't the moment to discuss this." "How often?" "Just once."

"How did it go?"

"Not well. She wasn't ready to leave her body."

"Oh." He closed his eyes. He smelled a happy failure approaching. They lay in silence for a while.

Keera said, "Take a deep breath. Pull it into the deepest part of your lungs."

Zach inhaled deeply as he could.

"Sense each particle of air, each molecule entering as you breathe. When your lungs are full, slowly exhale."

Like there was an alternative. He exhaled.

"Do it again and notice that you are sinking lower and lower into the mat."

Her voice became more distant. He inhaled again, his breath rushing through the air passage, a cold stream running over rounded stones. His body light, drowsy. Tingling in his fingers; his hands weighed forty pounds each.

A faint rumble in the distance. A passing truck. Couldn't be. The street way too narrow for large vehicles. The rumbling increased to a roar. Like standing in front of a jumbo jet without ear protectors. His body shook as an unbinding sensation ripped through him.

Hands wrapped around his wrists and pulled. Strong hands, not a girl's hands, not Keera's. A tearing sound, fabric shredding, and the room fell quiet again. Zach waited for the roar to return, but it didn't. He opened his eyes. He was staring at the ceiling.

It's failed. Terrific.

Wait, the ceiling hung inches away from his face. The ceiling? He turned his head to one side, and his whole being flipped over.

Below, him and Keera still lying on the mat.

But he floated above them.

In two places at once.

Outside his body.

Not possible.

A gray mist, steamy but not warm, not humid, half transparent and diffused, filled the room. He pulled a hand up to his face: it fluttered wispy around the edges. And as he watched, it grew wispier still. Unnerved, he looked away. He grabbed his leg. It felt solid but it, too, had little definition. Shit, Keera hadn't told him about this.

No sign of her floating with him. Maybe she was still in her body. Better be sure. The thought sent him hovering close above her. How did that happen?

Then he saw him. A small boy, about three years old. Dark hair, crooked teeth, drifting near the door. He grinned at Zach and made playful grabbing motions with his hands. Eager to play, it seemed, but a nanosecond later his face contorted in anger, and he flew at him. The boy smashed through him with a smacking bang that sent Zach tumbling around the room like a stray balloon.

He steadied himself to find the kid waiting, making the same grabbing movements, sulkiness darkening his face. Where the hell was Keera? She had warned him about the dead people and he'd laughed. Should have listened. The kid wanted to play a game Zach didn't recognize. The boy, too young to control his emotions, would throw unprovoked tantrums. Lashing out the only way he knew. Zach braced himself for another onslaught, a helpless target for an angry ghost child. Wished him gone.

He vanished.

Not even a puff of smoke, just nothing there anymore. Maybe that's how things worked around here. You think of something, and it happens. Like when he envisioned being closer to their bodies and, whoosh, he was inches away.

As if at the bidding of a higher force, he rose to the ceiling and kept rising. Through the dusty crumble of plaster followed by the denser fibers of the joists and floorboards. Each layer as detectable as if he could run his physical hands through them. An empty room lay above, and then more plaster and wood before he floated through the cool layers of a slate roof.

It couldn't be night yet, but a dim light bathed the city skyline. He tried to locate familiar landmarks, his car parked outside the house for a start, but a force swept him away with increasing speed. A darker void enveloped him as he sped forward. Wind buffeted him even though he hadn't a proper body to detect it. Another crazy contradiction to cope with. He waited for more bizarre encounters, but nothing materialized. Just the rushing wind in his face that probably didn't exist anymore. He tried not to make sense of it. Might damage his sanity forever.

He slowed. The void grew lighter. Grassy brown plains below him, low rolling hills in the far distance. A creek snaked its way through undulating ground and joined with a smaller one. Trees and small bushes clustered on the banks and past them, in a hollow, a bare-chested man lay under another tree, dressed only in fringed pants.

He flew at the figure without slowing, collided with violence, but no pain, no smashing together of limbs. The body jerked and a flailing arm struck a tree. He felt that. And the spiky grass under his bare back. And the warm breeze that bent the leaves.

This was no vision—this was a new reality.

He'd gone mad.

CHAPTER 10

Zach's head reeled; nausea swirled through it. He sat up to inspect his surroundings, and discovered his jeans missing. He wore fringed buckskin leggings, decorated moccasins encased his feet.

Not his feet, not his legs!

Sweat streaked his temples, the sun needled his skin. The sun? The day had been rainy, cloudy only minutes earlier. Not now. He palmed his chest and recoiled. Not his flesh. This chest was nugget brown, hairless and scratched like he had run through bushes half naked. Where was his shirt?

He stood up and fell again. These legs refused to work. He crawled back to lean against a tree, and two thick braids of black hair swung loose past his shoulders.

"Holy shit," he cried.

Footsteps swished through dry grass. A young woman stumbled out from behind a tree. She wore a long deerskin shift, belted at the waist with a leather thong and fringed at the bottom. A leather knife handle protruded from a sheath strapped to her waist thong. The knife was big enough to saw a log in half. The woman approached with halting steps, half sliding down the incline. He wanted to run. Wanted his own legs back, the ones that could outrun a pursuing defense all the way to the touchline.

The woman stopped and spoke. "How kola," she said with a twisting smile.

Keera.

Not the same Keera as before; her voice was flatter and more guttural. But he'd understood her. Hello, friend, she had said. What fresh madness was this?

The woman put out her hand to help him to his feet. "Welcome," she said.

Zach struggled upright and locked his knees.

"Is that you?" The words came out thick and slurred. He stared more closely at her. Short and broad-faced, the woman looked little like Keera.

'Yes, it's me in here. Ignore the external appearance if you can."

The Keera woman smiled again. More a friendly grimace than a smile. He leaned against the tree. It scratched his back. He flinched and stayed away.

"I can't ... I can't." He stopped. His mouth not forming the words right, he swallowed and licked his lips. Tried again. "I can't ..." This was the worst dream ever.

"It'll take you a while. Your body hardly speaks, isn't used to forming words. Keep trying."

He took a breath. "I can't accept we're here and not in your room." That was better. A complete sentence. "Is this a hypnotic illusion? An extra vivid dream?" He heard himself speaking in a monotone.

"You'll soon find out it's not." Keera directed an arm over a shoulder and pushed the elbow with her other hand. Like she was warming up for an athletic event.

He bent down, hoping he wouldn't fall over, and tore up a handful of grass. It felt like grass. A slight breeze ruffled it and brought the fresh smell of open land to his nostrils. He smelled his arm, not as funky as he expected, but not his smell. He pinched his skin.

"Where the hell are we?" His voice, stronger now, even carried nuances.

"The early eighteen hundreds. We're in what will become South Dakota one day. Over the rise behind you is an Oglala camp." She stretched her arms to the sky and lowered them, showing more control over her limbs than he could his. "We'll join it when you can walk."

He slapped his knees. "These aren't mine. I'm pretty creeped out about it."

"None of that body is yours, Zach. I explained that before." She eyed him warily. "You aren't going to pieces on me, are you?"

"I didn't figure on all this." He wriggled his toes. "These moccasins are not a great fit."

"You expect a shoe store around here? Tighten the cords." Keera moved her head from side to side.

"I wasn't complaining actually. I'm still amazed I can talk. No need to be snippy about it."

"Sorry. Taking over a body is hard work. You may have noticed you're not doing so well yourself yet." She windmilled her arms for a few seconds, one after the other. "How did you manage out there?"

"Freaky shit. There was this angry kid. He charged me—not nice."

"I've seen him. He's not so bad if you can talk to him. The living child was willful, and still retains that personality." Zach shook his head. "I can't believe I'm having this discussion while thinking I'm trapped in a guy's body from two hundred years ago." He laughed, but it sounded more like coughing. "I don't know what substances you used on me, but I suggest you get a medical patent on the mixture. It works so well. This could revolutionize travel. Visit the world from the comfort of your home. Includes Smell-o-Vision and Touch-a-Rama."

Keera stopped her stretches. "This is no acid trip, no mescaline-induced alternate world or anything like it. You have left your ordinary world behind. You are experiencing a whole new facet of reality."

Zach shook his head. "I know what reality is, and it's back in Chicago, driving in the rain, interviewing people who should be in restraints and dealing with a boss who wants to humiliate me. This ..." he waved his hands around, "is a damn dream. A very vivid dream, but still a dream."

"This isn't a dream," she said with growing exasperation. "You've left your normal body to take over another one. You're really here. You can feel hunger, pain and joy. I thought we had this straight."

"No. I still don't believe it. This is too weird."

"You want to go back? Already?" Her lips curled.

He tried to make sense of all this. He was in a freaky dream, or he wasn't. If he were, then he would wake up in that room with Keera sooner or later. At worst he might have a nightmare to get over. Nothing serious. If this wasn't a dream, he ought to investigate further. Insisting on a return to normality mean one thing —he'd never see her again. She'd made it clear she had no time for wimps.

He cleared his new throat. "What about my normal body, my personal body, my extra-favorite one? What's it doing now?"

"Nothing. Like I told you. It's just lying down."

"Is it safe?"

"The house is secure. If your body is touched or moved, you'll leave this one and go back to it."

"I still can't believe I'm in this body," Zach said. He ran his fingers along an arm.

"Why not?" Annoyance darkened her face. "I explained everything to you."

"You did, you did. Sort of. But you know what I do for a living?"

"You're a writer, reporter, something."

"That's right. You know what happens to a reporter every day of his life? He gets lied to. All the time. He also has to listen to hundreds of unbelievable stories. I thought your story was another one. I didn't believe a single word, and now I am inside some other body." He locked onto her eyes. "I'm very, very nervous about this. I could be in a psychiatric ward somewhere, and all this is happening in my mind. Please say it isn't so."

She patted his shoulder. "You're not going mad; you've passed into a new world. Soon you'll return to your familiar one. In the meantime, I need your help. I need you to see what I am talking about, and to tell the world about it later. Nobody will believe me, but they'll listen to a skeptic like you."

Not the longest motivational speech he'd heard, but it calmed him. Especially the bit about her needing him. Zach was taking control of his new body. Even the mouth, thank God. Bardo had been right: he adapted fast to changed circumstances. He was also quick to assert himself. She took over before he derailed the project.

"Touch your nose with either hand," she said. He tried but jabbed his cheek instead. Tried again, and his finger slid past his nose.

"I'd do better drunk."

"Sorry, we're in an alcohol-free zone. Can you walk?" He took a single step and fell over again. He pulled himself upright by clinging to the tree. Tried another step and one foot tripped over the other. "This is useless. Have I taken over the body of a cripple?"

"Your man walked here from the camp, and he'll walk back. You have all afternoon to learn to use his body. Do as I do. Raise your arms above your head and touch your shoulders."

"This is a hell of a time to play Simon Says." But he followed her instructions. "Your actions are jerky, but you'll improve fast now."

"I feel like a puppet whose master has cut its strings."

"The body you're wearing has a neural memory. The same memory that lets you ride a bicycle twenty years after the last time. It never forgets. Stop forcing this body to do things the way you are used to, the way you walked, reached for something or sat. Allow it to be itself."

Zach staggered to the next tree. "This guy takes shorter steps; that's why I'm having trouble."

"The local diet doesn't create big men."

"You're a lot shorter, too. And your hair's in braids, a broader nose, and your eyes ... they're almost black. Also, you look starved."

"You're in pretty good shape yourself," she retorted. Only minutes into a strange new world and he's already checking out my figure.

"Yeah? Where's a mirror?"

"There are no mirrors here. Find a still pool of water."

"I can't wait." He stretched his arms. Ran his hands down his chest and belly. "Hey, I've got great pecs. And what a six-pack." He fingered the clothes he wore. "What's this outfit? These leg things and this cloth?"

"They're leggings so you can ride a horse without chafing, and as protection in the scrub. The loincloths protect your modesty. They're called breechclouts if you want to get technical."

Zach slid a hand down the front of his breechclout.

What? "Have you found anything interesting?" she asked. "You won't find underwear."

He fell silent as he explored.

"The hell are you doing?"

"A man has to be sure of certain things, Keera." He removed his hand. Gave her a big smirk

"And?"

"It's not what I'm used to, but it'll do."

I told you he was adaptable. Bardo cutting in on her thoughts.

Her face flamed in anger. "You won't do anything. Not here. Not with anybody. Not even if they are as beautiful as Venus and naked in your arms. Got it?"

"Okay, okay."

"We have a duty to these bodies. We cannot abuse them or force them to do things they wouldn't normally do. Is that clear?"

"I said okay, didn't I? But it'd be an amazing experience to make love with someone else's body." Grinning like a damn schoolboy.

"No!" But he kept that goofy grin, and she had to tamp down her anger before they were both screaming at each other. "One other thing," she said as calmly as possible. "The Oglala do not express feelings openly. No hugging, no hand holding, and no kissing, not even cheek kissing."

"Can you stop with the finger-wagging stuff? I got it. A real anal society."

"No. A society that has to repress itself to live peaceably to-gether."

"Whatever." He flicked at his braids. "These have to go. I fancy a Mohawk style."

"If you turn up with that hairstyle, the Oglala will take you for a Pawnee and kill you. We're supposed to blend in, not stand out."

"Fine. Don't I wear any shirt, a buckskin tee?"

"It's summer. Haven't you noticed?" She forced herself to stay patient. He'd have hundreds of questions, and it was in her inter-est to keep him committed. He wasn't waiting for instructions, but kept moving around, becoming more sure-footed. This was good. They couldn't afford for Zach to stagger into camp like a walking wounded guy. Dozens of eyebrows would rise. Urgent, anxious eyebrows, fearful of news of a hostile raiding party.

CHAPTER 11

Bardo had chosen their channeling ground well. They were concealed from curious eyes by a stand of cottonwood trees. In a depression that cut between rises a hundred yards apart that reached as high as two men. Nobody could see them unless they breasted the top of a hill.

"The air. It's warm and smells good. Clean," Zach said. "Back home, warm air smells of fried food and car exhaust. And it's so quiet here. All I hear is the leaves rustling." He touched his chest. "Shouldn't I be wearing armor? Those bone things that hang down in front. They're so cool."

"If you were wearing a breastplate of bird bones you'd be going into battle and ready to die."

"Really? Well, maybe not."

"You can put a deerskin shirt on later. It'll be cooler when the sun goes down."

"I have a wardrobe?"

"You have a shirt."

He shuffled to a tree twenty yards away and returned without stumbling. "I can do this, I reckon."

"Good," she said. "We'll walk into the camp. If you stumble, I'll explain that you tripped and hurt yourself earlier."

"Love the way you make me sound like a cool guy."

Her earlier exasperation with him had softened. Zach was accepting the situation faster than she had a right to expect. He was cooperating, even if his attitude leaned to an immature, jokey take on events. If he kept his mouth shut, they could do this. If.

"The band is further east than normal," she said. "This part of the year, they prefer the Black Hills, their spiritual grounds. They must have followed a buffalo herd this way. By the look of it, the two of us have been gathering berries."

Rain Bird hadn't resisted her entry at all this time. The integration process was as easy as slipping on a tunic. After several body sharings the woman had stopped the questioning had acquiesced in this unfamiliar presence, and, as far as Keera could tell, was an eager observer of her adventure. How long Rain Bird would remain quiet was an unknown. Keera had no experience in struggling to remain in a body when the original habitant wanted to resume control. She walked to a deerskin bag on the ground, her steps slow but steadier. She picked it up, checked inside and with a jerk of her head indicated they should climb a rise.

As they crested it, Zach drew a sharp breath. In front of them and two hundred yards away, a shallow creek, twenty yards wide. Fifty, sixty horses grazed on the other side. Women were tearing strips of bark from trees and throwing them down for the horses. The women dressed like her, in long buckskin dresses.

Beyond them stood a few dozen tipis, some set along the banks, others further back. A large clearing in the center. Children darted about, dogs followed, occasional shrieks of laughter split the air. At the shingled bank, two women knelt and filled floppy containers with water.

"This is incredible, amazing," he said, his voice cracking disbelief. "Will the US Cavalry come charging around the bend any moment?"

"It's the wrong year for that, and you're not in a movie house," she said. "The white presence here is minimal, just a few traders coming through."

"This is more than a dream, isn't it?"

"If you start losing it, pretend you're filming a secret documentary. Nobody knows what you're doing except you and me. It'll give you a focus and stop the heebie-jeebies grabbing hold."

"The heebie-jeebies?" He laughed aloud.

"You know what I mean." She scanned the camp. "It's quite empty, the men are hunting."

They stepped stiffly down to the creek and stopped opposite the women on the other bank. The breeze carried their chatter. One of them nudged another. "It's Rain Bird with the quiet one again. What do you think they were doing in the trees?" She burst into a giggle.

Her companion flashed teeth. "Whatever it was, it took a long time to explain." The women snorted and snuffled with suppressed laughter.

Zach said, "Hey, I understood that. Something about a long time."

"Of course you can. You're Oglala. Your name is Slow Hand."

"Slow Hand?" His face lit up. "You mean this guy is a ladies' man?"

His enthusiasm is encouraging, isn't it? She ignored Bardo and gave Zach a megawatt smile before she poured acid over him. "Not exactly. You're named Slow Hand because you're a slow learner, dim-witted even, a backward child."

"I'm a what?" She didn't soften her words, a little piece of revenge for his aggravating manner earlier. "And you're clumsy. In the modern world, you would have been classified as schizophrenic because of the voices in your head. They make it hard for you to communicate. When still a boy, you mostly gave up speaking."

"I'm a schizo?" He was shouting and didn't care who heard him. "Shh. You talk little, remember."

The two women on the bank looked over with surprised faces, chores forgotten.

"I don't believe this. I trusted you, wanted to help, and you turned me into a head case."

She lowered her voice. "I did what was necessary to regain the stone. Your new body gives you brilliant cover. Whatever, whenever, however, you mess up, nobody here will suspect anything but a crazy guy doing his crazy thing."

"Yeah, but—"

"No buts. I've spent a lot of time on this. I've taken over this body before. It works for me, and your body will work for you. Believe me."

He shook his head in distaste. "I'd prefer to be a major player here, not a sap who walks around drooling."

"You don't drool." She shot back. "You spend most days listening to voices."

"Jesus, the poor guy." He tilted his head. "But I hear no voices."

"They aren't talking to your spirit; they're talking to his."

"That's a relief. But why doesn't this Slow Hand object to being taken over? I can't feel his presence at all."

"He's used to being told what to do. His spirit is totally subdued by yours. He is an uninvolved spectator of what is happening to him."

Zach watched the women watching him. "Hell of a trick to play on a guy. What's your name, anyway?"

"I'm Rain Bird, widow of your older brother Eagle Chaser. He was killed in a raid by the Crow a few months ago. She's distraught with grief, which made it easy for me to take over her body."

"Why am I hanging about with my brother's widow? Doesn't this break a taboo?"

"It's the custom here for men to add the new widow to their wives to help look after them."

"You ... you mean I've got two wives, and you're one of them?" His stupid grin surfaced again.

See how he bounces back?

She allowed Zach several seconds of hope. "You have no wife. Your brother and I looked after you, and we all lived in my family's lodge. When Eagle Chaser died, you stayed with us."

He considered this. "Does this mean we sleep together in the same tipi?"

"The whole family sleeps together. All families live like this."

"How does anybody have sex, then?"

Did he ever think of anything else? "They manage. Sex here is less ritualistic, it's more basic than what you're used to."

"How do you know what I'm used to? You don't know me. Maybe when this is over, we'll find an enchanting resta—"

"Shut up," she said. "You're talking too much, and they're watching and wondering." She stepped off the bank and splashed across the creek. He followed her. The women never took wide eyes off him.

They drew closer to the tipis, and Zach asked her, "How do I present myself? What do I do if someone talks to me? What if they challenge me to a fight?"

Keera hadn't expected so many questions. Couldn't he be quiet and observe, and not act the inquisitive reporter? "You'll understand them," she replied. "Fighting? Forget it. You're not a warrior. Other men would be ashamed to fight you. Best of all, stay silent."

"Not happy, Keera. It's embarrassing to be a loser."

"Put your male ego aside for a teeny bit. You'd like it a lot less if you had to prove your bravery every day. Or forced to prove it by risking your life."

Zach was finding it difficult to shut up. Lucky the camp was empty of most men and half of the women. Nobody close enough to overhear them. It wouldn't last. He had better learn to hold his tongue before they had to answer awkward questions. She pointed ahead to a tipi. "My father Three Dogs, and my mother Looks Back Woman, are in there. They know Slow Hand very well, so please try to be as unobtrusive as possible."

A man leading a piebald appeared from behind a group of tipis and approached them with the languid walk of a master of his domain. He was bare-chested, his body hard muscled, as if it did all the tough yards but enjoyed no soft rewards. A face chiseled from mahogany; long, braided hair decorated with three feathers at the back. Whitish remains of scars on the brave's chest and shoulders. Battle scars.

Crazy Elk. The young warrior Bardo had warned her about. The one who regarded Rain Bird as his future wife.

"How," he said, stopping in front of them. His horse edgy and stepping sideways, like it sensed something strange about the two of them.

"How," she replied. "The camp is empty. Where have the men gone?"

"Claw and Little Man found the buffalo trail. It was not far. Everybody has joined the hunt." Crazy Elk fastened calm, dark eyes on Zach. "Maybe one day you will join us and seek your food among our four-legged friends instead of among the groundlings you pluck." He swung onto his horse. Zach stepped back as the animal pranced closer.

"I seek where I choose, fella," Zach snapped.

The words came out in fluent Lakota. Crazy Elk's eyes widened. Keera stiffened.

"The berries have at last given you quick speech, Slow Hand." Crazy Elk grinned back at him without mirth. "But be careful how you address your brothers. We have proper names, earned names, and they deserve respect."

"Slow Hand meant no insult," she said. "Words are hard for him, and he is still learning to choose them." For God's sake, Zach, keep your freaking mouth shut.

Crazy Elk didn't take his eyes off Zach. "Words are dangerous things, Rain Bird. Slow Hand should think before using each one of them."

"He will," she assured him, laying a warning hand on Zach's arm. The warrior held Zach's gaze for a few seconds longer before he dug heels into the horse's flanks and wheeled away. Horse and rider picked up speed as they passed the last of the tipis, the sound of hooves fading to silence.

"Don't forget, Zach," she said with compressed lips. "Silence is the best option here."

"Sorry. I can't ignore a put-down. It's a fault of mine, I know. Anyway, why was he left behind when the others went hunting? Was he a guard?"

She released his arm. "Crazy Elk is a suitor for Rain Bird. If he was still in camp, then he was waiting for us to return."

"A stalker?"

"No, he's not like that. More protective than menacing, but he's jealous. He had wanted Rain Bird before she married Eagle Chaser and now he wants her even more. She's been too distracted to pay him much attention, but he's waiting for her to come out of mourning."

"Is he jealous of me?"

Maybe, I hope not. "No, you're not a warrior, nobody takes you seriously."

"Why?"

"Because you're not safe to take into a battle. You are too unpredictable, and the voices tell you to do strange things. So, if you can't show your mettle, your bravery, you can't be a warrior."

"I knew it," Zach said. "I'm a lover, not a fighter."

"Same reason you don't go on buffalo hunts. You might do something nutty."

He ran his hand over his hair. "Why don't I wear feathers? It goes with the territory, doesn't it?"

"You earn feathers. Crazy Elk has three. They mean he's killed three of his tribe's enemies. In fact, he may not have killed them, merely slapped them with his lance to show his contempt. Killing's considered the easy way to count coup."

"Count coup?" "You count the times you slap the enemy and you get a feather for each time. It's French for a blow."

"Jesus. Why don't we take that idea back to the twenty-first century? No countries nuke each other. Nobody kills nobody, just slaps the enemy. The team with the most slaps in forty minutes gets to win."

"It's too advanced for the twenty-first century," she said. "Let's take our berries to our lodge."

They drew further into the camp. The tipis wore individual decorations. One showed drawings of horses; another a scene of men on horseback chasing buffalo. Snakes and deer were popular choices also. Some tipis displayed only abstract patterns in blue and ochre as if the owners had simply splashed colors on instead of spending painstaking hours on hunting scenes.

A young girl emerged from one of them. Thin, tired and pregnant. She gave Zach a disinterested glance but nodded at Keera as she passed.

"Has somebody been contributing to the delinquency of that minor?" He said, looking back at her. "Any concept of an age of consent in this place?"

"The parents decide when a daughter gets married," she replied. "That's Stays Alone. She's older than she looks, about fifteen."

"Still a kid, for Chrissakes."

"I know how you feel. It seems more shocking when you see it for real rather than reading about it. But we can't change anything; we're here to get that stone and vanish."

"Yeah, but ..."

"Keep in mind that the survival of this tribe is the most important thing. When a girl is sexually mature, she gets a husband to look after her. Otherwise, she starves."

"That one seems to get zilch at the dinner table even now."

Two dogs dashed up and eyed them with excited curiosity. Their ribs showed, their rough fur a haven for every bug in the world. One dog approached Zach and sniffed him all over. Not big, just a rangy, yellow-brown, starving cousin of a coyote. He took a step back. The dog growled a soft warning as if it sensed someone it could dominate.

"*Wahampi*," she shouted. The dogs shied back, collided with each other and fled.

"Thanks," he said. "Dogs are not my favorite animals. Especially unwashed ones."

"You'll find plenty here, so get used to it."

"What did you yell at them?"

"*Wahampi*. A useful Lakota word I picked up. The dogs always run off when they hear it." She stopped outside their lodge. Like others, the sides were rolled up a little for ventilation. "It's time to help my mother prepare the evening meal. Remember to keep quiet."

"Got it." Zach patted his flat stomach. "I feel a bit peckish now that you mention it, and I love ethnic food. What's on the menu tonight?"

"A special treat—*wahampi*. Boiled puppy soup."

CHAPTER 12

Keera had to be kidding about the meal, but already Zach knew she wasn't much of a kidder. Puppy soup, Jesus. "Can't I get out of it? Tell them I'm on a diet or something."

Keera set her jaw. "Nobody diets in the modern sense of the word. It's hard enough to stay alive. To refuse food is unthinkable."

"But I'm supposed to be crazy. Maybe I can get away with it. I'll do anything not to eat a puppy. Watching will be bad enough."

She considered this. "Maybe you can avoid the meal. You're so weird nobody expects a sensible act." She nodded as if agreeing with herself. "Let's go in."

She pulled open the entrance flap of the tipi, and ducking her head, stepped inside. He followed, and immediately his nostrils filled with the tang of smoke and dogs. A fire pit in a ring of stones lay a couple of steps in front of him, directly below an opening in the tipi. Behind it, an old man, Three Dogs, he guessed, holding a decorated pipe. The yard-long stem was a flat piece of wood with a carved stone bowl at the end. Quillwork, feathers, and colored designs marked its length.

Beside Three Dogs sat a pair of rangy dogs who rose at Zach's entrance, but a middle-aged woman slapped back. Only two dogs. Maybe the old man couldn't afford the upkeep of his heritage.

Maybe he had eaten one of them. The woman dressed like Keera, but with several rows of white lumps sewn on the front of her shift. Lumps? They looked like animal teeth, for God's sakes. Keera took her place next to her.

Three Dogs acknowledged Zach and waved him over, tapping the ground next to him. "How goes the day, Slow Hand?" the old man said. "Did you walk far to find the berries?"

Zach shot Keera a pleading look, but she occupied herself with examining her moccasins. He had to say something, right? Nothing complicated, something normal? He cleared his throat. "No. We got tired and lay down to rest."

Three Dogs stared at him. "Un hee!" he cried, rubbing his nose. "Slow Hands speaks! It is a good day."

Looks Back Woman sank onto her haunches in astonishment. Keera glared at him. What the hell? I just made small talk, that's all. I'm supposed to do only that much, right?

He said, "What's the matter?" It came out pretty good, not real smooth, but like a guy who hadn't spoken for a while.

The old woman clapped a hand to her mouth. Three Dogs smiled, his weathered face creasing into deeper lines. "Nothing is wrong, my son. You spoke well. We didn't expect it."

"We're all surprised," Keera said, but sounding displeased.

"That's a truth," said Looks Back Woman. "Slow Hand speaks twice in one day. A thing to behold."

Keera blazed an angry look at him, and he understood. Shut up for the rest of the night. One dog stood up and sniffed his chest and his face. Three Dogs pushed it away. "Even the dogs are surprised," he said. "Slow Hand speaking is an unexpected thing for them, too." He said to Keera, "You still sound different, Rain Bird. Your voice is deeper, a hoarseness in it."

"There might have been bad medicine in those trees, Father," she replied. "My throat is scratchy."

Three Dogs nodded, satisfied. "If scratchiness stays, I'll fetch Red

Leaf."

She inclined her head in agreement.

Zach surveyed the tipi. Rawhide lines strung between the poles; bags of different sizes hung off them. A deerskin garment draped over one line, and he guessed it was Slow Hand's. Two shields were attached to the poles. Bows, quivers of arrows and lances gathered in one section of the lodge. Above these, dangled objects with black hairy tails. Must be dream catchers. Not pretty ones either. Not like in street markets. As he stared at them, he changed his mind.

Not dream catchers.

Scalps.

Scalps of shriveled skin, caked with dried blood, sporting lank hair strands. Scalps he would sleep under that night. Not exactly a chocolate-on-the-pillow kind of welcome.

Looks Back Woman left the tipi and returned with a hot rock gripped by a cleft stick in her hands. She dropped it into an open-topped, rubber-looking bag supported by sticks. The buffalo bladder Keera had mentioned. The rock sizzled as it hit the water. How long before the puppy appeared? He hoped it wasn't too cute, and a sudden unease gripped his gut.

Both dogs scrambled to their feet and growled. Faint cries from a distance. Three Dogs stabbed a lance into the ground and struggled upright with Looks Back Woman and Keera helping him. Once standing, he shuffled out of the tipi. Zach waited for the women to pass before him, but Keera waved him on with a quick gesture. Their group moved in a slow procession to the center of the camp where others gathered.

Thirty or more warriors rode in. A long way behind them in straggling lines came their women leading horses. Raw meat bundles, tied with strips of hide, covered the backs of several animals. Other horses dragged loaded travois.

"A successful hunt," Keera whispered to Zach. "No boiled puppy tonight. We'll have buffalo instead."

His immediate relief was tempered by the thought of eating buffalo. Hell, it couldn't be as bad as puppy. One rider peeled away from the rest and rode up to them.

Crazy Elk.

He slid to the ground, slipped a knife from his belt and hacked at his meat pack. He pulled free a slab of fresh liver and offered it to Keera.

"A gift for you, little one," he said.

Zach watched with incredulity as Keera accepted the offering. She brought the liver to her lips and bit. Chewed steadily until the mouthful slipped down and stayed down. Not a single flicker of repulsion. He couldn't have done that; how did she manage it? There was a steeliness to her he hadn't expected.

Crazy Elk smiled at them and walked away.

"Was he playing with us?" Zach demanded.

"No." Keera wiped her chin. "Every Oglala has a duty to help those who can't help themselves. He's happy I accepted his liver. Soon he will offer Father a horse or two for Rain Bird."

"She's bought? Just like that? This is very primitive stuff."

"He won't ask unless he thinks she'll go with him. Her accepting his gift was a step towards that. I hope Rain Bird approves. I also hope our mission is over before he gets too encouraged."

Three Dogs was talking to another old man. A stocky guy with a necklace of bear claws around his neck; squat, wrestler legs balanced, ready to grapple anybody, anything. A strong nose dominated a face sun-etched with thick lines.

"That's Red Leaf," Keera said. "He and Three Dogs are the elders here. Red Leaf is the war leader and a healer. He has the stone."

"Him? He's the friendly medical type who hands out herbal remedies, works the Sacred Stone and chants?" he said, turning so that the other two couldn't see him talking. "He looks like he takes lives rather than saving them."

"Correct. He's merciless. He's killed a man for every year of his life."

Zach stared at the old man again. This man, who reminded him of the sour-faced guys that stood behind liquor store counters, had racked up enough felonies to be serving a couple of dozen life sentences. "Why is he called Red Leaf? It's a girly name for a warrior type, isn't it?"

She made a face. "It refers to the blood sprayed over nearby bushes and trees when he kills."

Red Leaf turned to them as if he had heard her words. Turned Zach into a schoolboy caught talking in class. "Why do I feel he's no pushover to steal from?" he whispered.

She bit her lip. "He'll be wary of us now. Three Dogs is telling him of the changes in us. Crazy Elk may have told him about you challenging him. He'll speak to us soon; he won't leave it be."

"Let's move," Zach said, walking away. Keera followed him. "What will he do about us?"

"He'll try to find out why we have changed. He needs a satisfactory answer he can announce to the camp."

"So, what do I say when he talks to me?"

"To be honest, I don't know."

"Thanks for the detailed briefing."

Keera grabbed his arm and stopped him. "I told you I didn't have a complete plan. We're going to wing it. Okay?" Her eyes were sparking with annoyance.

"Okay, okay. So Red Leaf is the boss here?"

"Yes. My father was the war leader until a Crow arrow damaged a leg tendon."

My father. "So what Red Leaf says, goes?"

"Not necessarily. The Oglala don't follow orders blindly. If they can't respect their war leaders, they find another, or they pack up their homes and leave the band."

Zach looked around, still half believing this was all a crazy dream. "How do you know all this stuff?"

"It's my specialty, remember?"

"You know the lives of specific individuals, too. A helluva detailed specialty."

The women unloaded the travois and carried meat chunks to their tipis for cooking and curing.

"I made a few trips here before to orientate myself. If I were confused as you, we would be in real trouble."

Looks Back Woman came up to them carrying pieces of raw meat, each the size of a small briefcase. "Take this, Rain Bird. I'll get some more."

Keera added her slab of liver to the new load and carried it toward the lodge. She didn't insist that he come with them, so he stayed. Industrious women stoked the fire higher; the sun died soft and orange behind the hills, and he shivered at the encroaching chill. Tomorrow looked to be a fine day.

A fine day to steal from a man who had already killed sixty people.

CHAPTER 13

Men gathered near the fire, began drumming on logs and shaking gourds. Other men and women approached, and ranged themselves on either side, in separate groups. Both groups launched into a song. Three Dogs and Looks Back Woman returned and Keera stopped alongside Zach. She handed him a buckskin shirt which he slipped over his head. The garment hung to his knees, softer than he had expected, smelling of smoked game.

He couldn't locate the healer. "Let's move around and try to spot Red Leaf. Once we know he's here, we raid his tipi. Which one is it?"

"It's near the edge of the camp, with elk decorations," Keera said. "But we ought to formulate a plan first."

"A plan? We grab the rock and figure out where to hide it. At least the tricky part's done. The part where Red Leaf discovers us and shears off a major part of our coiffures."

She shook her head. "Once we have the Stone we have to get out. He'll notice it missing almost immediately. Why don't you just watch the show and leave the plans to me?"

The flames danced lights over the singers turning them into pulsating wraiths. Steel fingers clamped his arm.

Red Leaf.

"Rain Bird, join your sisters," the healer said. "Slow Hand stay with me."

Keera walked away with a solitary backward glance; anxiety painted all over her face.

Red Leaf inspected Zach. The old warrior's chest thrust forward, challenging, his air suspicious. Zach braced himself for tough questions but kept in mind Keera's admonition to say as little as possible.

"Three Dogs says you've received good medicine. You talk like a warrior." Red Leaf plainly didn't believe a word of it.

Zach's mind tumbled with thoughts, too many to form a smooth answer.

"If you can speak you must speak. It is a curse to treat the Great Spirit's gifts lightly."

Zach cleared his throat. "It comes hard for me."

Red Leaf grunted acknowledgment of his difficulty but stayed on point. "What happened in the cottonwood grove today? It's plain you're not the man you were before."

Zach shrugged. He worked his mouth through several silent syllables before uttering the words. He didn't want to appear too fluent. "Ke—Rain Bird and I fell asleep while picking berries."

A smile grew slowly across the healer's face. A walnut prized open. "The gathering of berries is hard, I know," he said with some sarcasm. "A man must rest when he can." He grabbed Zach's arm. "What did you dream? What did you see?"

He'd put a great store on a dream; Keera had told him that. Every detail important, and minutely inspected. He fought to clear his mind, to construct a story that would explain why Slow Hand was different. A story to satisfy this unhesitating killer.

"What did you dream?" Red Leaf repeated. "If you didn't dream, then I know what's happened."

"What ... what do you mean?"

"Walk-in spirit. You've been invaded by a walk-in spirit."

What new weirdness was this? The guy was searching for something he could announce to the others, but how bad was a walk-in spirit?

"If so," Red Leaf continued, "you know what comes of this."

"I become a new man?"

"Yes, but a dangerous one. Too dangerous to live with us."

"You will send me away?"

"I'll put you to death."

Holy shit. Slow Hand dead through no fault of his own. "Are you certain I have a walk-in spirit?"

"I make sure with a sage bundle. The smell of burning sage makes evil spirits crazy. They flee. If they don't, we kill the body. Take away their home."

"But if they flee, this saves the person."

"It's best to kill him to be sure."

Jesus. He'd better think of a dream fast. He searched for lies sound enough to stand up to further questioning, lies simple enough to remember. It was no use. No way he could come up with a plausible story in his current mental state. He decided only the truth would work. "I dreamed of another man flying in the sky, and he entered my body," he said.

Red Leaf released Zach's arm and stepped back. "What happened after that?"

"I woke up, and this body was new to me. I talked without other voices in my head." Zach had long learned the best lies relied on telling the truth but omitting the crucial, damning element. Technically, these weren't lies at all.

"What did this other man look like?"

"Tall, strong, handsome and fleet of foot."

Red Leaf dropped his gaze from Zach's and pondered this information. "An interesting dream, Slow Hand. Any birds, or any four-legged beings in it?"

"No, just the man from the sky. It has puzzled and confused me, too." Red Leaf might take days to figure out an interpretation. By then, he would be back home.

"What about buffalo or thunder? Did those things enter your dream?"

He shook his head. Behind him, a new sound burst into the air. The men were singing, a full-throated booming, dozens of voices in unison. His skin goose-bumped a little.

Red Leaf gave a triumphant shout. "*Un hee!* I understand it." He laughed, delighted at solving the puzzle. He poked Zach in the chest with a gnarly twig of a finger. "The Great Spirit has taken pity on you and made you a warrior. Your dream tells me you've been given new strength to fight our enemies. You're still a small man, true, but inside, your spirit is now that of a big one. Strong and fast."

This interpretation was as bad as the first one. "But I know nothing of being a warrior," he protested. Unpleasant images came to mind. Him wielding a bloody tomahawk; him running from a stream of arrows; a feathered lance spearing into his side. "You must be wrong. I'm not a warrior."

Red Leaf's face darkened. "Do not insult me. I understand your dream, Slow Hand. You're now a warrior although you haven't been tested yet. You'll not hide with the women anymore."

Zach stayed silent. The men's voices now replaced by women's, higher and keening. What would Keera say when she found out? He looked over to the singing, swaying women but couldn't see her.

Red Leaf spoke again. "Today we found Crow tracks. They were following the same herd. They'll be camped not more than a day's ride from here. In the morning, I send two scouts to find them. Then we fight them and steal their horses." Red Leaf slapped Zach's shoulder. "You'll come."

Oh good.

The healer started to walk away then turned back. "And you'll take your first scalp," he added.

Even better.

"I see you're pleased with the thought of it," Red Leaf said. "But remember this: if you don't perform as a warrior should, then I'll know I was mistaken. We will burn the evil one out of you, and then make you vanish from the earth."

Best news ever.

The drumming stopped as Keera came toward Zach, her face loaded with questions. She grabbed his arm and whispered, "What did Red Leaf want?"

"He said I'd changed greatly in just one day. Wanted to know why."

"What did you say?"

"The truth."

"What!"

"I knew he wouldn't understand. He'd interpret my experience in terms of his own culture, and I was right."

"What exactly did you say?" Keera wasn't willing to accept his take on the conversation.

"I said I dreamt a man, big and strong, took over my body." Best to omit the handsome part.

"And?"

Zach laughed.

"He thought about my dream and he figured it to mean I now possessed the soul of a warrior."

She chewed her lip and looked off into the crowd. "Well, I suppose it could have been worse."

"There's a complication."

She swung back to him. "Please tell me it's not serious."

Some ten yards away two warriors were tearing buffalo meat off the bone with their teeth, and talking at the same time.

"He's decided since I'm now a warrior I'm not to hang out with you anymore," he said.

Keera grimaced. "It won't matter. We can't take the Stone while Red Leaf is discussing Slow Hand's transformation with the others. They'll notice you missing right away. But, at dawn, when Red Leaf is in deepest sleep, we'll have a chance."

"And then?"

"We'll ride off and bury it along this creek somewhere we can find two hundred years from now."

"And then?"

"We return home."

"Hallelujah. I was getting worried about my neck."

A long, ululating howl burst from a man near the fire. Zach flinched, but no one else reacted. The warrior finished his ode to joy and resumed gnawing meat.

"Your neck?" she asked. "How's that in danger?"

"The buffalo hunting party spotted Crow tracks. Red Leaf says we're to find them and fight them."

"Shit." Keera scowled. "I didn't expect that. Still, we should be out of here by then." She searched his face. "What did he mean by 'we'?"

A lump in his throat interfered with his reply. "I'm to come along and take a scalp."

"Double shit," she said with some force. "It's nothing, as you say. We'll be gone by then."

"We better be, because there's an extra complication." She didn't speak, only waited as if she had guessed this could be the worst of all complications. "Red Leaf has also decided that if I don't make like a true warrior, then I must be inhabited by a walk-in spirit."

"Shit. That means he'll kill you."

"That means he'll kill Slow Hand, actually. Poor guy."

"You'll feel Slow Hand's pain, Zach. The trauma of it will stay in your own spirit forever."

"Oh."

She laid a hand on his arm. "Don't worry, I'm not letting that happen to you."

He laid his hand over hers, and she didn't pull away as he expected. "I'm relying on you to take me back in the same cheery, healthy condition I left."

She squeezed his arm and released it. "That's my plan; you better be worth it."

The celebration fire had subsided; fewer people milled around it. Looks Back Woman walking Three Dogs to their lodge, steadying him as they limped away.

"Let's go," Keera said. The darkness brought a new dimension to the camp. Fires blazed inside tipis, the glow of the flames turning the lodges into giant lanterns. Laughter came from many of them, a low buzz from all of them as the people kicked on with their celebrations in a more private mode.

Inside the lodge, Three Dogs eased onto a bundle of hides and Looks Back Woman pulled a robe over him before lying alongside.

Three Dogs struggled upright again. "Daughter, I spoke to Red Leaf about you. How you and Slow Hand had returned from berry picking no longer the same as you ventured out."

"What did he say?" she asked.

Zach glanced at her impassive face. How much influence did the healer have over Three Dogs?

"He said if you were infected with walk-in spirits he would have to act."

"What would he do?"

"It's best to kill those troubled by this condition, but I told him I would not allow him to do this. If you have a walk-in, I will deal with it."

"By killing?"

Three Dogs lay back on his bedding. "I do not kill daughters."

The old man pulled a buffalo skin over him. He didn't mention his son-in-law. Keera turned to Zach and pointed to another pile of hides. He lay on it, and she drew more skins over him. She dragged more bedding over and lay beside him. Close enough to caress. He caught her eye before she closed hers with emphatic finality.

Zach dreamt of horses running over him, and Keera tending his wounds and kissing them better. He awoke to find himself still in the tipi. He raised his head and made out the old couple sleeping across the other side of the embers. Keera close and facing away.

He slid his hand under her hide blanket and worked it along her hip. Her breathing steady and slow. He inched towards her breast and touched warm, firm flesh—her hand.

She grabbed his and thrust it back.

"Stop it," she hissed.

Zach grunted disappointment and rolled away. Across the tipi, the old woman chuckled softly.

CHAPTER 14

Keera shook Zach awake at dawn. "Now," she whispered. He rubbed his face and sat up. She picked up a food bag and pushed through the exit flap. He followed, quieter than she had expected.

She couldn't ignore his pass of the night before. Say nothing, and it might tempt him to try again. In the wrong place, at the wrong time. She took him toward the creek. The sun glimmered over the horizon; the dew soaked her moccasins. A grand, crisp morning. One to savor, but no time to savor it.

A young guard sat on a horse near the main herd. "How goes it?" Keera addressed the teenage boy. He looked familiar, and she realized he'd been the one Red Leaf had healed. How long ago was that? She couldn't tell. It had to be weeks, in Oglala time, because the boy showed no frailty, no fever now.

He replied with studied gravity. "The horses are quiet; no enemy near." He glanced at Zach but didn't speak to him. A young boy should be tucked in bed, dreaming of mighty deeds in battle. Not staying up all night, every sense alert to a strange sound. A sound that might be the last one in his life.

"They say you'll be a fine warrior," she said. The boy's smile split his face.

"Claw warned me to be watchful," he said. "The hunters found

Crow signs yesterday."

"If they located the same herd, they have eaten their fill and be sleeping, not raiding." She sniffed the morning air; even the horses smelled good. "We're looking for cherries. We'll return before the sun is high."

"Is it normal for young kids to stand guard?" Zach asked her as they walked away.

"Definitely. The Oglala live by their courage and their readiness to die in battle. Soon, that boy will guard the horses during an armed conflict before he takes part in the real fighting." She pulled a knife in its sheath from the food bag. "Put this on, you're a warrior."

He took the weapon and tied it to his waist. "This makes me feel a lot better. Armed with a knife I wouldn't know how to use on any living thing."

The two of them skirted the creek bank until a swale hid the camp from view. Keera switched her direction to bring them away from the creek and to the rear of the camp. They walked in silence and mounted a small rise. Nothing but more grass, and more undulating country. Zach had coped better than expected. Facing off Red Leaf was an unexpected success; he was a quick thinker, like Bardo had promised. If he could repress his boyish enthusiasm for constant fun, they'd run less risk of wrecking their plan.

Still, he'd gone too far in the tipi. "What the hell were you thinking last night? In a tent full of people? In other bodies? Didn't I give you the speech about no personal displays of affection?"

"Was it the tent full of people that bothered you?"

"You're going to argue with me? Here? Now?" The guy was impossible. Her alarm, and her disappointment, must have been obvious.

"I apologize," he said, startling her with his fast backdown. "We've been through so much together, in such a short time, I felt close to you. Overstepped myself. Won't happen again."

What was this? Some ploy to get under her guard? She searched his face but found no sign, no inkling of deceit. No half-concealed smirking either. She saw nothing but genuine contrition. "Okay. As long as you know." Maybe all the scolding she had laid on him was taking effect. It better have. They stared at each other for a few seconds, but she couldn't get a stronger take on his thoughts.

He changed the subject. "The sky is amazing, isn't it? It goes all the way down to the ground. No buildings to block the view. Nothing here but earth and sky."

"I love it, too, and the clouds that warn you of an approaching storm miles away." Faint thunder sounded. Not thunder—horses. "Get down." She dropped, pulling him with her. She slid down the slope to the bottom, Zach right behind her. "Strangers. They're coming close, and they won't be Lakota. Friendlies don't arrive at dawn."

She pressed her ear to the ground. He flattened himself further into the grass. She peered through the strands. A dozen or more warriors topped the crest of the rise a hundred yards away. They remained silhouetted against the sky for an instant before they disappeared into a gully, its curve hiding them.

Keera wriggled toward the bend to get a better view, her head low enough to scrape her chin on the ground. One of the Indians gathered the reins of the horses while the rest crawled to the crest on their bellies. At the top, they paused for several minutes, their heads down, their feathers showing above the grass. Then, like a family of oversized, scuttling lizards, they disappeared down the other side.

Zach sidled up next to her. "Shouldn't we be crawling the other way?"

"We have a problem," she whispered.

"I can see that," he whispered back. "Let's crawl away and run."

"We can't. It's a Crow raiding party after the horses. We have to stop them."

"Stop them? How? We're two city slickers, and they're armed killers."

"The horses are too important to us to lose. We have to warn everybody."

"It's too late. The raiders will be in amongst them in a minute," Zach said.

"You're right. You have a knife—get it out. We'll charge the horse minder, screaming. That'll wake everybody." She started to her feet.

"Wait!" Zach grabbed her arm and forced her down again. "I've never wielded a knife in my life. And I'm against killing."

"It'll happen this way. We charge towards the guy screaming and yelling. The Oglala guys jump up out of bed screaming and yelling, too, because they think they are under attack. The Crow will assume they have fallen into an ambush and flee."

"Yeah, back toward us."

"They won't know you're a pacifist, Zach. They'll do their best to stay out of your way. Ready?"

"I'll never be ready for killing."

"You have a knife. That man over there doesn't know you won't use it. And, as we'll be making a lot of noise instead of sneaking up on him, he'll guess more of us are coming. He'll take off. Only a fool takes on overwhelming odds." Zach stayed still. They had only a couple of minutes to stop the raid, and if he didn't move, she would have to charge the guard alone. A guard wouldn't be worried if he saw a single woman running at him. Zach had to join her.

He said, "Can't I just slap him like you said before?"

"This is not a time to count coup; you don't have the skills or the moves to get away with it. Just make a hellish racket and the entire camp will be at your side in minutes."

"Minutes!"

She rounded on him, thumping his shoulder with an open palm. "You've no choice. If you stay here, the Crow may find you on their way back and scalp you. That's if the horse herd doesn't trample you. We have the element of surprise; we can do it."

"Dammit. It's not our fight."

"It is now." She jumped to her feet, raised her hand in the air —shocked that she gripped a knife already—and shrilled *"Hoka Hey!"* The keening scream split the silence. She ran along the gully towards the guard.

"You're crazy," Zach yelled, but she heard him scrambling after her. He had committed. Whew. He yelled again, a piercing, whooping sound, and answering whoops came from the camp. With Slow Hand's short legs pumping like crazy, Zach closed the distance between them.

Ahead, the guard dropped the reins and lifted a bow from a horse. Zach passed her, his feet thudding into the ground. The distance between him and the guard only twenty yards when the Crow fitted an arrow to his bow and drew it taut.

Zach flung his knife at him, but the warrior sidestepped it with unmistakable contempt, and the knife struck a horse's head. The animal reared, and skittled sideways. The animal crashed into the guard, jarring the arrow launch off course, straight into the ground.

Undeterred, like he was used to calamities on the battle field, the Crow dropped his bow and tugged at his knife. Zach five steps away and coming at him, an enraged buffalo with speed and fury. He let loose another whoop and, a second before impact, turned his shoulder into the warrior's chest. Knocked off his feet, the guard landed on his back, arched his spine in desperation, his lungs begging for oxygen. Zach stood over him, his fist clenched, chest heaving.

Keera caught up. The Crow twisted on the ground clutching his chest, only seconds away from recovering his wind. Rain Bird would have plunged her knife into him, but Keera couldn't. Her earlier certainties evaporated at this moment.

Arms brushed them aside; an Oglala bent over the fallen guard, raised a war club and smashed in the Crow's forehead.

Crazy Elk greeted Zach with a grimace. "You acted like a warrior, Slow Hand, but if you want to be an old warrior, you must finish off."

Zach didn't answer, transfixed by the crushed face on the ground.

"It's your scalp, Slow Hand." He shook his head.

The Oglala knelt over the body and drew his knife. Working with quick precision, he scored a line around the top of the Crow's head. He grasped the hair and ripped off the scalp with a sucking, tearing sound that Keera would never forget for the rest of her life. "*Aaaieeeh!*" Crazy Elk cried, thrusting the matted hair and flesh into the sky.

She fought the gagging in her throat. Crazy Elk looked Zach over, gave her a slightly longer inspection, and darted back toward the camp. Warm vapors rose from the scalped head, evaporating in the cold morning air.

She placed a hand at the small of Zach's back. "Are you okay?" He'd been scared, had wanted to run, but had followed her to protect her. There would have been no internal Slow Hand urging him on. His decision was a Zach decision.

"Yeah, I'm fine," he replied, turning to her, his chest still heaving. "I've helped Crazy Elk smash a man's head open and scalp him. I feel great."

Several more Oglala warriors came over the crest and ran up to the fallen Crow. They lashed the body with their bows.

"The hell they doing that for?" he snapped.

"They're counting coup," she said. "As you were the first to strike the enemy, you get the first coup. You're entitled now to wear a golden eagle feather."

"Jesus, that makes me feel complete." He kept staring at the dead, hairless body, but she pulled him away.

"It's better if you don't look. Let's get out of here. Where did you learn to knock a man down like that?"

"Football," he grunted.

More warriors joined the first group, grabbed the Crow ponies, and ran them back to the camp.

Zach and Keera topped the rise to an appalling vista. Several warriors were locked in combat, struggling and twisting on the ground in front of the horse herd. Other Crow were astride ponies and urging them forward with screams and slaps.

One Oglala darted towards the rearmost Crow and delivered a crunching blow to his spine. The wet thud of stone against bone and the warrior slipped from the pony and disappeared into the melee. Keera slid her hand into Zach's, gripped it like an emergency escape handle. A horror scene in front of them. There was no escaping it.

The herd now disintegrated; the horses cannoned wildly into one another before racing for open spaces. Crow braves, all hands and heels, forced captured Oglala ponies into a sprint for safety. One Oglala appeared in the clearing. He notched an arrow into his bow and let it fly. The arrow slammed into a Crow's throat. His hands flew up, scrabbling at the shaft, and he tumbled off his horse backward.

Zach and Keera watched, frozen in place. Watched the warrior's grip on the arrow shaft falter and the hands fall away. Watched the blood run rivulets across the throat and into the grass until his heart stopped pumping it out. She gripped Zach's hand tighter.

More Oglala running from tipis. A volley of arrows followed the first, but the excited arrows never found a target. Most of the

Crow were already a hundred yards away and riding for their lives. The group wrestling separated; two Crow pulled free and ran for horses, any horses.

They found Red Leaf instead.

He held an iron-bladed tomahawk out from his side and waited for the right instant to move. As the first warrior closed in, Red Leaf sprang forward. The tomahawk slashed down and across, and split his opponent's face into diagonal sections. The Crow dropped sightless to his knees. Red Leaf swung again, the blade bit into the skull like it was a sapling trunk.

The second Crow threw himself at Red Leaf with a hoarse yell. The tomahawk rose in the air again, and the blade sank into the Crow's chest with the force of a pile driver. The smell of blood and raw human flesh caught at Keera's throat.

She closed her eyes and waited for the killing to end.

CHAPTER 15

Keera tugged at Zach's hand. Women were kneeling over a small body a short distance away.

"They're not mutilating another Crow, I hope," Zach growled.

No, Zach. It's worse, much worse. A sobbing wail carried to them, a group of women around a child. The young herd guard, his head mutilated in black and red. Healed, then killed. Who could figure out God's plan?

"Oh, Jesus," Zach said. "That kid. The bastards scalped a little kid."

The women, still wailing, picked up the body and shuffled with their wrenching burden into the camp interior.

"What kind of hell is this?" Zach demanded of her. "Noble, courageous warriors murder a child?" He pulled his hand away from hers.

The boy she'd seen healed back to life, rubbed out in seconds, and sent on to the next one. She'd explain it to Zach once she figured it out for herself. "They wouldn't want to," she replied, "but if he appeared dangerous, they wouldn't hesitate. He would have been proud to kill a Crow. It's hard to judge if we're not them." She scanned the area. No more bodies on the ground. Two warriors limped past, one grinning despite the streaks of dried blood on his shoulder.

"Final score: five Crow dead, one Oglala child mutilated," Zach said. "That must count as a successful day."

She said nothing, hoping his bitterness would drain away. He would need years to understand the nature of life here, and she was tired of lecturing.

"Why are we helping these people?" he asked. "If somebody tried to swipe my car I'd yell, push maybe, throw stuff at them. I wouldn't slice them open with an ax."

"You might kill if the ownership of a car meant the difference between living and starving. Anyway, there'll be more killing now."

"Why?"

"The Oglala will want revenge. A war party will form."

"How soon?"

She looked away. "The men will talk about it already, but they won't move until they find the Crow camp. That'll take days, if not weeks."

"And we'll be out of here by then, you mean." It was a mistake not to answer him promptly.

"What are you thinking?" Zach's voice rose. "I had a clear understanding that we tarry not a short second longer than we need to. Right?" He moved around her until she lifted her eyes to his. "You're not delaying our departure just because you find it exhilarating to be living this life?"

"It's difficult for me." How to explain to a guy who dealt in the here and now. "I may never come back again. So much to take in and we're here for such a short time."

"A short time. That's exactly right. That's what I was promised. That's why I'm here. A short time, the crucial part of the contract as far as I'm concerned." He stared at her, demanding a response. She refused to oblige him. "Here I am," he continued, "wondering, wondering how is it possible to be in somebody else's skin and bones. Also wondering how long before I wake up in an institution wrapped up in a tight white jacket. I was just getting used to this nightmare, and now I find there are more nightmares inside the first one."

She couldn't think of a suitable response; he was right on every level. It was a marvel he'd hung in there so far without cracking up. Since his first minutes of panic when he arrived at the camp, Zach had performed beyond expectations. Sure, his joking around was wearying, but he understood what was expected, and he stayed supportive. More than that. She could have caused the death of Rain Bird by acting instinctively, but he stepped in and saved the moment. "You've done well. Incredibly well, for someone who had no idea what was in store. I heard you were adaptive, but I didn't listen. I was wrong."

He ignored her conciliatory words. "While I stagger about, wanting to be home again, you're reveling in this experience. You're loving it."

He was right again. Immersed in the biggest event of her life, how could it be wrong to extend it as much as possible? But Bardo said two nights only. They were to return by the end of tomorrow. Wishing wasn't the same as getting. Never was.

She said heavily, "We're delayed, that's all. We'll try tonight."

He didn't continue, but he didn't believe her, she knew.

The chase party returned, Crazy Elk at the front. He dismounted with a flourish of a man on an exhilarating high. "The Crow won't stop riding for many moons," he announced to the group who responded with laughter and whoops.

He placed a hand on Zach's shoulder. "This one was the bravest of us all." More warriors gathered. "He refused his weapon and knocked the guard down with his shoulder."

How did Crazy Elk know that? Did he follow them from the camp?

"He showed his contempt by refusing to even use his hands," Crazy Elk added. More laughter from the group. All of them still charged up from the battle.

"He should change his name," somebody shouted. "We should rename him Fast With Shoulder." Much laughter.

Crazy Elk held up his hand. "Slow Hand will ride with the war party." A general nodding of heads. "We shall avenge the death of Little Bear, rub out many Crow and take their horses. They will not be far. We find them tomorrow. Slow Hand." Crazy Elk lifted his hand from Zach's shoulder and replaced it again. "Slow Hand has found good medicine. It made him a warrior and gave him speech. We thank Great Spirit for looking after our brother."

"Such unusual medicine," said a voice in the crowd. Red Leaf strode forward, the men parting in front of him. "Slow Hand has gained the mind of a warrior just by dreaming. His body has become a warrior's as well. All of us are stronger with our brother fighting alongside."

The men whooped and cheered as if Red Leaf had announced another nation was joining them. Crazy Elk clapped Zach's shoulder once again before heading for the center of the camp. A large fire already constructed and flickering. Chattering warriors surrounded it.

"Funny thing," Zach said, as the two of them walked back to their lodge. "I feel so bad about the kid, such a pointless killing, but I feel very vengeful towards the Crow. They're enemy and not people."

"The longer you stay in that body, the more you'll become like a real Oglala."

"I'd like that. So many wonderful things here. The dishes created from family pets, the rustic garments, the choice of one hairstyle, the spacious lodgings, the do-it-yourself hot water systems, not to mention the killings and the fear of starvation if no buffalo turn up. Hmm, yep, I could settle down here."

"Notice something, Zach? They don't kill animals for pleasure or profit. Everything in it, they believe, has been created by the Great Spirit for all to share. The people, the animals, the trees, the rocks even. You believe this lifestyle is worse than yours? Have a deeper think." She stopped before her words became counterproductive. Some people were blind to what was in front of them.

"Yeah, well," he said, then changed the subject. "Why is Crazy Elk so happy for me to become a warrior? I assumed he'd be jealous of the time I spend with you."

Keera watched the warriors swapping battle stories around the central fire before replying. "If you're now one of them, you don't need me to look after you. Crazy Elk can approach me for marriage without taking on the burden of an extra and useless mouth to feed."

"Or maybe he's hoping I will get killed in battle."

"No. No chance of that."

"Look at the facts, ma'am," Zach said. "Novice warrior goes into battle, can't tell his ass from his elbow. The guy collects a stray arrow from his own side. Body brought back to camp with much sorrow. End of the rival for Rain Bird's attention."

She swung back to him. "Don't believe that of Crazy Elk. He's a warrior and generous. Of course, jealousy is a big part of O-glala life, like anywhere. But Crazy Elk wouldn't do a dishonorable thing. No Oglala would allow one of their tribe to kill their own."

"Sure, but he might be hoping."

"Impossible, these people bond in concrete. Lose that thought." Zach had a long way to go before he became Oglala.

They entered their lodge. Looks Back Woman and Three Dogs were waiting.

"Your bravery is the talk of the camp," Three Dogs said to Zach. "It is strange you could knock down a Crow like that. You never even wrestled with other boys when you were young."

"Something came over me," Zach said. "I had no control."

Three Dogs nodded. "The Great Spirit works in strange ways when he wants a life spared. Maybe you should prepare yourself for this coming fight. A sign may show itself to guide you and keep you from harm."

"I hope so."

"You have no experience of taking scalps, but if the Great Spirit wills it, you will gain your first one." He leaned forward with a serious face. "You must cut evenly around the bone of the head and pull strongly."

Keera fought down the rising bile in her throat.

"I shall follow your instructions," Zach said. "But first I must rest. This fighting business is new to me. I have to dream on it."

He crawled to his pile of bedding and lay down. Keera covered him in more skins and, as his eyes closed, she slipped out of the tipi.

CHAPTER 16

Outside the lodge, she found Red Leaf waiting for her. An immovable brown boulder. This would not be a passing conversation.

"Slow Hand learned how we fight together today," he said.

"He is gaining confidence," she replied. "His becoming a warrior changed his outlook on life."

"You were far from the camp when you saw the Crow approach. You were not frightened?"

Red Leaf wasn't wasting time with chitchat. He wanted answers. "We didn't plan to go so far."

Red Leaf searched her face. "Perhaps you both needed privacy."

Was that all he wanted to know? If they were fooling around or not? "As I'm still in mourning, I cannot go with another."

"It's not unknown for a woman to seek solace during this time." At least he didn't smirk when he came out with this.

"You think that after my marriage to Eagle Chaser, I'd be satisfied with Slow Hand?" Sorry, Slow Hand.

"Perhaps your mating instincts overcame your pride?"

"Perhaps you're quick to see what isn't there."

Red Leaf took this in without anger. Then he delivered the bad news. "Your husband has been in the land of many tipis for plenty moons. The mourning is over." He pivoted on his heel and walked away.

"But I think of Eagle Chaser every day," she cried after him, but he didn't turn back. His pronouncement cleared the way for Crazy Elk to press her father for her marriage. No one else had made advances. None dared cross him. Would Rain Bird agree to the marriage? No matter. The widow would need to wait until she possessed her own body. There would be no proposal acceptance by proxy. It was all too weird.

Keera reached the perimeter of the camp and stopped. What now? She asked Bardo.

You've made good progress. Trust in yourself.

Everything is more complex than I expected, she said.

Act soon, and leave.

I'd like to stay forever. Months, at least.

You are not on a study trip.

But I'll learn so much. It's an incredible experience.

You've learned enough.

But I can add priceless firsthand information to our knowledge of these times.

Could you explain how you came by it?

She couldn't. She'd be laughed out of her career, credibility gone. Damn. Double damn. Keera thought of her other pressing matter. Will Zach stay the course?

He will not willingly leave your side.

The unexpected glow within her was a surprise. Sure, he was easy to look at. Not controlling, fun, in an irritating sort of way. But not her type. Too superficial.

The two of you have a strong bond.

I hadn't noticed.

He trusted you and woke up in the body of another. When he was scared, you calmed him. He is gaining control of his situation which helps you. He is not a lapdog, he is not a servant. Work with what you have, and you know have someone special.

Yeah, well. How do I avoid this marriage to Crazy Elk?

I'll repeat. Act soon, and leave.

Thanks a bunch. I was hoping for more detail. Suggestions even.

The task is yours, not mine. You must take the lead. How you resolve the issues will affect your future.

Bardo was clamming up. She recognized the signs. He would deflect any more questions, his way of saying that she knew what to do next. Let's hope so.

As she neared her father's lodge, women gazed at her with new curiosity. The few men that passed her found other, more interesting things to look at. The word was out—she was Crazy Elk's woman now. She hoped Rain Bird felt the same. Flinging aside the entrance flap, she stooped and entered.

"Ah, Rain Bird," Three Dogs greeted her. "Crazy Elk has waited for you."

Crazy Elk sat next to Three Dogs, and expelled a stream of tobacco smoke from her father's pipe. Zach still slept on the other side of the lodge.

"Sit with us, daughter," Three Dogs motioned with his hand. "Crazy Elk has offered me five of his best horses for you."

No, no, not already. Frustration welled, making her snap back. "Five horses? That's not much for a widow of the finest warrior this band has seen since you were a boy."

Crazy Elk flushed with anger. "You speak like a man looking for a battle," he said, stabbing a finger in her direction.

"I speak like a person who reflects the truth," she replied. "A brave man does not fight it."

"That's true," he acknowledged, "and I don't avoid the truth. I never run. I'm afraid of nothing. The widow of the bravest warrior we once knew deserves to be married to the bravest warrior now."

Ignore the boasting, she reminded herself. It's normal for Oglala, keeps their morale high.

"Crazy Elk speaks wisely," Three Dogs said.

Crazy Elk was the perfect match for Rain Bird, and the whole camp agreed. It didn't matter. She couldn't make a promise that bound Rain Bird. "I cannot enter a new union while I still dream of my husband."

"Red Leaf proclaimed your mourning period over," Crazy Elk said, with triumphant finality.

"What a man says is not what a woman feels," she shot back.

"What a woman feels isn't as important as an elder declares."

Keera flared with anger herself. The nerve of the guy. "Do you wish to marry a woman who spends all her dream hours seeing the man she lost? When she cries out a name as you are taking her, do you want to hear another's?" She leaned forward. "Do you wish to wake in the morning and wonder if the sharpness in your stomach is hunger or her knife?"

Before she finished speaking a rush of energy rose in her—a spirit coming in. Rain Bird reclaiming her body. No, no. Not now. Especially not now.

Do not reject him. Rain Bird's voice clear and firm. Not frightened.

I can't accept him while I have your body, Keera replied. You know he can take me to his tipi immediately. The energy surged, and she fought to lower it.

I want him for my husband. Do not reject him. He has to propose to the real you, not a false version of you. At this moment, he sees my nature, not yours. Tomorrow will be different.

Three Dogs grunted with ill-concealed glee as he tapped the remains of the burnt tobacco into the fire. "Rain Bird has discovered a new way of seeing things, Crazy Elk."

The warrior's chest was rising and falling. No women ever spoke to him like this, she was sure of it. He took several minutes to calm himself. "Rain Bird, you're the best woman in the camp—"

"The best woman! Am I a dog, or a horse to be ranked in this way?" Within her, the energy surged again as Rain Bird struggled to reclaim her body.

He turned in bewilderment to Three Dogs who concentrated on refilling the pipe. He tried another approach. "I didn't mean you were a dog or a horse. You skin buffalo, and you cook and you—"

"Cook!" She erupted again. "Your mother can cook! Why don't you stay with her if you want good cooking?" He stared back in confusion. "Because she's not a wife. Rain Bird, why do you say strange things?"

Let me be. I wish to speak. You've no permission for this. I agreed only to help you. I didn't agree to lose another husband.

Keera struggled to stay in control. You'll have your husband, just not today. I need more time. I cannot be hampered by someone who will control my movements. A series of sharp pops erupted in her ear. Rain Bird venting.

The woman's anger brought home to Keera how careless she had been with Crazy Elk. Her words couldn't fail to alienate him if she continued this way. She had allowed her emotions to ride over a sensitive situation and jeopardized Rain Bird's marriage hopes. Time to backtrack.

"I speak strangely because I feel strange," Keera said to Crazy Elk. "The past few days have been wearing." She waited for Rain Bird to butt in again but her energy presence had waned.

He relaxed. "Three Dogs? I offer five horses. Is it not enough? I can give a soldier's jacket. With metal buttons."

Three Dogs said, "I have to smoke on this. So many things to think of before I can answer."

"It's unusual to consider if a woman needs a husband to hunt for her." Crazy Elk knitted his brow. "All females need a husband."

And all males need wives, even uppity ones like Rain Bird, it seemed.

Three Dogs drew smoke deep into his lungs. "These are unusual times. Rain Bird is not the same as she was before. She's been a good daughter, and I want the best life for her."

"Red Leaf has ended the mourning, and I want her. I'm the bravest in the camp, and I give horses." Crazy Elk shifted his legs, getting restive.

A new voice broke in. "I'll give you much more for Rain Bird." The three of them swiveled to Zach, who pushed himself upright. Keera speared horrified eyes at him, but he crawled over to them and seated himself opposite Three Dogs.

"I wish to marry Rain Bird," he said. "I will give you more than anybody."

CHAPTER 17

Keera watched Zach settle opposite Three Dogs, her hands gripping each other tightly. Had he gone mad? Was this some stupid joke?

Crazy Elk laughed at him. "What do you offer, Slow Hand? You've only one horse, and that came from me. You never even stole it for yourself."

"Three Dogs, I can tell you the future," Zach said.

She groaned. Please shut up. He didn't look at her.

"How can you do this?" Three Dogs asked.

"As you've seen, I've become different these past few days."

Crazy Elk snorted. "The whole camp talks of it."

"There is a reason." Zach ignored Crazy Elk. "I've had a dream. I dreamt of the Crow arriving and their defeat. I dreamt of our warriors taking revenge, and of other things that will help you. I can tell you of the *wasichu* coming in great numbers to take our land."

She wanted to knock him unconscious. Both men regarded Zach with increased interest.

"The dreams commanded me to rise and take my place with other warriors, not to spend my time playing as a child."

"Dreams are powerful, Slow Hand," Three Dogs said, "and you

must follow them."

Crazy Elk grunted in disgust. "My offer of five horses and a soldier's jacket is a good one, Three Dogs. His offer may be as permanent as a fresh wind. What do you say?"

"Slow Hand brings something new. I'll have answer when I've thought on it."

Crazy Elk pushed brusquely out of the tipi, the flap slapping back. She fixed her gaze on Zach, willing him to stop his nonsense. He still refused to look at her. The three of them sat quietly around the fire. Even him. Maybe he was done for the day.

"What else did you dream of, Slow Hand?" asked Three Dogs.

"All of the dreams will be revealed in full at the right time, Three Dogs. So much to tell, too much for one person to remember."

How much worse could he make it? Was he thinking of making a speech to the whole camp?

"Is it true the *wasichu* will come in great numbers?" Three Dogs asked.

"As the night follows the day. More *wasichu* than water drops in a creek."

If Zach had a plan, she couldn't see it. The cheesy nonsense he was sprouting would only make it harder for them to move freely.

"We'll beat them like we beat the Crow, the Shoshone, and the Pawnee." Three Dogs airily dismissed Zach's warnings. "They are poor hunters and poor riders."

"They have mighty weapons," Zach said.

"I've seen their fire sticks. True, they hit a target from a long way, but they also take much time to shoot again. Our warriors can unload a quiver full of arrows between their firings."

"Soon, they'll make better weapons, ones that fire as fast as ten men."

Three Dogs pondered. "Why will they come here?" he asked after a while. "They eat little buffalo. Red Leaf told me they prefer the stinking meat they call bacon. And they drink their mysterious water, which makes them fall over. What is here for them?"

"The yellow metal in the Sacred Hills. It's precious to them."

"The yellow metal? I've seen it." Three Dogs sneered. "It's worthless. Much too soft for an ax head or a knife, and too heavy to fashion into containers. And it's not bright and pleasing like shells or the beads we trade for."

"They'll also come for the buffalo."

"Have you seen the work of their buffalo hunters?" Three Dogs' eyes widened. "They take the tongue and the hide, but leave the meat to rot. Is there so much food in their world they can dump most of it for the insects?"

Zach pressed on. "Soon, the hunters will take more hides. A great iron horse will enter the buffalo grounds and men will shoot buffalo from inside it. Just for fun, not for meat or hides."

Three Dogs nodded. "I've dreamt of this iron horse. So have others in this camp. Strange to us. Shiny black, releasing a smoke signal as it passed and pulling many boxes on wheels. It was strong, but it ran only in long straight lines, on metal logs. It couldn't chase a dodging animal."

"It won't need to. The buffalo are many and easy to shoot. More and more *wasichu* will come. By the time the last child in this camp dies of old age, the buffalo will have vanished."

"Vanished?" His voice broke with disbelief. "It cannot be. Some days, I've stood on a hill and couldn't see the grass for the buffalo. In every direction, buffalo all the way to the horizon." Three Dogs drew on his pipe and sat without speaking for many minutes. "What people are these?" he said finally. "What people destroy the buffalo, the thing they need to live on?" A breeze billowed the tipi walls. Three Dogs' scalp collection swayed from its pole.

Keera remained still; her hands clasped in her lap. If word got out that Slow Hand had future visions, he'd have everybody following him day and night. Good work, Zach.

Zach said, "They do not consider their children's future, they think of money. *Wasichu* want money, and plenty of it will come for buffalo hides."

"I've seen this money. There's a picture of the White Father on it. It's decorative and good to wear, but you cannot eat it."

"I'm sorry to tell you this, but even our own people will kill buffalo for trade, for guns, for metal."

Three Dogs sucked on his pipe again before speaking. "Slow Hand, you know we Lakota are many. This camp is just one small band of the Oglala. We have many such bands. The seven tribes of Lakota: Oglala, Sicangu, Miniconjous, Hunkpapa, Sihasapa, Itazipacola, Oohenupa; they can hold as one. Together, we'll destroy our enemies when they come. A pity, for they make valuable items to trade."

Zach shook his head. "Even if all the Lakota joined together, they would be as seven birds with broken wings fighting a hundred wolves."

Three Dogs knocked the ashes out of his pipe. "What you say is hard to hear. Yet, it came as a dream, and we all know dreams are powerful. I have to listen and take notice." He picked up his stick and struggled upright. Keera stood to help him. "I have to walk and think. I pray for guidance." He pushed aside the flap and shuffled out.

Keera waited for Three Dogs' footsteps to fade away before she unleashed her pent-up fury on Zach. "What in holy hell are you doing?"

"Helping you get out of marrying Crazy Elk for a start," he said.

"I was handling that myself, thank you."

"You were not. You were giving them a feminist rant—getting two hundred years ahead of yourself."

He was right. She had slipped out of Rain Bird's character and back into her own without thinking. Wouldn't happen again. She couldn't be responsible for Rain Bird losing her chance of a husband. "Okay, I forgot myself."

But Zach hadn't finished. "I don't see them treating their women badly. They're only normally sexist—"

"Only normally sexist?"

"Okay, okay. Wrong choice of words." He waved a hand from side to side as if wiping away his words. "Our mission isn't to bring twenty-first-century enlightenment to these people, is it? The idea is to stay focused on the Stone."

"Exactly, and the plan was for you to shut up while we waited for dark."

"I couldn't. If Three Dogs agreed to the marriage, you could have walked out of here by now. With Crazy Elk. The plan in tatters."

He was right again. He had seen the same mission-wrecking possibility she had. And acted on it. No faulting him for that. Still, there was another issue. "Why did you tell them their future?" she asked. "That's messing with them in a big way."

"Is it? Don't psychics tell the future every day?"

"That's different."

"It's the same. They tell the future, and the world doesn't get weirded out. People carry on like always. I know what Three Dogs will do. He'll try to get his head around what I've said because he feels he should believe a dream. You told me yourself the Oglala put great stock in them. But it's too much to take in. He'll decide I've misinterpreted what I saw, and he will come up with something that makes him feel comfortable. That's not Oglala nature—that's human nature."

"You're so sure of this."

"The truth is too much for Three Dogs to believe. I can tell him everything, and none of it will help these people. Nothing will happen. The time frame is too long for anyone to take in. Three Dogs can reveal my dream to everybody, but they'll regard it as interesting, frightening maybe, but irrelevant to their needs here and now. Anyway, he won't want to spook his people." He settled back on his elbows. "I thought it was a master stroke myself, bidding for your hand. Don't you agree?"

She stabbed at burning chips with a stick. "We don't need Crazy Elk to regard you as more of a rival than before. He'll watch us even more closely." She looked up at him. "We have another problem. Rain Bird's spirit is struggling within. She wants her body back, wants to marry Crazy Elk now."

He sat up again. "Really? Jeez, that could cause trouble. I haven't felt a peep out of Slow Hand."

"He's watching and learning. He's a reactive guy. Also prefers to avoid any conflict if he can."

Zach said, "This plan to steal the Stone, I have issues."

Great. I can't wait to hear them. "Tell me."

"The Stone can't be easily taken. Red Leaf carries it around most of the time, except to sleep, you say."

"So?"

"To get it off him, somebody has to kill him, and I don't know about you, but after seeing him fight, I'm not volunteering for the job. Not to mention ethical problems I have with killing."

"Who said anything about killing?" she said. "When he's asleep, you sneak into his tipi and snatch it. I'll keep a lookout."

"Sneak past that guy? If he woke up, he'd disembowel me quicker than I could say 'sorry, wrong tipi.'"

"For God's sake, Zach. He's an old man asleep. The Stone will be in a bag, hanging off a pole. You take it, we leave. We ride out, follow the creek to an obvious bend, we bury the Stone near a tree and mark the trunk. We then go home."

"None of that plan I like except the bit about going home. Not crazy about me sneaking in, either."

"You're right. I'll sneak in. It's sexist to think that sneaking is a man's job. You can help by rolling up the sides of the tipi and keeping watch."

Zach back-pedaled, trying to settle her down. "Maybe a better way ..."

"A better way? I can't think of it," she said. "We have to move tonight. It's a full moon. Red Leaf has fought in battle and he'll be exhausted. You coming, or not?"

"Can't we think on this for a while?"

"No." She slammed a fist on her knee. "I'm trying tonight, with or without you." His motivation was flagging, and she understood why: he didn't understand the whole of the mission.

"Look," she said. "The Stone is more than a medical marvel—it's a talisman. If we can take it back to the future, and it continues to heal, it'll become a focal point for all Lakota."

"They'll worship it?"

"No, they'll revere its power, and that alone will bring them strength and pride and the energy they need."

"Wonderful, but why us?"

"Because we were chosen." Before he could roll his eyes, she hurried to explain. "Any Oglala would be too sensitive to handle this. We *wasichu* have to do it." He remained silent as he digested this. "You owe them something,' she said, adding a little pressure. "Crazy Elk saved Slow Hand's life, which you put in danger."

"Hey, no fair. I was trying to look after you."

"Good intentions don't always have the right outcomes. Let's complete what we set out to do, and you'll feel a warm glow for the rest of your days." He digested this as well. "And, you'll have one hell of a story."

Zach surrendered. "Okay, I'll come, I'll come."

The lodge flap opened. Three Dogs stepped in. "Rain Bird," he said. "Your marriage. I have thought on it. The vision of the future that Slow Hand brings isn't just for me, it's for all of us.

Therefore, I have accepted Crazy Elk's offer. You'll marry in the morning."

CHAPTER 18

Keera, Rain Bird, to marry tomorrow? A snake crawled up Zach's stomach and jammed itself into his chest. Not Slow Hand trying to get out, but jealousy. Plain, simple, savage jealousy. Keera, another man, together? No way.

"When will the marriage ceremony be held?" He asked Three Dogs. Maybe he could object when the moment came.

"Rain Bird goes to Crazy Elk tomorrow, in the usual way, dressed in her finest skins, and she'll stay in his tipi as his wife." He turned to her. "Do you have something to say? When Crazy Elk was here, you spoke plenty."

"The decision is yours, Father," she replied, her face giving nothing away. "You always choose wisely for your family and your people."

"Don't worry, Slow Hand," added Looks Back Woman, who entered behind Three Dogs. "We'll care for you."

"The man needs less looking after than before," Three Dogs said. "He's thinking of a wife, and we have several prospects ready."

Keera didn't look put out to be marrying, in fact, she looked quite pleased. Hell. Might even look forward to a night with Crazy Elk. Then he remembered. This was their last night. Three Dogs' decision didn't matter; it was irrelevant. His heart lifted, an eagle finding an updraft. Still, the way Keera had accepted her father's decision without protest, that was biting.

"Yes, it's time to find a wife," he told Three Dogs. "If I cannot have Rain Bird, then I must look elsewhere. Someone younger perhaps." Keera's frozen eyes warned him off the topic, but he ignored her. "Tell me which of the young ones would be suitable. I have little knowledge of these things."

"Crying Wind is an excellent choice," said Looks Back Woman. "Seventeen summers—old for a first wife, but she's strong and makes good jerky."

He stroked his chin, suppressing a ribald laugh. "A perfect companion." He glanced in Keera's direction and wished he hadn't. Her face glowed with enough fury to force a grizzly back.

Three Dogs creaked and settled in his favorite place. "Dim the fire, we sleep. Tomorrow Rain Bird gets a new husband." Looks Back Woman separated smoldering buffalo chips, and smoke billowed before escaping through the tipi's top vent.

The parents lay down at the back, opposite the entrance, while he crawled to his previous bed. Keera joined him, her face hard as a battle-ax, and she lay with her back to him. Her taut body shrieked a message—don't touch me!

The fire was still radiating a faint heat when a poke in his ribs roused him from sleep. Keera crouched over him. She jerked her head at the entrance and crawled toward it. He followed, blinking to clear his eyes. Once through the flap, he stood and stretched. She put a finger to her lips and walked away.

She guided him out of the camp, steering wide of the horse herd this time. He increased his pace and caught up with her. Tried to catch her eye, but she made with the finger again and gestured to continue forward. The tipis disappeared behind them as they climbed a small crest and down the other side. The night was quiet enough to hear the silence breathing and the stars squeaking past overhead.

At the bottom, she stopped and faced him. Drew her hand back and cracked him across the face with an open palm. He stumbled backward from the blow, his cheek hot and stinging.

"Wha—?" He took another step back as she raised her hand again.

"That's for thinking of having sex with one of these girls." Her face dark and intense.

"I was only joking." He pressed cool knuckles to his cheek.

"That's why I hit you only once."

"Jesus, Keera. You're such a piece of work. Crying Wind wasn't underage or anything like that."

"You do not touch any Oglala girls. Got it? Or do I have to explain with a blackboard and chalk?"

He ripped up cool, damp grass and held it to his cheek. Keera's ability to swerve violently from being a Nordic ice maiden to a fiery Latino type was unnerving. "I was peeved at the idea of you marrying Crazy Elk and liking it, that's all. A bit jealous, even."

"And I was maintaining our cover, you ape, while you acted as dumb as the schoolboy you are, and nearly made me act out of character."

"So you felt a teensy weensy bit jealous, then?"

Her face darkened further. "What do you think is going on here? Are you taking this to be some holiday jaunt now, with a touch of romance? Well, you can tear that idea right out of your mind. We're here for one reason only, and that is to retrieve the Stone. Whatever it takes."

"Yeah? You sure got steamed at the thought of me with a young wife."

"Because we don't need that kind of complication. Don't mistake it for jealousy. It doesn't exist."

They stood there, in the prairie, in the night, glaring at each other, both hearts pulsing in anger. He didn't believe her entirely, but understood she'd stand firm against any move on his part to forge a closer bond. At the moment. For the sake of the mission, she was implying. So, what was she implying when she gripped his hand during the battle? Such a female thing: to hold two contradictory ideas simultaneously.

Keera said, "I'm sorry I hit you so hard." Then she touched his flaming cheek. "I keep forgetting how much I've put you through."

What?

"I've no right to expect you to cope with everything. It's difficult enough for me, it must be overwhelming for you."

"You're not angry anymore?" She tilted her chin toward the top of the hill. "We have a job to do, the trickiest part. Let's refocus."

Refocus. Like he was so in the let's-be-quiet-and-sneak-up mood. Good thing she only wanted the impossible from him.

She pulled his knife and pouch out of her belt and handed them over. He'd forgotten to bring them. Such a warrior. She tramped back to the top of the crest, and he scrambled after her, his cheek still burning.

"Red Leaf's tipi is the second from the right," she said. "He has no dogs, he's known to sense intruders without them."

"What makes you think he won't hear us, then?"

"There is no choice. We have to try. Red Leaf will be sleeping close to this side of the tipi, away from the fire. If we undo the straps that hold the sides and roll up the hide, I can wriggle through and grab the bag."

Clouds passed in front of the moon, darkening their surroundings. Tension worked into his neck and shoulders, welding them into one semi-rigid unit. No dogs barked. As many dogs as people in the camp, but none of them stirred. Maybe they ignored familiar footsteps.

Twenty yards out, Keera slowed and placed her feet with care.

Avoiding twigs, he guessed, and did the same. The air grew thicker, grabbing at his throat. She knelt at the rear of the tipi, motioned him to join her. She pointed to the straps, and he pulled on them gently. She located the adjoining set and worked on it. Constant winds blowing against the hides had pulled the straps tighter, making their task harder. Each finger scraping on the hide seemed louder than a shouted warning.

His straps came free, and he looked over at Keera, who waited. She made rolling motions with her fingers, and they both took up the edge of the hide and rolled it up to ankle height. A mix of burnt wood and herby aromas rushed out with the warm air. She propped up the hide with a twig.

They flattened themselves and stared inside the tipi, like two starving prairie dogs. The fire still glowed near the entrance, Red Leaf's head only inches away, his chest barely moving. A medicine bag hung from a slanted pole above his head. Zach nudged her arm and pointed. Keera nodded, and her lips parted in anticipation. The deerskin bag close enough to snatch. Straps tied it to the pole, but it didn't matter. Easy to take the Stone and leave the bag; give them more minutes to escape. Precious minutes.

She reached out, but he stopped her. His honor; he'd done the harder yards, taken the bigger knocks. He shifted a few inches closer and stretched for the bag. Shallow breathing as his fingers slid along the beadwork to the flap. There was no fastening, and his fingers wormed their way inside toward the stone. Below the bag, Red Leaf's face, a death mask of sleep.

His fingers found something cold and feathery. He drew out his prize—a dried-up bird.

A rustling sound.

A hand slammed on his wrist like a shackle.

Red Leaf rolled out of his bed, never slackening his grip on Zach's wrist. "How, kola," he said, the traditional greeting now laced with sarcasm. He pulled Zach inside with an effortless yank and dumped him like a helpless puppy. Zach released the dead bird and wiped his palm on his leg. Red Leaf picked up the bird with tender reverence, threw an angry look at Zach before pulling down his medicine bag and replacing the bird.

He beckoned to Keera. "You enter, also." She crawled through the gap, and he kicked away the twig holding up the hide. Zach and Keera sat close together. Red Leaf picked up his knife in its pouch and, sitting opposite them, laid it on his lap. Zach heard Keera's heavy breathing and placed a reassuring hand on hers.

"The two strange ones visit. A peculiar hour, but you're welcome." Red Leaf sounded genuinely pleased. "Curious times. A man-boy who has hardly spoken from the moment he learned to talk is now a great speechmaker, one who tells the future of our people. He who always played by himself and avoided fighting becomes a warrior and has counted coup."

He faced Keera, "And the silent, mourning widow, one who sought solace with a man-boy who also didn't speak, now talks like a warrior, and even disdains a marriage to Crazy Elk, the bravest in the camp. You two creep into an old man's tipi and try to steal medicine that is not yours. No Oglala ever dares to enter this tipi without my bidding, but you have no fear. This old head is puzzled."

The healer sounded like he'd been expecting them for some time. Had a speech prepared and everything. Which way would the night end? Punishment, banishment, death?

Red Leaf turned back to Zach and pointed to his medicine bag on the pole. "What did you seek?"

What to say? Keera wasn't talking; no sign of how to play this.

"The Stone—" he started, and Keera's knee banged into his. He fell silent.

"Even old men can see you want the Stone," said Red Leaf. "You think you'll possess its power? The strength of the Stone does not pass with a change of ownership. Only one can use this force."

"Yeah, right."

"You agree, then. Yet you come to steal." Zach shook his head. "I mean that I don't believe you."

"But your words have a different meaning. What person uses words that convey the opposite meaning to the original thought?" Red Leaf unsheathed his knife and pointed it at him. "Are you wanting to trick me with words?"

"No, where I come from—" He stopped when Keera kneed him again.

"That's the question, Slow Hand. Where do you come from? A child born and raised in this band of Oglala, but you act as if you're from another land. What happened when you went berry hunting?"

How to answer that? He had enough trouble trying to keep his own head together without constructing an explanation that might satisfy Red Leaf. Keera wasn't helping; she was scoping the entire tipi.

"Your nurse is more interested in finding the Stone than speaking," said Red Leaf. He searched under his shirt and withdrew the fist-sized Stone. Zach sensed Keera tense beside him. It looked hardly all the bother. Bluish with orange coloring, pretty but not awesome.

"I was at one with the *Wakan Tunkan* tonight when you came," said Red Leaf, his hand pulling brown cloth from under his blanket. He wrapped the Stone with concentrated solemnity, then placed it in a small pouch on a leather string around his neck.

"This power should be shared by all," Zach said.

"I help those who need it," replied Red Leaf. "That's the Oglala way. That is why those who have plenty give to those who don't. We value a person who does this. You know this."

"What about the people in other bands?" Red Leaf was confused. "I cannot be here and over there at the same time."

"Lend it to others, to help the sick." He tried to sound like a tribal elder, but he sounded more like a mother imploring her child to share his toys.

"Your mind is muddled, Slow Hand. The *Wakan Tunkan* came to me in a dream and guided me to where it lay. When I awoke, I searched and found it. My gift of power from the Great Spirit. Because you've not gone on your Vision Quest you fail to understand. What a man dreams of then, becomes his power source. Men dream of buffalo, the eagle, the swallow, or the elk as I did long ago. Now I've dreamt of this Stone; it's mine, and its power is for me alone."

So much for negotiating. Was the alternative feasible?

"Do not think," said Red Leaf, somehow reading his mind, "that you can knock me down and steal it. I have killed many men, and you've killed none. My knife will find your heart before you find your feet."

"I know that," replied Zach. Whose idea was it to steal from this killer?

"Know this also. You haven't come here to take my Stone because that's not possible. You've been brought here by the Great Spirit so I can discover the secret of your new medicine. How a backward child becomes a warrior in a day. That would be a great thing to learn, eh?"

"It's not a secret for me to tell."

"But you'll tell it all the same."

Shouts penetrated the tipi walls, and Red Leaf lifted his head to listen. "Not an attack," he said, "but something has happened." He gripped his knife blade between his teeth and picked up rawhide thongs. Within a blurry second, he was behind Zach and binding his wrists, the hide sawing into his flesh. Keera attempted to move away but Red Leaf grabbed her hair, and she stopped. He lashed her wrists and sheathed his knife. He removed their knives from their belts, stuffing them into a bag that hung out of their reach.

"Wait for me without a sound. If you cry out, I'll return and kill one of you instantly. The other will die slow. Nobody in this camp will believe your story, or feel mercy for thieves. Your deaths will not be honorable ones."

CHAPTER 19

K eera woke when the morning light penetrated the lodge skins and flooded the interior in warm amber. The cheerful glow belied her foreboding. Red Leaf would be merciless in extracting the information he wanted. Information, that even if supplied would be incomprehensible to him. And if he couldn't grasp it, he'd assume he was being given the runaround and get angry. Armed and angry.

Noises from outside, a buzz of voices. Zach stirred. Raised his head and looked around, orientating himself. Closed his eyes, his face despairing.

"Sit up," she said. "We have to talk."

He kept his eyes closed. "Can you teach me a death song? I think I'll need it soon."

"We have little time. Move."

He struggled upright, twisting his wrists to loosen the bindings. "These are hellish tight."

"Red Leaf has more problems than he first thought."

"How so?"

"He's finding out I've been promised to Crazy Elk. He'd only heard of my initial refusal."

"Does it matter?"

"The shouting. We've been discovered missing. On Rain Bird's wedding day. Everybody must think they've run off together, or Slow Hand has abducted Rain Bird. Obviously they have to be brought back. Red Leaf is in a bind. If he doesn't admit he holds us straight away, then he has to hide that fact until he gets us out of camp."

"So, it's in his interests our capture here remains a secret." "Yes."

"Why don't we holler and scream and get freed by the good village folk?"

"Because everything will become very unstable. Red Leaf may fight with Three Dogs; he might flee. He could kill us anyway, and nobody here will stop him."

"So ... if we're killed," Zach said, "it's unfortunate for Slow Hand and Rain Bird, but Zach and Keera wake up back in Wonderland. A place with hot and cold running water, where people can purchase sensible footwear and frown upon the daily use of personal weapons."

"Put the idea right out of your mind. We need to stay until we get the Stone. I won't be pleased if you throw away Slow Hand's life cheaply. I'll—"

"Got it, you'll make my life hell. Chill. I'm only throwing ideas around."

"Because you haven't met the real Rain Bird and the real Slow Hand, you can't think of them as actual people. Is that true? Because you're pretty free and easy with their destinies here."

Zach leaned back as if she would strike him. "I'm working through some possibilities, that's all. It doesn't hurt to be thorough. I don't want anybody dead, not on our account anyway. Certainly not these two burdened carriers of our consciousness."

Good to hear he understood the situation. She changed tack. "Cast back to when we found Red Leaf."

"I'm casting. He was asleep, we were almost on top of him."

"He wasn't asleep."

"Well, I know that now."

"He was in a trance. I saw the signs. He's figured out how to leave his body."

"A neat way of watching over yourself. No wonder he doesn't need dogs," Zach said. "What does this matter anymore?"

Time for a quick lesson. "It means if these bodies of ours die and pass into the non-physical, he can follow. If Red Leaf is killed, it's worse because he'll gain more powers and cause us, the real us, severe psychic and psychological damage."

"I don't want to be more damaged than I am already. I've had enough. Can't you make us, like, jump out of these bodies and slip into something more comfortable, like our own?"

Stay with me, Zach, we're close to the end. Whatever it'll be. "The Stone isn't ours yet, you notice? Red Leaf will keep us until he finds out what your medicine is. He's a power-grabber, and he's intensely interested in your secret."

"Trouble is, he won't believe me if I tell the truth."

"There's the problem. He might get nasty if he thinks you are holding out on him."

"How nasty?"

"He'll torture you."

"Torture? He'll torture me? One of his own?" His reaction startled her. Maybe she shouldn't have brought that up.

The tipi flap flew open and Red Leaf entered. He crouched close to her face. "You did not tell me you had agreed to the marriage," he said, inspecting her face like she was trickier than he'd thought.

"You didn't ask."

He nodded as if he were blaming himself for an oversight. "Crazy Elk is mad with the thought you ran away with Slow Hand, and has vowed to kill him. He's ridden out with a band of warriors. Three Dogs is ashamed because you gave your word."

Keera sat straighter. "Tell him I would have kept it, but we were tied up here like a pair of prairie chickens."

"Thieves are not honored like guests." Red Leaf settled on his bed and lifted a pipe hanging from a pole. He packed the bowl with tobacco and used a forked stick to light it with an ember from the fire. After the offering to the four directions, he drew smoke in and exhaled.

"What will you do with the Stone when you die?" Zach asked. Red Leaf drew more smoke before answering.

"The *Wakan Tunkan* gives me the power to escape death."

"Are you positive? You must die to find out for sure."

"I've left my body behind often and gone to another place. Many of my departed friends were waiting for me. They explained how I'll live even when my body becomes a feast for insects."

Keera straightened a leg. "You took a journey to a new world."

"Many creatures did not welcome me, but I was not afraid." Red Leaf poked his pipe at her. "You, Rain Bird, have been there too."

"All of us dream of strange places, and sometimes these are not dreams. The spirit is not always dependent on the body."

"I'm not the camp idiot requiring careful instruction. I know who you are."

Keera waited.

"You're not the people you seem," Red Leaf pronounced. "Slow Hand and Rain Bird have been invaded by walk-in spirits. I didn't understand at first, but I thought on it, smoked on it and dreamt on it, but I was still not sure. However, when I left my body, the truth lay in front of me."

Red Leaf owned more than warrior cunning. He was a thinker. And a killer. A combination she never expected to face.

"What brought you to my lodge?" Red Leaf said after releasing a slow stream of smoke. "The Stone? But a spirit has no need of a healing thing. This puzzles me, but I'll find out the answer."

Red Leaf's complete certainty wasn't calming. "You can't take the Stone with you when you travel to this place where you never die," Keera said. "What will happen to it when you no longer return?"

Red Leaf waved his hand. "The *Wakan Tunkan* occupies your mind like a fever takes hold of a body. It has taken me to many places, and it will be a long time before it passes from my hands."

"Where does it take you, Red Leaf?" she asked, folding her leg under her and stretching the other one. If the chance came to grab the Stone and run, she wanted to be sure her limbs would be ready.

"To a place where I watched my people fighting many *wasichu*. The yellow-haired one led soldiers into the Sacred Hills. Angry warriors surrounded them and rubbed them out. I understood at first that this was the greatest victory of the Lakota with their friends, the Cheyenne. But this victory was a mistake, because afterward the *wasichu* never rested until our nation gave up their hunting grounds and became farmers." Red Leaf looked disgusted enough to spit. Zach moved his leg out of range.

"You know then," Keera said, with gentle pressure, "the Lakota will one day lose their lands. That the *wasichu* will overcome." Red Leaf's face grew pinched and drawn, an acknowledgment she was right. But he answered with defiance.

"That day was proof that we can beat them when superior leaders appear. An old man Hunkpapa and a young Oglala controlled the warriors until the time was right to attack. I did not know their names."

"Sitting Bull and Crazy Horse," she said.

"You were there, too?" Red Leaf wide-eyed with surprise.

"Others can see the future as well."

"You saw what I saw?" He seemed pleased she had confirmed his dream.

"That battle is hundreds of seasons in the future; it will never concern you."

"The future always concerns me. When I discover the nature of the spirit within Slow Hand, how it made him a warrior, then I can turn the most timid man into a fearsome attacker. With such strength, my nation will destroy anybody who comes to our lands without a welcome."

"Jesus wept," muttered Zach.

"I've never heard of this person Jesus, but many *wasichu* women wept after that battle."

It was impossible to shake Red Leaf's view. A healer's calling was to interpret dreams, and his band relied on him for that. But he could only comprehend the images in terms of his own world. That hadn't mattered before; their world hadn't changed for eons. But the future approaching was a tsunami of unimaginable proportions for the Oglala. Guns, alcohol, and starvation would sweep away the old certainties. Their reason for existence gone, they would exist only as wreckage.

Red Leaf emptied his ashes into the fire. He reached into a soft bag hanging off a pole and pulled out a smaller one. "Crazy Elk and the others return soon. I must talk to them. Both of you will sleep the day away." He crouched next to Zach and shoved powder up his nose. He covered Zach's mouth and nose, forcing him to breathe in the powder. Within seconds Zach drooped, and Red Leaf pushed him over and away.

He stepped over to Keera. "Your stay in this body may be a short one. Make sure your next dream is pleasant." A breath later, she was unconscious.

CHAPTER 20

Zach woke to the damp odor of moving horseflesh inches from his nose. He lay across a horse's back, like a saddle roll, face down, hands still bound behind him, fingers numb. To the rear, the vague shapes of tipis receded with each step. Twisting his head to the front, he made out Red Leaf leading the horse, and another, alongside. Keera lay across that one. The moonlight, dimmed by wispy clouds, showed a creek ahead, and the horses splashed through it; the same creek he and Keera had crossed on that first day—two centuries ago.

When trees surrounded them, the horses halted. Red Leaf tied them off to a branch. He padded over to Zach and pulled him down. Zach groaned as his head struck the earth and promptly received a kick in the ribs.

"Do not wake the night spirits," Red Leaf said. "Their anger isn't easily abated."

Zach heard Keera being lowered to the ground. Lowered, not dropped. She was probably still unconscious. He tried to sit up but, another kick stopped him.

"Be still," ordered Red Leaf. "I'm not a herder."

He dragged Keera to a tree trunk and propped her up. Faced Zach. Question time. And just one way out: to tell the truth, tell all the truth, the whole damn truth and nothing in between. Might mess with Red Leaf's head long enough to allow them a way out of this. Red Leaf squatted in front of him.

"It's time to talk."

"Yes," Zach replied, "and I'll tell you everything."

"I know that already."

"Let me sit up. Even a chicken won't squawk when it's lying down."

"You speak as a warrior, not afraid. You shall sit." Red Leaf stepped behind him and dragged him to another tree. The man was powerful as one thirty years younger.

"Thanks, man," breathed Zach. Red Leaf struck him across the face.

"Be respectful; you know my name."

A salty taste filled Zach's mouth. His vision blurred for a second. That's for forgetting how proud this bunch was. "Sorry." He grabbed several more breaths and considered asking for his hands to be untied. Maybe later, if the chat went well. "What is it you wish to ask?" he asked as politely as he could.

Red Leaf back on his haunches again. "Where are you from?" Picked up a stick and tapped it on the ground.

"Another place, like you've seen."

Red Leaf brightened. "I figured that. Where is Slow Hand's spirit?"

"Within me, but it sleeps."

"A spirit always as dormant as possible." Red Leaf apparently regarded the original Slow Hand as a waste of space. "Why are you and the other spirit here?"

"To retrieve the Stone."

"It cannot be taken. I've told you this."

"It can and must be taken." Zach surprised how sure he sounded.

"What would you do with it? Are you a healer in your world? Are you a wise leader, a warrior person? Do people respect you?"

The guy was getting personal. He went for the lofty tone. "The stone can help the Oglala for many years. If you keep it to yourself, it will be lost to your children and your children's children." This was supposed to be Keera's pitch, not his. He was only along for the ride.

Red Leaf waved a dismissive hand. "The Great Spirit will take care of the years to come." "How can you be sure?" "He ordered this world and placed the birds, the animals, and the trees in it." Red Leaf waved his hand around. "He allowed the Oglala to dwell in his creation, and he'll not allow the Oglala to be cast down and be oppressed by their enemies." Red Leaf pushed his face closer. "He'll guide me in my actions."

Zach tried a new approach. "Do you want me to teach the Oglala how to become mighty warriors? My people are the greatest. We have power over the whole world."

Red Leaf grew skeptical. "What can you teach us? A man's strength comes from within, from your spirit and your medicine. It is not a skill you pass on to a seasoned warrior or even a novice boy."

"I can show new moves."

"Moves?"

"Yes. How to dodge, turn and tackle."

"No warrior dodges. Only elk dodge. Warriors don't turn away from battle or enemies. You say many strange things. What is a tackle?"

"A tackle is when you run at the enemy, put your arms around him and drive him into the ground."

"And then you kill him?"

"No. It's unnecessary."

"Of course. Someone else can kill him, and count coup."

Zach rolled his eyes. "Jesus Christ! Can't you let the enemy go with a warning?"

Red Leaf lashed him across the face with his stick. "My name is not Jesus Christ."

"It's just an expression," Zach said, his face flaming, eyes watering. "Sorry."

Red Leaf said, "If we don't kill our enemies, they'll come back. Kill more warriors, steal horses and women."

"I see you put horses ahead of women," cried a furious voice from the next tree.

They swung around to find Keera glaring at them.

"Can you shut up?" Zach snapped at her. He didn't need her ranting at Red Leaf. Not now. Not with him tied up and helpless. Keera ignored him and twisted her body to ease the pressure on her bonds.

She addressed Red Leaf again. "The Stone gives you the health and strength of many men. Use it to increase the power of the warriors in your band. Let them share in the power."

Red Leaf blinked at the unimaginable. "How is it possible to share this gift from the Great Spirit? He gave it to me, not to anybody else. Only I can control it."

"Only you have controlled it so far. Allow others to have the same medicine."

"You're like a quarrelsome warrior. But you're just a woman and an annoying one. I'll speak with you when it's time." Red Leaf turned back to Zach.

"I'll speak when I choose, Red Leaf," Keera returned. "I'll not be silenced like a noisy child."

"Be quiet, woman," snapped Red Leaf, head down, staring at the ground, steaming.

"Give up the Stone," she said. "It belongs to the whole Lakota nation, not you."

"Silence! Or you will receive the punishment you deserve."

"You can silence me, but you'll never silence the thoughts I've put in your mind."

Zach had stopped breathing. Please, Keera, stop. Her words must have reached Red Leaf because he appeared to be more contemplative. Like he was turning over Keera's words in his mind, and finding fresh questions.

"You place so much regard on the *Wakan Tunkan*," he said to her, "that I wonder if I have missed some of its qualities. Perhaps you know more of its powers than I do. Perhaps you should share them with me."

"The more people that have access to it," she said, "the more its qualities will come to light. You alone cannot grasp what you have."

"I have the understanding of ten people. Everybody knows this. I think, I smoke, and I am guided. What need is there of others?"

"There are many others such as you; if you all work together, much can be revealed. The future of the Lakota depends on this."

"You talk a lot of nonsense, even for a woman."

"One who so frightens you that you bind her before you speak with her."

Way to go, Keera. Insult the guy some more.

Red Leaf slammed his stick on the ground. "Enough of your irritating words. You know nothing but how to scold a man."

"Real men need no scolding," she shot back. With a frustrated roar, he drew his knife and ran to her. Their eyes locked as he raised the knifepoint to her nose. Zach froze in terrible anguish, expecting the blade to drive deep into a nostril and slice it open.

Instead, he heard a gurgling, a choking, overlaying the sound of wet air venting from tubes. The knife dropped as Red Leaf tore at the stone arrowhead protruding from his throat. Legs buckled, eyes without focus, dark bubbles on the lips. He fell forward on his knees as if praying to a favorite spirit before toppling sideways across Keera's legs. She jerked them free and tried to wriggle further away.

Crazy Elk stepped out of the bushes and stood over the body. His face as impassive as a cliff, but his previous certainties now shredded.

He had killed the most acclaimed of his band.

The man who'd kidnapped his wife.

CHAPTER 21

Crazy Elk stayed still for a long minute, clearing his thoughts, Keera guessed. He'd unleashed a new future on his band, and it couldn't look good to him.

"I swore to your father I would protect you always if you were to be my wife," he said. He lowered his bow, producing a knife, and cut her free. He pulled her upright, rolling Red Leaf's body away from her with his foot. "How much did he harm you?"

"He only bound us," she replied, rubbing her wrists. Pins and needles started their cursed work, and she shook her hands to distract from the prickling. "I saw you in the bushes. Why did you wait so long? If you had acted earlier, this death could have been avoided." She glanced at the body, the neck a hideous pulp.

"He was speaking of his powers. A warrior does not intervene when an elder goes about his business. I killed him only because of my vow."

"Can you both chat later?" Zach asked, working himself upright. "My hands, I got no feeling."

"Free him, Crazy Elk."

He didn't move. "If Red Leaf bound him, it was because he was dangerous. Red Leaf feared nobody, but he bound both of you." He riveted eyes on hers. "When did he kidnap you?"

Kidnap. Crazy Elk thought the whole thing was a kidnapping,

not a capture. A lucky break, if she could deliver a convincing story to back up his impression. "I took Slow Hand outside during the night to explain to him I would leave my father's lodge and join yours."

"You needed darkness for this?" This, with undisguised scorn.

"I didn't know when my father would take me to you in the morning. I used the time I had."

"Looks Back Woman said you both crept away like thieving wolves."

"Not like thieves," she said. "We didn't want to wake them." He would try to get her angry with wild accusations, she knew, hoping she'd stumble over her story. One thing was in her favor: Crazy Elk hadn't seen countless crime movies to know that it was a smart idea to separate two suspects. Before they got their stories straight.

"Red Leaf found you explaining matters to Slow Hand and tied you both up?" He furrowed his brow in mock astonishment.

"When we walked past his tipi, he was waiting. Like he knew we were coming."

Crazy Elk nodded. "He always knew things the rest of us didn't."

"And asked us to join him in his lodge."

"Of course. He wanted to be sure you both were in good spirits after the Crow attack. Red Leaf always considered the hearts of his people."

He seemed to be justifying Red Leaf's actions to himself, working through the narrative. Encouraging.

"We had a long talk. He was curious about the changes he saw in us. I asked him about the *Wakan Tunkan*, and if he would share it. He grew angry."

"Anybody would be annoyed with such a stupid idea. So he tied you then?"

"Not then, later. He heard people shouting. It must have been

159

when we were found missing. He bound our hands and said if we made a sound, he would kill us."

"Like chickens, he bound us." Zach supporting her version, finally grasping what she was doing.

Crazy Elk glanced at him. "Why would he bind you?"

"We didn't understand either," Zach said. "But when he brought us here, all he wanted to know was if we were walk-in spirits."

"He was wary of such spirits," Crazy Elk said. "We all are."

"We explained that we weren't, but he wouldn't free us."

"A man has to be sure. It's an important matter."

"Well, he's no longer interested," Zach said. "Are you going to cut me loose or not?"

"I was thinking of leaving you here. Three Dogs wants to speak with you, and I have to take my wife to my tipi."

"Your wife?" "Yes. Rain Bird has been my wife since her father announced it, as you know. It took longer than expected to bring her to me."

"How did you find us?" Keera asked. Leave the wife stuff alone, Zach. We're in a delicate situation as it is.

"When Three Dogs told me you two were gone, I counted the horses. None were missing, so you couldn't be far." "Red Leaf said you went looking for us, and you meant to kill me." Crazy Elk glanced at Zach. "It is true I was angry, and I kept my anger close to me. But we found your tracks stopped at a rise and returned to camp. I lost them after that because of other tracks. By then I understood something unusual was happening."

"You suspected Red Leaf?" Zach asked, trying to slip his hands free. "Nobody from this band believes ill of him."

Crazy Elk shook his head at the absurdity of the idea. "But when I suggested we should look in the tipis, he opposed this. I didn't agree, but I stopped the search and smoked on this. Then I understood to wait and watch. After dark, I hid at the camp perimeter to see if you two sneaked away when people slept. Red Leaf came out, leading two horses carrying a body each to this stand. I followed and watched and listened until Rain Bird was in danger."

"You saved our lives, and we thank you. Can you cut these damn thongs?" Zach said, trying to stretch them loose.

"Free him. He will come back and speak to Three Dogs," Keera said.

Crazy Elk inserted his blade into Zach's bindings and sliced them apart.

"Thanks," Zach said as he inspected the welts on his wrists. He lifted a chin at Red Leaf's body. "What are we going to do with him?"

Crazy Elk walked over to the horses and untied them. He bent over the body and jerked his arrow free with a single movement, wiped it clean on the grass and replaced it in the quiver. He picked Red Leaf up like a baby and draped him over a horse. "I'll tell his family I killed him for taking my wife, and I'll give them three horses to show my sorrow."

"They'll be satisfied with three horses?" Zach turned to Keera in amazement.

Crazy Elk gave the reins to her. "The family may seek revenge later, but I shall be watchful." He motioned towards the camp. "We'll lay Red Leaf in his lodge; I'll tell his son in the morning."

He walked ahead, Zach followed a few steps behind him, while she brought up the rear leading the two horses. Her new husband didn't for a moment question that his wife wouldn't obey him. This wasn't the time for her to protest. As they splashed through the creek and approached the horse herd, a slim youth stepped out of the shadows.

"How kola," Crazy Elk greeted him. The boy offered the briefest of glances before staring at the ground. "Shy One, where is your friend?"

Shy One pointed up a tree. "Burns Fast is watching for Crow," he said. "He perches in the trees in case we have another visit."

The boy must have recognized Red Leaf's body, but he stayed impassive. Crazy Elk didn't bother with any explanation, and the boy didn't ask questions. Crazy Elk hefted the body onto his shoulder. In death, Red Leaf seemed to weigh less than a pillow. Keera handed to horses over to Shy One, and Crazy Elk led the way to Red Leaf's tipi.

He dropped the body not so gently on the bedding and turning to Zach, he said, "We talk. Rain Bird make the fire."

The men settled near the smoldering chips while she added pieces to it and blew until sparks flew and tiny flames formed. Crazy Elk fished a small pipe out of his bag and pushed tobacco into it. He drew long on the pipe after the traditional offerings and passed it to Zach. She sat away and a little behind Crazy Elk.

Crazy Elk said, "You and Red Leaf were talking of the *Wakan Tunkan.* I didn't understand. Why do you wish to take another man's medicine?"

"The *Wakan Tunkan* is strong medicine," Zach replied after he released the tiny spool of smoke he had inhaled. "We must save it for all the Lakota, not just this band."

"It's arrived where the Great Spirit wants it. What argument can we have about this?" Crazy Elk was no more inclined to contemplate the impossible than Red Leaf.

"Who will keep it now?" Zach asked.

"This tipi and everything in it passes to his son. He'll decide what to do. Red Leaf never took another wife after his died of the smallpox. He always asked why the Great Spirit hadn't led him to the sacred stone earlier so she might have lived."

"Do you have healing powers? Do you sing healing songs for others?"

"For others and myself," Crazy Elk said. "A warrior needs to know how to heal and kill. The two are closely connected." He turned to her. "Cover Red Leaf in a respectful way, so his family are not angry when they see him."

She rose and busied herself with the body, her hands smoothing his clothes, her back to Crazy Elk, concealing her hands. She straightened Red Leaf out on his bed, keeping her eyes averted from his wound. The medicine bag, she removed from around his mutilated neck and drew a buffalo robe over the whole body. She picked up his weapons and placed them alongside the unstrung bow, a quiver of arrows and the killing tomahawk.

"Dancing Arrow will have to make a wise decision," Zach said. "I hope he considers that not only Oglala should enjoy its benefits."

She slid her hand into Red Leaf's bag and gripped the wrapped Stone. No jolt, no tingling. An inert rock like any other. For now.

"It's now his medicine," Crazy Elk said, "and his choice. Save your pleading words for the morning. Perhaps Dancing Arrow will agree with you, but I doubt it."

She pulled her dress away from her chest and slipped the Stone into her medicine bag. Shook her shoulders and patted between her breasts, the Stone secure. Red Leaf's bag lay alongside his body, visible to Crazy Elk. He couldn't tell it now lacked the stone. She crawled over to Crazy Elk's side and sat. Inspected her moccasins. Calmed herself. The three of them sat in silence while the warrior pondered their explanations. He'd need a second opinion, she suspected. And a third, and a fourth. Too much thinking for one man. Crazy Elk stretched and yawned.

"Time to sleep." Zach said. "Rain Bird and me will return to our tipi."

"Rain Bird sleeps with me tonight. You go alone."

Zach reddened with anger, fierce enough for her to recognize its heat. A growl of frustration in his throat. Zach at breaking point. It was written over his whole body. He wouldn't move, and she knew it. Crazy Elk watching him, expecting trouble but not afraid of it. No foretelling how this would end.

"Go to your lodge," Crazy Elk repeated, his voice soft and steely at the same time.

"No," Zach growled.

"Anger makes children of us all." Crazy Elk rose to his feet, Keera with him. He jerked his head towards the entrance. "Leave. You cannot stay."

Zach sat still and obstinate. Crazy Elk leaned over to pick him up by the arms. Zach grabbed his wrists instead and launched himself upward—his anger channeled in one direction. His forehead smashed into the warrior's nose. Crazy Elk staggered backward before toppling over, his nose spattering blood.

Zach stood over him, one foot drawn back, ready to slam into his belly, but Crazy Elk was unconscious. Keera pulled their knives down from the pole. "It's time," she said.

CHAPTER 22

Outside, the dawn light caught them by surprise. Nearby, a woman removed jerky strips from a drying rack. Several tipis vented smoke as the camp woke. Keera ran past the other lodges, past the meeting place, to the horses. Zach stretched his short legs and caught up with her. Shy One sat on his horse observing them.

"We need two of my father's horses," she said, her chest heaving. The kid didn't move, stared at her. "Oh hell," she said and reached for a pony. It shied away, but she grabbed its mane and jumped high enough to grip its back with her thighs, and struggle upright.

"Don't just stand there. Get yours," she yelled at Zach.

"There's no saddle stuff."

"You don't need them. Be quick."

At that, she cut another pony out, shorter than the rest and placid in the face. Zach wrapped his fingers in its mane and hauled himself astride.

"Hang on with your knees and thighs. Slow Hand can ride, so can you." She pounded her heels into her horse's flanks, and it leapt forward. She snatched a look back. Zach unsteady, but hanging on, Shy One running into the camp.

Pony muscles stretched and contracted under her, the hooves

thumping the ground, sending tom-tom signals back to camp. She kept the creek on their right. When the camp disappeared behind a rise, she slowed to a walk and let Zach catch her. His pony cleared its head with a shake and a snort.

"Why did you land that tirade on Red Leaf?" he asked her. "You were so close to disfigurement, if not death."

"I spotted Crazy Elk hiding. I felt he wouldn't act without an imperative reason. Red Leaf is not one to argue with."

"So, you made like a nutty feminist?"

"I said what I knew would enrage Red Leaf. It worked. You did a pretty good job of enraging him yourself. I worried that he'd stop beating you with that stick and pull his knife out."

"My annoying him was accidental. I was trying to placate him. I see we were working against each other."

No Zach. Everything worked as it was meant to be, but you didn't see it. She changed the subject. "Where did you learn that head butt?"

"Football. I've never done it without a helmet before. Works even better."

"I hope he'll will be okay."

"His nose will be more battle-hardened than before. That's all." He seemed cheery at the thought of it. If Crazy Elk caught them, he'd need more than cheeriness to save him.

"How long do we have before he comes after us?"

"A normal guy takes fifteen minutes to get his head clear after a blow like that. Maybe five more to stop the bleeding. But they make the men of titanium here, as far as I can tell. Less time than that, I guess."

"Let's slow him down." She jerked her horse's mane and led it into the creek. Zach followed her.

"I reckon he can hear us from his lodge," he said as the horses splashed the shallow waters.

"Not once he's riding flat out in the direction Shy One tells him. If he figures we've changed course, he'll look for fresh tracks near the camp. It's hard to find them under water. He'll have to search both banks to spot where we left the creek. We may have a lot more time than five minutes."

The water ran clear through reeds and over stones. A lone eagle drifted high above, waiting for prey to break cover. Distant clouds hovered, picture-book fluffy and white. A wonderful moment, if they weren't escaping a murder scene.

"Where are we going?" Zach asked.

She pointed forward. "To bury the Stone and leave."

He swiveled on his pony. "You have it?"

She patted her medicine pouch, allowed herself a tiny smile.

"We're done here, then?" His joy obvious. "We just catch a passing cloud back home?"

"After we bury the Stone."

He faced the front again, beaming from ear to ear. "Your words make my heart sing. What happens to the bodies?"

"Their original owners will reclaim them. They'll be confused, but as far as the camp is concerned, they'll be regular people again. Some may assume walk-in spirits had messed with them, but for the rest, their normal behavior proves the walk-ins have gone."

"Rain Bird will get a shock when she finds out she married Crazy Elk."

"She knows. It's what she wanted, the perfect union." Rain Bird hadn't uttered a single protest since her first hot-tempered one. That was acceptance enough.

"What about Slow Hand?"

"When Crazy Elk finds them, they'll be dazed," she said. "That'll spook him. Slow Hand will have reverted to type, Rain Bird no longer so feisty. He'll have much to think about."

"Hope you're right. I don't need the blood of innocents on my conscience."

"It won't happen. I've thought very hard about it."

"One more question. Where do we hide the stone?"

"This land is part of the future Pine Ridge Reservation, near the junction of the White Clay River and Black Tail Deer Creek. These places still exist in our time. I checked a map of the region."

"You just checked a map? No proper reconnoiter on the ground?"

"What's to check? We'll follow the creek until we find a prominent landmark and mark a tree. It takes hundreds of years for the mark to fade."

"Are you sure?" He waved a hand at the trees. "These aren't redwoods around here."

"All trees live for ages. We follow this creek until it changes direction west. There we bury the stone."

"I've got a question," Zach said. "How can you be sure we can find it when we come back?"

"It's impossible to guess how much this countryside will change," she admitted. "But this will be reservation land. Farming and cattle ranching the prime land use apart from a few dwellings. I'm banking on this creek staying here. When we find a distinctive part of it, a major bend, and mark a tree, we should be able to recognize it when we return."

The horses plodded through shallows for five more minutes before she took them out and back onto the left bank.

Zach said, "One massive storm, and dozens will pass through here in the next two hundred years, could reroute this tiny stream, uproot the trees and remodel the whole terrain."

"Shh," she said. "I'm sensing something. I can't concentrate with your jabbering." She looked behind her again but saw only the grassy undulations, picking up golden tops as the sun rose. The creek corkscrewed south for another hour before it swerved to the west and stayed that way. A stand of cottonwoods sprouted at the curve. Keera stopped and studied the terrain. "Let's ride further and see if the creek turns again."

Five minutes later, the creek still kept its course, and she wheeled her horse around. "Go back." Back at the earlier bend, they dismounted and examined the hard ground.

"Did you bring a shovel?" asked Zach.

"The hardware store was closed. Loosen the earth with your knife and we'll scoop it out."

"How we get to 'X marks the spot'?"

"Walk over to where the bend starts and pace along the bank to the first tree. Score it with a deep X at knee level. Make the cuts wide; it'll take longer for the X to close up. Count another hundred and fifty paces away from the water's edge. Thats the spot. It should be far enough from the creek to avoid minor floods. The ground is rising here. That'll help."

Zach gazed around; his doubt obvious. This bend wasn't as distinctive as she would like. But she'd rely on her psychic senses to locate the Stone more precisely on their return. "Shall we get on with it?"

"You're so strict," Zach said. "I like that in a woman."

Keep your mind on the job, Zach. They paced along the creek. After fifty strides they reached the first tree and he marked the trunk. An X, deep and wide. How long did cottonwoods live, anyway? They walked the hundred and fifty steps uphill.

"Here," he said, and scratched out a mark in the sparse grass.

Both of them stabbed knives into the soil and loosened the earth to scoop it out.

"Is that enough?" he asked when the hole was two feet deep. "This is murder on my manicure."

"It'll do. We'll put your knife in with the Stone."

"Why?"

"If we have trouble locating this exact spot, then leaving metal in the bag will allow us to use a metal detector." She pulled the medicine bag from around her neck, unwrapped it and took out the Stone.

"Doesn't look much, does it?" Zach said. "A chunk of weathered rock."

She closed her eyes. Still no vibes.

"Keera? Crazy Elk is closing on us all the time."

"You're right." She re-wrapped the Stone and placed it back into the bag. Zach added his knife. She lowered the bag in the hole, and they both pushed the dirt over it. The filling stood three inches proud of the surrounding ground.

"Dead giveaway, isn't it?" Zach said. She stamped on the mound until it was closer to level, then kicked away the loose earth.

"A zillion acres of grasslands in this area. Nobody will stumble on this. In a few weeks, with rain, God herself will have trouble locating it. Let's go." As they collected their horses, she said, "We need to back track so that Slow Hand and Rain Bird are found nearer the camp, not so close to the buried stone."

They retraced their tracks along the creek for a few minutes before stopping and dismounting. The air still cool, sweet almost, inhabited only by occasional birdsong. A new sound joined in, swelling louder by the second. A horse, galloping.

Crazy Elk, delivering revenge and retribution.

CHAPTER 23

A lone rider shot into view around a stand of cotton-woods; coming at them like a cavalry charge.

Crazy Elk.

Zach fumbled for his knife before he remembered he'd buried it. Keera laid a hand on his arm. "Let me do the talking."

Crazy Elk didn't slow when he saw them, but rode his pony harder. He pulled up next to Zach and leaped off his heaving horse. Clutching his knife.

"Why did you attack me?" he shouted. "In my lodge. Where I smoked with you."

Zach took a step back to keep a safe distance between the knife and his belly. Crazy Elk breathed through his mouth. His eyes bounced from Zach to Keera. Seething, confused and unpredictable. His nose a swollen lump pushed to one side and discolored yellow. Dried blood trailed to his neck.

He stepped closer to Zach and jammed his knife against his stomach. "Slow Hand, you ran, and took my wife with you." He was shouting again and didn't wait for an answer. The knife hand whacked Zach across the face, the blade angled not to cut, but to deliver a stinging blow.

Zach stumbled back a couple of paces, hand to his cheek. The rough blade had broken his skin, no more. Only a smear of blood

171

on his fingers.

"Stop it," Keera shouted. "He's not armed."

Crazy Elk swung around to her. Zach grabbed his chance. He drew on his football training. Maximum force is transmitted to the point of impact by planting your feet, transferring the turning force of the body through the knees, thighs, chest, and shoulders. He added his fist to the end of the power stream and slammed it into Crazy Elk's chin. The Indian buckled, and Zach hit him again. Crazy Elk staggered away from the attack but still gripping his knife. Zach should have hit him once more, but waited.

Big mistake.

Crazy Elk blinked a few times, then launched forward with a battle yell. This was no school-yard brawl, this was no on-field burst of anger, this was Crazy Elk's world—a fight to the death. With the man who had dishonored him.

Zach backtracked fast. He should have grabbed the knife hand and pounded Crazy Elk unconscious. He should have placated the guy as earnestly as he could. He should have done a lot of things. Keera shouted something at them, but he had blocked her out. Nothing mattered now but to survive the next couple of minutes. And then the next couple.

Crazy Elk came at him, the knife carving slices out of the air like he was practicing on imaginary flesh. He lunged at Zach, who sidestepped and kicked out at Crazy Elk's knee. The Indian wobbled for a few steps but didn't fall. Turned with renewed ferocity. The only hope was to find a rock to club the guy with. He searched with his feet as he back-pedaled. He found one. The wrong one. The one that rolled his ankle and landed him on his back.

Crazy Elk dived on him for the finishing blow. He straddled Zach and raised his knife.

Stopped.

Keera's knife lay across his throat. "Throw your knife away," she cried. "A man who would kill a fellow Oglala, an unarmed man, disgraces all of us."

Crazy Elk stilled. Zach couldn't tell if he believed her or not. He could easily knock her aside and still have time to kill his wife's abductor. But he stayed frozen. The possible consequences of his action had to be tearing at him. The death of Red Leaf would already turn many of the Oglala against him. The killing of Slow Hand, a bewildered weakling, would be a crippling blow to his prestige. His band would not follow him anymore. He had to know this.

Crazy Elk pushed himself off and tossed his knife away. Keera edged back, Zach scrambled to his feet and grabbed the discarded knife. Much better odds, two knives to none. If he could bring himself to stab anybody. He wasn't sure Keera had the same qualms.

Crazy Elk wasn't much subdued. He pointed to Zach and shouted again, "What is he doing out here, alone with another man's wife?"

"As you know," Keera said, "Slow Hand is new to the ways of men. He doesn't always know how to act."

Crazy Elk spat on the ground. "He knows to hit me hard enough to make me dream, and how to steal my wife."

Crazy Elk didn't know that they had taken the Stone. All he cared about was that Slow Hand had taken his wife.

Keera placed herself before him. "Slow Hand didn't want to. The spirits took over, he said. Strange spirits that used his head as a weapon."

"Walk-ins? You told me Red Leaf was wrong."

"When I saw you asleep, I knew it was a sign. Never has anybody hit you so hard. That's when I thought Red Leaf might be right. Walk-in spirits were forcing Slow Hand into wrong actions."

Crazy Elk waved an angry hand at Zach. "Slow Hand has taken

my wife, and I will punish him for this."

"Slow Hand took nothing," she said. "It was me who suggested we go. Return in the morning, I need to help him today."

Crazy Elk swallowed. "A wife does not spend the night away from camp with another man."

"Your wife will do what she thinks is right, and she'll not dishonor you."

"Of course she won't because she'll do as I say," he shouted.

"She's not a dog you order about," she snapped back.

He howled to the sky, bewildered by the wife he'd long awaited. A wife he couldn't control.

"I cannot go, Rain Bird," Crazy Elk cried. "I cannot leave you behind with him. A man does not do this."

"Just go," she said, more gently this time.

He didn't obey. "Why are you here? Tell me again."

"Slow Hand has not been a warrior long. A part of him is still a boy who wants his mother, and I'm the only friend he's ever known. He's frightened by the changes he's experiencing. In the tipi, he didn't attack you—the walk-in spirit commanded him. That's why we ran away. To rid ourselves of these spirits."

Crazy Elk was incredulous. "This is healer's work, not a woman's."

"Yes," she shouted in his face. "But we have no healer."

Good work, Keera. Let him suck on that. Crazy Elk considered her words, weighing them against his fury.

"We'll try to banish these spirits," she said. "Watch, but do not interfere until it's done."

Crazy Elk gave up. "I will stand off and see this banishment. Then I take you back." He pointed again to Zach. "But this one will have to resolve matters with me."

Very impressive. The guy had resolved an impossible situation with no loss of honor. He walked to a small rise where he sat below the top.

"Lie down, Zach." Keera placed a firm hand on his chest. "It's time to fly home."

He stretched himself on the ground, and she joined him alongside. "Nice work," he said. "You spoke powerful medicine."

"I told the truth, you notice? Something I learned from you."

"I feel so vindicated now. But I could have taken him, if you failed to convince him."

"No unarmed man beats an Oglala with a knife."

"Yeah, well. What's he doing now?"

"Still watching, but he won't let us lie together for long. Start your breathing."

He drew a deep breath. "One thing."

"What's that?" he said, as he wiggled into a comfortable position. "Red Leaf is out there."

"Nooo! Is this ever going to end?"

"This part might be rocky, I have to admit," she said.

"I can handle it," Zach said. "Sure, you're a resilient guy. Whatever happens, ignore it. Pretend it's a bad dream, we'll get through, don't worry."

"Yeah, but in what condition?"

"Close your eyes."

"Closing tight."

"Clear your mind."

"Is Crazy Elk creeping up on us?"

"I can't see. Take a deep breath and exhale slowly. Feel every molecule of air passing through your lungs."

He drew breath as instructed. The darkness behind his eyes resolved into something deeper, and he was back in the rushing void. A bear claw necklace whirled toward him, an evil spinning thing. Red Leaf's sign. It caught him around the neck, a quoit finding its target. The claws dug deep, his flesh shredding but no pain. He couldn't escape, he'd arrive when he arrived, and not before. The old warrior alongside, grinning like never in real life. Drawing a finger across his brow in an unmistakable scalping gesture.

He closed his eyes, but the vision remained. It wasn't a physical reality, but it was impossible to ignore. The claw necklace spun around his neck. Spun faster and faster; the claws tearing at flesh. Immense heat filled his head, and he feared it would separate from his body. A silent scream tore out of his chest. Red Leaf vanished. The black universe around him exuded an unexpected calm. Then that, too, vanished.

Zach woke in the room where they had started their journey. When he tried to stand, his legs weren't ready. He crawled to a wall and propped himself against it. Keera's body lay inert on her mat. As he watched, it jerked into life. One, two convulsive jolts ripped through it, then nothing. She opened her eyes, blank and confused until they met his and recognition flooded in.

He asked, "Have a nice trip?"

CHAPTER 24

Zach stayed on the ground and watched Keera push herself to her feet. "Hell of a ride, eh?"

She eyed him reflectively. "You've returned in one piece? Everything good?"

"Oh yeah. It was fun. You wanna go again?"

"In a heartbeat."

Not me. Not ever again, not for love or crazy money. "Me too," he said.

She threw him a disbelieving look and passed her hands over her body as if she was washing.

"What are you doing?"

"Cleansing. Removing any entities that might be attached. Please do this."

Zach climbed to his feet and copied her motions. "This, of all the stuff I've done with you, is the most stupid."

"Do it, or you'll have trouble from mischievous beings following you. When you're finished, try to walk."

He took a step forward, swayed, but regained his balance.

"It takes a few minutes to get used to your body again," she said, moving around the room. "The first time is the worst."

Her face was soft and sleepy. "The modern look suits you better."

No response. "What happens now?"

She stopped at the door. "What do civilized people do after the excitement's over?"

"They hold each other close, grateful that they've survived such traumatic events?"

"They share a calming pot of tea."

Of course. How stupid to think otherwise. She led him into the hall, where she stooped to plug the phone back into its socket, and switched on the front door intercom before taking him to the kitchen. Big enough to hold five servants holding two pots each. A roughhewn refectory table, bearing the marks of cutlery through the ages, dominated the middle of the room. A counter ran along the longer wall, and a Victorian sideboard completed the décor. Daylight poured in through large windows.

"The cups are over there." Keera suggested a cupboard with her head.

He padded over in his socks, opened the door and selected two mugs from a choice of chinaware.

"Not mugs. Tea requires cups and saucers."

He drew out two cups and matching saucers designed by a gardener on a bad acid trip. Flower petals adorned the rims and edges; the handles fluted into graceful stems. "These okay?" This tea thing was getting worse by the minute.

"They're fine." She plugged in a stainless steel, electric kettle. "There's a loose connection somewhere. It's not coming on." She smacked the side, and a blue spark shot out from the base with a snapping crackle.

"Whoa," Zach said. "Leaking electricity and metal is not a clever mix."

"Doesn't matter, it's going now." The kettle hissed and bubbled.

"Why don't you replace it? No need to die because of a faulty household appliance. Wouldn't look impressive in the obituary."

"I don't have the time or the inclination to shop for these things," she said. "But you're right. I'll be so embarrassed when I'm dead."

"No need to be like that. I was just trying to be helpful. You know, showing manly concern that a woman might not understand electrical stuff."

Keera regarded him for a second. "I'll take that as a jokey guy thing. Something guys say to get a reaction. I'm not biting."

"And I'm not kidding. Please replace it."

"Okay. Okay." She changed the subject. "How was your trip back?"

"So so. The usual death threats and other moments of blood-curdling terror."

"But your sense of humor survived intact. That's good. Did you see Red Leaf?"

The kettle boiled, and she poured water into a chintzy teapot.

"Yep. He wasn't fond of me." He could have added more, but it was like admitting you were terrified by a dream.

"Nor me." Keera filled the cups. "Sugar?"

Zach spooned two into his cup and stirred. He remembered the earlier cup, and added another two. "What did he do to you?" he asked.

"Not a lot. I've learned to protect myself."

"Isn't that a secret you should have shared before I was let loose out there?" He took a sip. As horrible as before. The extra sugar didn't work.

"No time, not with Crazy Elk itching to get his hands on you. I was confident you'd be fine. After so many knocks, mental and physical, you were still standing."

"You're right, I'm fine, I dealt with weird stuff, and came out the other side sane and whole. But I'm surprised, all the same." He checked his watch. "How long have we been away? I counted two sleeps back in Oglala land. What day is it?"

Keera checked the kitchen clock. "We've been away twenty minutes, I'd say. Give or take."

"You're kidding. How does that work, then? One set of time rules for now, and another for then?"

She sipped her tea with the delicacy of a kitten. "Often I have felt I've been away for ages and come back to find the clock's moved forward only a few minutes. It's like a dream where time stretches to fit."

Time stretching. Time travel. "Know what? I can't figure out if what I experienced actually happened, or it was an extremely vivid dream. How can I prove it one way or the other?"

"You can't, you'll go crazy trying," Keera said. "Trust me; you did incredibly well. I have to thank you for staying with me through all those difficult moments."

Difficult moments, she called them. Freaking nightmares more like it. "It was nothing."

"You were brilliant."

That smile again. Could fire up a furnace. Did as much for him.

"I couldn't have done it without you," she added. "Stop it, you're making me blush."

"I didn't see why I needed anybody at first. I even argued against it."

"You're kidding. Little introverted you? Arguing with somebody?" Her normal spikiness had softened. Must have been something in the air back there.

She said, "You saved me from a marriage that could have derailed our plans big time."

"Yes, I did."

"You stopped me from charging that Crow, and took over." "I did that, too. Heroic, wasn't I?"

She stopped there. It must have been a big thing for her to admit she had needed him. "And," he said, "our adventure is not over yet. Who knows what dark dangers lurk ahead? I may have to save you a few more times yet." He sipped the disgusting tea. "I'd like that."

She laughed this time. A deep, mannish chuckle. "Well, I hope so. The next part of this adventure, as you put it, might be more fraught than the first part."

"How so?" "We're back in the physical world now. With real pain and death."

"Keera, we're going back to dig up the Stone and knife. How hard can that be?"

"I'm not talking about the excavation. I have a growing sense that the people there will be hostile to us."

"Why would that be? We're not tearing up a treaty, or planning to trick anybody out of land. We're just a couple of city folk, tourists, admiring nature's beauty and the culture of its original inhabitants."

She finished her tea and pushed the cup aside. "We're going there to take something away. Something important. They will sense this, they're more attuned to feelings and thoughts than you think."

"I'll keep my thoughts blank, then. That'll fox them." He pushed his own tea away, unfinished and happily so. "When do we go back?"

"Tomorrow, when we've rested and calmed ourselves." "Good idea." He waited for the offer of a bed for the night. Even a sofa. "How early do we leave?" His voice sounded funny.

"Very early," she murmured. "It's a long trip."

A chime from the hall. She rose. "A delivery, I won't be a moment."

He watched her walk, a movement of rare grace and beauty. The beginning of something wonderful.

Maybe.

◆ ◆ ◆

Keera opened the front door a chink, leaving it on the chain until she knew who was outside. It didn't make any difference. The door crashed open, and a big man stepped inside. He had snapped the chain with one shove. Behind him stood a smaller man, natty in a suit, and smiling. The big man turned her around, gripped her elbows, and propelled her down the hall toward the kitchen.

Zach came to the door just as they reached it. She was thrown violently at him, and they collided and stumbled and regained their balance by gripping the table.

"What the hell, Feliks?" Zach yelled at the smaller man.

"We're in time for tea, excellent," Feliks said. "Make mine with lemon, please. Boggie won't want one. He has a weak bladder."

Keera edged away from them and tried to recover her composure. An unexpected slice of Zach's past had walked in and taken over. She needed the atmosphere to calm down so she could sense the way forward.

"What's with this heavy stuff?" Zach asked, spreading his hands in emphasis. "I told you I'd pay. I just need more time."

"Zach, Zach." Feliks soothing him. "In America, time is money. If I let you be late, then other clients will ask for time. I've come for your car. Before we leave, Boggie will enjoy your company for a while." He said to Keera, "One tea, please, with lemon." She hesitated a fraction but moved to the cups cabinet.

Feliks returned to Zach, "Boggie will have a personal conversation with you. You've caused trouble I don't need. Please, sit."

Zach sat.

She tried to calm herself, to grasp what all of them were thinking. This Feliks wanted money, also to inflict punishment. Zach, empowered by his Oglala experiences, wouldn't back down. He intended to fight. *God.*

Zach asked, "How did you know I was here?"

"You always take car for journeys. We watch, and we follow. We give you time to say hello to nice girl who lets you in, and now we are presenting ourselves."

How easy had that been? She caught Zach's irritation at his stupidity.

"I'll pay next week, and I won't tell anybody how nice you were. I promise."

"Words are cheap, my friend. My time is not. I am simple money-lender, but you have made me a repo man. A car dealer. A change of career. I don't like it, Zach."

Keera busied herself making a fresh pot of tea for their captors: Feliks the sharp moneylender and his enforcer Boggie, with arms as big as railway sleepers encased in a rumpled hoodie. She poured a cup of tea and fished a lemon out of the refrigerator, sliced it thin with a utility knife from a magnetic knife rack, and put slices on a side plate. "How much does Zach owe you?"

Feliks looked at her and back at Zach. "Is this your financial advisor?"

"A friend," Zach said. "She stays out of this."

Keera said, "I'll pay you what he owes, plus the outstanding interest, plus an extra fee to save this conversation Zach needs to have with your colleague."

Feliks glowed with the pleasure of a con man spotting a fresh mark. "Who's your father?"

"That's none of your business."

Feliks nodded. "I understand. I'll accept a financial settlement instead of car, but Zach still needs to talk to Boggie. It's an important part of my operation."

"That's rubbish," Keera said. "You'll make more money if you leave Zach alone."

"Not so. If I accept only cash when a late payment occurs, then many people will be happy to borrow to pay the extra charges. This increases their debt, and it grows and become unmanageable. Then they run away. The credit card companies have this problem, not me. But fear is a wonderful incentive to keep your finances in order." He picked up a cup and dropped a slice of lemon in it. He took a sip.

"Interesting flavor." He put it down. "Boggie, take Zach into another room while I discuss the refinancing details with his friend."

She didn't know which of them was worse: the moneylender who treated a beating as a normal clause of a financial arrangement, or his enforcer who seemed primed for destruction.

Boggie, smiling like a kid at Christmas, seized Zach's arm in one hand and pulled him off the chair as if he was a small child. Zach pushed back, but it was easier to push back a locomotive. He dug in his heels, but his socks slid along the tiles. Zach scrambled to get his balance and grabbed Boggie's arms for leverage. He threw all his weight into a head butt, but the big guy slid his head aside, and they grazed cheeks like clumsy dance partners. Boggie's fist pounded into Zach's gut, and she saw his resistance vanish in an instant.

"No," Keera yelled. She leaped forward, but Feliks pushed her back.

"This won't take long," he assured her. "The quicker it is, the less pain, the less to forget afterward."

Zach's breathing turned to strangled spasms. She picked up the utility knife and launched herself at Boggie with a reckless fury. Her knife hand raised up to drive the blade deep into him, her whole body propelling the onslaught, but Feliks intercepted her. His deft wrench of her wrist brought a searing pain. He ripped the knife from her fingers and pushed her aside.

"Your financial adviser values you highly as a client," he laughed.

She steadied herself against the kitchen counter, already looking for another weapon. Feliks giggled again and then choked.

Boggie asked, "You right, boss?"

Feliks was not right. He clutched his throat and his legs buckled. He slipped, his left elbow bashing the table top, his right hand still gripping the knife.

Boggie rushed over. "Boss, boss? What's wrong?"

Feliks continued to choke; his arms flailed like a broken doll's.

Boggie shouted at her. "You poisoned him!"

She shook her head in fierce denial.

Feliks regained control of his legs and straightened. His eyes rolled before focusing. They rested on Boggie holding his arm. Feliks' mouth twisted into a snarl and he broke away.

"Boss! It's me," the bewildered Romanian cried.

Feliks's arms jerked, and his knife hand came up in front of his face. His fingers tightened around the handle, and he rammed the blade home deep under the big man's ribcage and up into the heart.

Keera shrieked. Zach couldn't, his mouth frozen half open.

Feliks yanked the knife free. Boggie crashed to the floor like a sack of concrete mix. Blood spilled through his punctured hoodie, running over the slate. Feliks bent over him, swaying, and with two deft strokes of the knife, sliced around the top of the head. He gripped the hair and ripped away a hank of it still attached to a bloody scalp and stood, shakily triumphant. He raised his trophy to the ceiling and unleashed his cry, chilling and primeval.

"*Aaaieeeh!*" he screamed. "*Aaaieeeh!*"

CHAPTER 25

Feliks' head rotated as it took in Keera, Zach, and the kitchen.

"Who are you?" Keera asked, focusing on the problem in front of her, trying to ignore the one leaking blood on the floor.

Feliks said, "I am Red Leaf. Who are you?" His voice had changed. No longer graced with European phrasing, but harsher and guttural.

"Keera, and this is my friend Zach."

"Now you have different name," said Red Leaf, assembling the words like building blocks. "But you walked into the body of Rain Bird. I recognize you, spirit. You change bodies, but your fire stays with you."

Red Leaf swayed as he tried to bring Feliks' body under full control, his eyes blinking, his mouth working. It would take him an hour. Best to jump him soon. Jump—an inadequate word for risking death in a split second.

"I watched you enter my new world." Red Leaf stretched out his leg and inspected the pants. "These are fine leggings. But sharp grasses and prickly bushes will shred them. Why do people here wear them?" He looked up at her. "I tried to keep you with me, but my powers were weak." He pointed to Boggie's body. "Did he walk into Slow Hand?"

"Ah, no—" Zach said, stopping as she shot him a look.

"Have I sent the wrong spirit to the next world?" Red Leaf pushed Boggie over with his foot.

The movement released the warm, suffocating smell of blood. Zach stepped back.

Red Leaf's eyes flicked in his direction. "I saw his thoughts were only basic things. That's why I made that mistake." He said to Zach, "You must be him. Your spirit needs the one that lives in the woman. I saw it before; I see it now."

"What do you want?" she asked. He'd come with a purpose, of course. Taking over a living body wasn't an afterthought.

Red Leaf cracked a grim smile across Feliks' face, which now, weirdly, displayed walnut wrinkles. "When Crazy Elk ended my life, I observed from my other world. You stole the *Wakan Tunkan* and hid it for yourselves. This cannot be. I'll remove you from this world, and you'll never claim it."

Speech seemed to irritate him; the words weren't coming smoothly enough for him. He spotted the kitchen knives on the magnetic rack and shuffled towards them. He chose the largest one. A foot-long weapon with a two-inch-wide stainless-steel blade that caught the sun through the window. A blade to bisect a buffalo.

She said, "You'd kill a fellow Oglala?"

"You're not Oglala anymore."

"Yes, I am. Just like you are always a part of whoever you were, in all your lives."

"I'll be Oglala again. I have been told this. Then I'll locate the *Wakan Tunkan,* and retrieve it. For now, I'll make sure you cannot take it before me."

His single-mindedness was insane. The Stone gripped him like a fever no argument could shake loose. He was immune to logic, to reason, to anything that meant giving it up. She tried another approach. "If you kill us then we renew our existence on the same plane as you. You can't kill us there, and we can obstruct you even more."

Red Leaf slid his eyes from her to Zach and back. "You might, you have the spirit of a zealous warrior. That one, his new surroundings will distract him. He hasn't the same passion for battle as you."

The Oglala was right. She had experienced other levels of reality, but Zach didn't. He'd be bewildered until he grasped his new situation. Time enough for Red Leaf to wreak his mischief and eliminate a shattered Zach forever. She threw Zach a despairing look, but he had no fresh arguments either. He'd swallowed Red Leaf's insult without reaction, but she knew he'd chew it over. Trying to figure out what death was like, planning to jump Red Leaf at the first chance.

"We aren't seeking the *Wakan Tunkan* for ourselves," she said. "When we find it we will use it to serve the Oglala. You can assist us in this."

"You have little power to help anyone, spirit. You ended my life before I was ready, with no chance to sing my death song. In my new world, I'll take what is due to me." His gaze roamed over the kitchen; he was in no hurry for reprisal. "Many metal things here." He tapped the sink. "A metal bucket fixed to stone? You can't carry it, what's the good of it?"

She twisted a tap handle. Water blasted into the sink. He jerked back. "You've tamed the streams, and brought them into your stone boxes. The *wasichu* always alter the earth to suit themselves. You're a sad people." He pointed at the stove. "What is this?"

She reached up to the pan rack and took down a heavy cast-iron frypan, both hands needing to hold it. "For cooking," she said, clunking the pan down and thumbing an ignition button. Gas jets burst into arcs.

Red Leaf shuffled closer to inspect this new marvel. "The fire is blue, not orange and yellow. You have changed the color of fire.

For what reason? Is there no end to your madness?"

Red Leaf was having as much trouble adapting to their world as Zach had to the Oglala's. Also, she realized, he no longer wore the battled, hardened body of a warrior, but a wiry citified one. A body he wasn't used to, and unlikely to win a physical struggle with Zach, an ex-footballer in good shape. Not if she assisted by swinging the heavy pan at Red Leaf's head.

The knife was a problem. Let him use his knife hand, and they'd be dead in seconds. Red Leaf wouldn't be very agile right now, but he was a seasoned practitioner in the art of killing. They weren't. His readiness to kill, they couldn't match. Zach moved closer to him as if to chat about the stove, but Red Leaf swiveled and thrust the knife to his throat. His hand as fast as a top boxer. The point indented the flesh without penetrating it.

"Stay back," Red Leaf warned.

Zach stepped back. Red Leaf returned to the flame, more fascinated than a moth.

She switched it off. "It is our custom that we welcome every new spirit in our world with coffee. Would you like to drink with us?"

"*Wasichu* gave me coffee once; it tasted like a gift from an earth spirit," he said. "Warm, nutty. They drank it often, but it didn't make them better soldiers. I didn't understand why they bothered."

She took out a can of coffee beans and an electric coffee grinder. Tipped a handful of beans into the grinder, and thumbed it into clattering life. Red Leaf raised his knife, ready to ward off something unknown, but she waved it away. The grinder shook and whirred, He watched like he was expecting an attack. She added water to the kettle and replaced it on its stand. Flicked the switch. The kettle fizzed, crackled and blue sparks shot out from its base.

Miniature thunderbolts streaking at Red Leaf.

The old warrior plunged his knife into the sparks. The knife point clanged off the metal casing.

"No!" she cried.

Red Leaf didn't listen. He backed off, paused, then slashed at the power cord, slicing it in two. That action released a hundred and ten volts from the mains and threw him backward.

Zach closed on him, right fist swinging in a controlled arc at his jaw. Red Leaf's head snapped sideways, his knees buckled and he sagged to the floor. Well, that was easy—Feliks possessed a glass chin. Maybe he owned a couple of dodgy knees also. Kick a knee, Zach, he won't get back up. Zach moved to grab the knife off Red Leaf, but he kicked back, and knocked him off balance.

Zach grabbed at the table, but his feet slipped on Boggie's blood and gave way beneath him. He twisted madly, scrambling from the knife he knew was coming. Red Leaf rose to his hands and knees, and flung himself at Zach. A war cry erupted in Red Leaf's throat, joined by her manic yell.

She swung the cast iron pan with arms extended to full length, aiming for his head. Red Leaf ducked, an arm raised to ward off the blow. The pan crunched into it and sent the knife skittering away. As she raised the pan again, Red Leaf crab-scuttled across to the knife, and fled through the door. His footsteps pounded down the hallway. The front door handle rattled furiously.

"He's escaping," she cried and leaped for the door. Hallway empty. Red Leaf gone. Front door shut. "He didn't know to turn the door knob," she said as Zach joined her. "He's still inside."

They stood, tense in the silence. Two rooms between them and the front door. One containing a killer with sixty scalps on his resume.   And a seriously lethal knife. Keera put a hand on his arm. "Did he hurt you?"

"No. I got the first whack in, and that messed his mind up for a few seconds. But, Jeez, he recovered fast. I didn't expect that."

His adrenaline was up, the energy curling off him in waves. The clash had sparked him into life. Not for him the patient deflecting of anger until it turned into something more useful. His way was confrontation. To crash through or crash.

"You were mighty quick with the frypan," he said. "You saved my life."

"I've saved nobody. This battle isn't over, and we'll need better weapons if we're going to survive it."

"You keep a spear in the house?"

"Take a guess."

"Think hard, Keera. We need something."

They both stared down the hallway, the silence growing thicker, threatening to suffocate their thoughts.

Zach said, "Boggie carried a gun."

CHAPTER 26

Keera asked, "How do you know about the gun?"

"I felt it when we wrestled," Zach said. "This changes everything."

It sure does, but not the way you think. "A shooting will bring the police. How do we explain this? Tell them Feliks was possessed by a long dead Oglala healer who scalped Boggie, then attacked us? Guess what? They'll decide that the guy who shot his moneylender also killed the enforcer found in the kitchen. Can you see this any other way?"

He pulled a wry face. "What about self-defense? They burst in and demanded money."

"You think you can construct a plausible story why one man was stabbed and mutilated in the kitchen, and the other one shot dead in a hallway? Looks like a macabre revenge killing to me."

"The alternative isn't looking too good either. You got any white light we could hide in?"

A soft sound from a room ahead. The left one. Followed by the chink of a belt buckle.

"Clothes," she said. "Red Leaf's stripping for battle."

"Wonderful. Look, the gun is all we have."

She brushed past him, back to the kitchen, ignored the Boggie mountain and opened a drawer. Pulled out thin sticks of bound dried leaves and twigs.

"Rather have a gun," he said, patting the body. "Red Leaf won't surrender just because you throw herbal remedies at him."

She ignited the stovetop flames and lit a handful of the sticks. Smoky trails rose into the room, bringing the dry smell of sage and fennel. Behind her, a new sound.

Bare feet slapping on the slate floor.

Red Leaf walked, wearing only Feliks' boxers, his knife gripped for a brutal thrust into a soft belly.

Eyes only for Zach.

Zach backed away, keeping the table between them. No gun in his hand; he hadn't extracted it fast enough. Red Leaf edged around the table, Zach able to keep moving, staying a safe distance from him.

Red Leaf stopped. His nose lifted as he detected the smoke. A ripple of alarm crossed his face, and he reversed his steps. He must have recognized the herb mix and knew he had to get away, to regroup for another attack. She couldn't allow it. She leaped at him, the smoking sticks gripped like a talisman.

"Go, Red Leaf," she shouted. "Go away from here." Thrust them forward, back and forth across his face.

Red Leaf slashed at her. The knife severed the top of the sage bundle, the smoky part fell to the floor. The real Red Leaf would have severed her hand, not the bundle. The Feliks version wasn't so coordinated. He raised the knife again, to drive it home.

Zach launched himself, a frenzied projectile vaulting the table and slamming into Feliks' wiry body, and sending them both crashing to the floor. They scrabbled to gain leverage over each other, but Zach was too strong. He clamped Red Leaf's knife wrist with one hand, and with the other one, he twisted the Indian's head and mashed his face into the smoldering sage embers.

Red Leaf kicked out before his eyes blanked, lashes fluttered, and his body flopped soft as a blanket. Zach knocked the knife away and stood facing her, chest heaving. He wrapped his arms around her. Her heart hammered against him, wild and furious.

"I thought you were going to die," he said.

"I thought so, too," she replied, and they lapsed into close silence again, their energies mingling and steadying each other.

"We even with the lifesaving stuff now?" he said after a while.

"Looks like it." She glimpsed Boggie over Zach's shoulder and pulled away. "There's work to do."

Zach squatted by the body and retrieved a revolver. "Might need this to make Feliks see sense. Red Leaf was bad enough, but Feliks isn't exactly Mary Poppins either." He groped for Feliks' pulse. "Steady and strong, he'll come round soon, I bet. What was the smoky stuff you used?"

"Sage and fennel. A smudge stick. Works pretty well on evil spirits, and I figured Red Leaf was one by now. He's lost a lot of higher spirituality."

"It works that fast?" Zach mock-slapped his forehead. "Why didn't you pull that out when he first appeared?"

"The second he saw me grab the bundle, he would have grasped my intentions. He would have killed me without thinking. I needed the right opportunity, and it came along, just not how I expected." She looked over at the body on the floor. "He was so close to stopping us. If even one of us was killed, the mission was over. You couldn't do it on your own, and I wouldn't."

"You wouldn't?"

"No." Don't press me for more, I'm not sure what I'm saying. He gave her a quizzical look but didn't ask her to explain.

"Will Red Leaf be back?"

"Not now that I'm ready for him. Not here." She waited for him to draw the obvious conclusion.

"Ahh, he'll be ready for us on the reservation."

"You got it. He draws his strength from there."

"So we bring a heap of those sage bundles. Wave them around fiercely." Zach's ability to resume his normal chirpy attitude only minutes after traumatic events was startling.

"He won't need to channel a body to attack. It's likely that he's played with the minds of local people who'll do his work for him."

"Acolytes?"

"Unwitting ones, but they'll be hostile."

"Sounds like a fun excursion." He surveyed Feliks lying before them. "This one needs to be out of our lives."

Our lives. Sounded like a warm place.

"He'll use you to get to me," Zach said. "I don't reckon that smoky, wavy stuff will stop him."

"It won't," she said. "We have something better." Keera placed her charred smudging sticks on the sink, and Red Leaf's knife on the counter, next to the first one, the killing knife. "A murder weapon with Feliks' fingerprints on it."

He sank into a chair, looking up at her. "You want to pin Boggie's death on him? Doesn't this go against your fair play principles?"

"Zach, I talked you into this mission, and I feel responsible. This event ends with you in the same condition you started it—in good health."

He raised eyebrows. "You saying you'll do whatever it takes to keep me happy, because happy was what I was when I first knocked on your door."

"Happiness is not the main factor, maintaining your former equilibrium is."

"I love it when you speak plainly. I'll figure out what you mean one day. Anyway, how do you intend to keep Feliks away?"

She washed her hands at the sink tap and looked around for a towel. "Well, you know, we both saw him go weird and stab his large friend."

"Isn't this against the rules of karma or something? I'm all for getting Feliks off my back, but I don't want him doing time for a murder he didn't commit."

"He won't. Feliks is clever, he knows when the odds are against him. A murder weapon with his prints all over it, a dead body, the word of two respected pillars of society against his. What do you think he'll do?"

"Respected pillars of society. I like that, except that I'm not one, and I don't think a medium is one either."

"Let's say we're higher up the pole than he is. He knows that, he'll leave us alone."

"Um, can you consult your spirit guide on this?"

"I hope you're not getting dependent on our guides."

"The more opinions the better, I say."

But she knew she was right. Feliks preferred to avoid authorities. His American papers might be fake for a start, and his tax affairs of interest to the IRS. Feliks wouldn't welcome any official contact.

Zach left the room and returned with Feliks' clothes. Worked through them, searching for a gun. No gun, just a slim wallet. She glimpsed a few bills and plastic cards. He put it back in the jacket. Feliks stirred and tried to sit. Zach lifted him up by the armpits and stood him up against the wall.

"How you feeling?" Zach asked.

Felix stared at him without comprehension, then suddenly slapped at his own head. Tiny sage and fennel embers dislodged from his cheeks and forehead, dropped to the ground.

"What did you do to me?" he growled. "Drug me and torture me with cigarettes until I faint? You think this changes anything?"

"No," Zach replied. "But your killing Boggie does." He waved Boggie's gun at the body.

Feliks twisted around and stiffened. "I killed nobody. You must have done this after you knocked me out. That tea tasted funny. Poison, that's why. It gave me strange dreams about being an Indian. An Indian, if you please." He studied the lacerated head with disgust. "When his family hear of this, you'll pay plenty. What a mess." Noticed he was half naked. "My clothes, why you steal them?"

Zach handed them over, kept the jacket. "Put them on, you might think smarter."

Feliks dressed with care and held out a hand for the jacket. Zach shook his head. "You going to steal it?"

"We need it."

"Sure you do. Wearing a high-quality item will make you a better person. Ha. Give me my wallet."

Zach handed it over, and Feliks flipped it open. "You took nothing?" he said.

"Listen to me. Who knows what meds you're on, but you went nuts for a while. Ranted at Boggie, grabbed the knife and, Jesus, what a fucking outcome."

"Knife? I have no knife." Feliks confused, but wary.

"You cut him with that knife." Zach waved the gun at the murder knife, still sporting blood traces, on the sink.

Feliks stared at it. "Not mine," he said with confident finality.

"But your fingerprints are on it." Keera watched the clouds part for Feliks and the sun illuminate every particle of nastiness in the room. The little moneylender got it.

"You're framing me for murder?" he said. "I never figured you possible of such a thing."

"Keera, could you put Mr. Feliks' jacket in a plastic bag? Also the knives in separate bags. Thank you."

She drew out a garbage bag from under the sink and stuffed the jacket into it. Pulled a plastic freezer bag out from the same place and turning it inside out, picked up the bloody knife with it. Reversed the bag, capturing the knife, and wrapped it up in paper towels.

"Do you know what she's doing?"

Feliks sniffed. "She's cleaning the kitchen like a woman should."

Keera stopped for an instant before resuming.

Zach said, "Watch your mouth, Feliks. You're in America now."

She dropped the cook's knife into a freezer bag and wrapped it like the previous one.

"My friend is preserving the evidence," Zach informed Feliks. "Both knives have your fingerprints. The smaller knife has Boggie's blood on it. The jacket, your jacket, has his blood spatters on it. Get the picture yet?"

"What do you want from me?"

Like she'd guessed, Feliks knew when to cut a quick deal.

Zach said, "My friend will leave the evidence with a trusted person, who'll have instructions to take everything to the police if anything happens to either of us. A note enclosed will describe what you did here today."

"Okay, I got it, I go now."

"There's more. The loan."

Feliks sneered back. "This is all about money? You killed Boggie for money? Zach, I thought you were a nice boy, from good family. I'm ashamed to know you."

"I didn't kill him, you did. Believe me."

Feliks turned away. He didn't believe Zach and never would. The truth was out there, but too far out there.

"I'm not keeping your money, Feliks, you'll just have to wait a while longer. We'll renegotiate the vig when the time comes. Make some sensible adjustments."

"A loan without end date or vig is not loan—it is gift."

"And a loan with a weekly interest rate of ten percent is a crime," Zach said. "One final thing. Come back tonight when it's dark. Ten o'clock. Bring one, strong friend, and take the body away. You can go now."

Feliks drew his car keys out of his pants pocket and stalked out of the kitchen, Zach following.

Well, that was easy. Kind of.

CHAPTER 27

Zach eyed Boggie's bulk. "Time for housekeeping."

Keera wrinkled her nose.

"Feliks might dispose of the body too well. We better have proof it existed. Let's take some snaps."

She rummaged in her bag on the counter and produced a cell phone. She knelt down and fired off two close-ups of Boggie's cruel haircut and a couple more from further back to show the scene. "I'll email these to myself." She swallowed a few times.

"Do you have a place to store the evidence?" Give her stuff to think about, stuff to do, leave no space to dwell on the killing.

"A deposit box at the bank, but it's too small for this."

"Rent another one, bigger." He squashed the jacket. "Let's hope the customers enjoy Calvin Klein's scent. Tape?"

She handed him a roll from a drawer, and he pulled it around the bundle several times until it resembled a hefty handbag. "Buy extra-strength document envelopes and stick this in. Add the knives. When you have the evidence safe, write a short note to your lawyer, the bank will have stationery, and enclose the keys with it. Post this to him. I'll prepare Boggie for travel."

She gathered up the parcel and knives and hesitated before she left. Zach expected a goodbye kiss on his cheek, but she murmured, "See you soon" and vanished. He knew little about auras, but hers he could read a mile off. Stay away from me unless I say otherwise. The kind that tried to control events but found it impossible to control emotions. The kind that drove him away to find less difficult arrangements with others. Not this time.

Drawn to her in a way he couldn't analyze, a primeval, chromosomal bond kept him desiring her no matter what she dished out. This was new: an unconditional commitment, and it surprised him how easily he accepted it. The power of love—must be something in it after all.

Boggie's scalp lay near a corner; he picked it up and dropped it on the body. "Sorry about the scalping thing," he said aloud. "Nobody deserves that. But your undertaker will do a magnificent job getting you presentable for the laying out." A distasteful rummage through the pockets produced just over a thousand dollars in a wallet. "Thanks." He stuffed the bills into his pocket. "You wouldn't believe the overheads I have."

He dragged a plastic garbage bag over the top half of the body and another over the bottom half. He rolled the body over and over as he taped the two bags together. An exhausting task; the limbs stiffer than he expected, with rigor mortis resisting every move already.

He found a mop in a corner closet and wiped the floor clean. The same closet contained a stiff brush. Wetting it under the sink tap, he scrubbed the slate tiles hard and mopped up again. A half hour later they were free of visible blood. A forensic guy might find traces, but it would never come to that. With luck.

He kept a small backpack of clothes in the Mustang's trunk for those times when it was handy. Now he retrieved it and located a bathroom upstairs. The shower was refreshing, luxurious, and he made cheerful use of expensive-looking gels, shampoos, and conditioners. Skipped the moisturizers. His old clothes he stuffed into a plastic bag and dropped them in the trunk. Made a mental note to dump them as soon as possible.

In the kitchen, he tried to switch the kettle back on before he remembered Red Leaf had severed the cord. He rummaged in the cupboards and grabbed a pot with a lid he could use instead. A coffee plunger sat nearby. He dropped Keera's ground beans in it, adding the water when it was hot enough. Poured the coffee into a man-sized mug and sipped the it, blanking his thoughts, letting his mind untangle itself. A single idea kept returning. It was the worst day of his life and the best. Even stranger—it was also the longest one.

A couple of hours later, the front door opened and Keera's footsteps sounded along the hallway.

"How did it go? Oh," she said as she spotted the neat, black pile in the corner. "How come you're so good at this?" Suspicion clouded her face.

"A journalist," he said, "knows a little about a lot of things. Once, I interviewed a hit man, and he explained how to clean up a s-cene."

"And you've showered, I see."

"There could have been blood on me after that tussle. I had to be sure. How did you do?"

"Fine. All done."

"Anybody say anything?"

"No. The manager hardly listens to me. He just stares at my breasts."

Who could blame him? "How gross. The letter posted?"

She nodded.

"You want me to brew tea for you?" The things a guy will do when he wants to be considered a helluva guy.

"No, I couldn't hold anything down right now." She gave him an appraising look. "Why do you owe Feliks money?"

He considered telling the truth for a whole second. But explaining yourself to somebody is a bad way to forge a relationship.

"Bad financial habits, a bunch of debts. Borrowed ten grand off Feliks to consolidate them. Not a problem to pay back, except I needed to fix my car. Fell behind in my payments, you know, the usual story. Or maybe you don't. You come from a wealthy family, as you said."

"We all have to play the cards we're dealt with at birth."

Good answer, if you're born rich. The doorbell sounded. She glanced at the kitchen clock. "It must be Feliks."

He left the room, his hand on the gun in his pocket, hoping not to shoot himself in the leg. Opened the door to see Feliks standing there with frozen eyes and a tight mouth. Alongside him, a bigger version of Boggie. Same slab of a face, same set of arm muscles looking for a violent workout.

"This is Anatole," Feliks moved his head to his left. "He's Bogdan's brother." Feliks more formal with family present. Anatole didn't bother with a greeting. Made do with a steely glare that promised sadism, torture and the slowest death possible.

"Come in," Zach said. "Lovely to see you all." He led them down the hallway to the kitchen. Keera standing ready, the knife rack empty. Somebody had had her fill of knives for the evening.

"There's Bogdan," Zach pointed with the gun. "We said prayers for him. A tragic loss to all."

Anatole picked up the body wrapped in black plastic, still in a sitting position. Rigor mortis had frozen its death tableau. Tears rimmed Anatole's eyes as he brushed past Zach and headed for the front door, Boggie's bulk draped over his shoulder.

Feliks held back. "I'll keep the deal, but I have not much control over Boggie's relatives." A pained expression. "Romanians, thick on family matters, but they don't care about other things. Like agreements they didn't agree to."

"They're your problem. It doesn't matter who comes after us. If we suffer, your life as you know it is over."

Feliks gave him a hunted look, as if to say I wish it weren't this way. Zach led him to the front door where Anatole waited, still cradling Boggie's body. The big guy refused to look at Zach. He went down the steps and straight to an orange Ford. Feliks unlocked the back door. Boggie was lowered gently onto the seat. Feliks pointed a finger and thumb at Zach, the cocked revolver gesture, before climbing in the front and driving them away.

Back in the kitchen, Zach found Keera surveying the space with a distant look on her face. She blinked and rejoined the here and now. "See anything I should know about?" he asked.

"The big man, he's gone. No residual traces left."

"No angry spirit hanging about, ready to destroy our peaceful evening?"

"Red Leaf isn't close by either, but let's not discuss him because our thoughts alone draw him back."

"I'm down with that. You know something? I've hardly eaten for a couple of hundred years. Got any food in here or just coffee, tea, and sharp knives?"

Keera opened the refrigerator. "Brie with French bread, washed down with a half-bottle of Chablis."

"The Chablis sounds good. Any roast beef or ham?"

"I don't keep meat."

"Why did I even think of asking that question?"

She placed in front of him a wooden board holding the French stick and the cheese. Added a serrated knife and a cheese knife from a drawer. She poured a glass each for them as Zach sawed at the bread. He took his piece and broke it apart.

"Any butter?"

"One doesn't add butter to bread and brie."

"That's right. I forgot."

How prissy could she get about food? They should discuss this one day. If he wasn't assuming too much. About there being another day. There had to be. The way she held onto him after Red

Leaf's departure. Like she never wanted to let go. Her heart thudding against him. Best thing ever. He spread brie over his unbuttered bread and bit into it.

"Superb, my compliments to the chef."

He tilted his glass and let the cold wine flow into his soul. It made for warm drowsiness. Nothing more to do but wait for Keera's offer to mingle their souls more effectively.

She said, "I don't believe your story about the money."

Uh oh. "What does it matter? I owed him money, and now I don't. Problem solved, situation dealt with, tomorrow will dawn a fresh day."

"Seeing as how we have a way to go before we're done, I think more honesty between us would be useful."

Zach swallowed more wine. Time to explain a few facts of life. "You know something? Honesty is overrated. The world gets by with very little of it. In fact, people are so conditioned to being lied to, that I have discovered it's easier to flummox them with the simple truth.","Fine. Flummox me."

"No. I don't see how this is any of your business. I don't recall having to pass any test to join up with you, or make any promises. All I did was show up, express skepticism, and, hey, I got the position."

"There were other factors at work. You had, and still have, attributes useful to the project."

"I bet honesty isn't one of them."

"It's become more important lately."

"Since when?"

She didn't answer, messed about with her bread and cheese without actually eating any of it. "You lost your money on a horse."

Jesus, no. She was working her psychic stuff on him. No fair, they were allies.

"I received confusing images when we first met, and now I understand more.

"What I don't get is how Red Leaf could take over Feliks like that. Did Feliks leave himself psychically open in some fashion?"

"It was quite a lot of money."

"It can't be that easy to channel a moneylender," Zach added

"The money wasn't yours, was it?" she said. "You borrowed it? From Feliks, of course."

"If Red Leaf tried to take over me, I reckon I could fight him off."

Her eyes widened. "Wait, you borrowed ten thousand dollars? For a single bet?"

He recalled the homeless woman who had accepted his twenty. "I didn't bet all of it. Some of it I used wisely."

"That's not—"

"Stop it. Just stop it."

"I need to—"

"No, you don't. You're taking advantage. You notice how I don't pry into your private life? But you question me on mine, just because you see things others don't."

Keera tore off another chunk of bread and spread brie over it. "I can't help what I see. When I'm shown images, I assume it's for a purpose, so I ask questions."

"Ask all the questions you like, but I don't have to answer them. Nobody has the right to demand answers of another, and don't confuse a desire for privacy with innate dishonesty." That didn't draw a ready response. She worked on her bread and cheese while she thought. When she bit off more bread, she was so delicate about it he was surprised any of it came loose.

She said, "I take your point, although you sound like a lawyer desperate to win his first case."

He let the slight insult pass. He was winning the argument.

"The thing is, we'll be operating in a physical world from now on. You're an impulsive risk taker on a major scale. You might find the consequences of being wrong more permanent than you thought."

"Can you put that in plain English?"

"We'll be dealing with people who are volatile and resentful of whites."

"But we're on their side."

"That may be so, but you represent centuries of oppression and genocide."

She sipped more wine, eyeing him in serene contemplation, her earlier heat gone. She must have also recalled when he'd saved her from Red Leaf. Every little bit helped. Her gaze dropped to his lips. This was encouraging. Evidently mashing an evil spirit's face into sage embers had made him more attractive. She constructed another chunk of bread and cheese, her appetite returning by the minute.

"All I'm saying is that you need to watch your step and mind your mouth," she said.

"Don't worry about my mouth. I'll keep it firmly in place."

"For how long?"

"As long as it takes." Her helping of bread and cheese disappeared faster than the previous one. She licked a stray piece of cheese off a finger and refilled her glass. Downed it. Pushed back her chair and stood.

"It's time for bed," she said.

Upstairs she flicked a switch in her bedroom, and two bedside lamps flicked on, bracketing a large bed. She drew back the white top sheet and the Navajo blanket that covered it. An ancient set of drawers stood against a wall opposite a lace-framed window. An equally ancient wooden chest at the foot of the bed. A solitary Persian rug adorned the floor.

She said, "Go to bed. I'll be back."

She kissed him on the lips. His teeth captured flesh, gently rasping, exploring. "Go to bed," she repeated huskily.

"You sure about this?" he asked, teasing her. "Fool around with a gambling wastrel like me?"

"We don't want to die wondering, do we?" She left the room.

Zach undid his shirt and pants. Tugged off his shoes and socks and dropped them near a chair against the wall. Drew back the covers and slid between smooth sheets. Bliss. Fluffed the pillows, caught the scent of her hair, and with it, the promise of a perfect evening.

Fifteen minutes later, Keera entered the bedroom. She wore a thin cotton robe and rubbed her neck with a towel. Inspected him with unnerving inscrutability while she dried herself and switched off the lights. Moonlight from the undraped window washed her in silver as she faced him, and let the robe slip. An intoxicating vision and she knew it—of course she did.

And it came with an unmistakable message: he'd better be worth it.

CHAPTER 28

Zach woke up alone. Early morning light streamed in through the window overlooking a small rear garden. A gray squirrel ran up a tree, paused to evaluate him, then flicked itself to the other side of the trunk. Somehow, God knows how, the skittish critter reminded him of Keera. He climbed into his jeans and tee, padded barefoot down the stairs to the kitchen.

Keera sat at the long table dipping a spoon into muesli. She wore an azure silk robe that underscored the darker blue of her eyes. So, this is how the rich live: one robe for the night and another for the morning.

"Want some?" she asked, pointing at the bowl.

He ruffled his hair. "Is it a big bother if I organize bacon and eggs and coffee?"

"I don't keep bacon."

"Of course."

"But you can have eggs on toast, and you know where the coffee is."

"Say no more." He opened the refrigerator and soon had two eggs sizzling in a pan. The coffee steamed in his cup, the first gulp already cheering his stomach. "So," he ventured after a while. "How are you feeling today?"

"Fine, thanks." She flashed him a small smile and returned her eyes to her breakfast.

"Fine? What about triumphant because we've almost accomplished our mission? Relieved because we overcame Red Leaf and Feliks. Spiritually fulfilled because we were finally joined as God intended."

Keera spooned the last of the muesli into her mouth and dropped the spoon into the bowl. "I think 'fine' sums up my feelings precisely. No more, no less." She glanced at the kitchen clock. "Time to move soon. The flight to Rapid City leaves at one."

"Rapid City?" She was closing the shutters on him again. Shouldn't have mentioned last night.

"The closest airport to Pine Ridge."

Maybe he hadn't fulfilled her expectations. Nope. He knew what to do, and she had enjoyed every moment, every touch. They had made love twice, in fact. The second time instigated by her. She was probably embarrassed at exposing her feelings. Retreating while she figured herself out. Needed time to deal with that. Fine, he could wait. She was worth it.

He scooped the eggs onto a plate. "What about driving there? In a splendid car, an American classic. Leather seats, terrific sound system, and an experienced driver. We wind down the windows, enjoy the breeze in our hair."

"The drive takes fourteen hours at least." "I can do it quicker than that, I bet."

"No doubt. We'll be riding horses along that creek again, and you need to be fresh. You take us to the airport." She patted him on the shoulder as she left the room.

Was she putting him back to first base? He rinsed his dishes and dropped them in the dishwasher. Picked up his cell. "Nicola? Hi, it's Zach."

"Are you all right?" The kid sounded concerned.

"Sure. Well, to tell the truth, I'm feeling downright poorly today, so I won't be in if anybody asks."

"You should know, Zach, two security guards are at your desk, dumping your stuff in a box."

"What?"

"We've been sold. The magazine, I mean. To this media corporation from Phoenix or somewhere."

Was this good news or bad? "I'm fired or something? Did Edwina make any announcement?"

"Um, she's gone too, Zach. They say there's a new editor soon. Younger, more in tune. Nobody asked me, and I know heaps of stuff."

Nothing beats being young and confident, except being young, confident—and rich.

"Edwina left this morning," Nicola continued. "The owner guy, Caspar something, came in and gave a speech. He said the magazine was interfering with his main business. Yeah, the HR guy is looking for you. Said you're terminated, but not to tell anybody. I'm sorry."

"It's OK. Did my name get mentioned anytime?" "Um, not so much. Some guy said your pieces killed advertising. Other guys said you were worth having around, just for the laugh factor, but I didn't get it. You were always nice to me, but you never made me laugh that much."

Killed advertising. I fucking hope so. Particularly the sugared water ads that deprived people of a life. Sorry about the laughs, Nicola.

"Zach? Do you mind if I take your chair? It's more comfortable than mine."

"Sure, it's yours." Nicola's grasp that the small things of office life were equally important as the big things was cute and childlike. Or maybe it was an accurate assessment of how to get ahead in that world. The morning was getting brighter by the minute. He was now free to work elsewhere. Plus, a hefty termination package to come that would sort out his immediate finances. "Tell the HR people I'll be in tomorrow. Gonna miss you."

"Me too, Zach. See you then."

He replaced the receiver to find Keera standing next to him.

"I sense you're fired, and you're happy," she said.

He wrapped her up in a hug. She didn't resist. "You are such a great psychic," he said, planting a kiss on her cheek. "Let's get that Stone."

"Yes, let's," she murmured. She broke free and took the stairs again.

An hour later, Keera let him open the passenger door for her.

"It gets stuck sometimes," he said.

She spotted the lie; he was trying to impress her. Sweet.

He scowled at the bird droppings on the roof before ducking into the driver's seat. "I can't believe this didn't get towed for over-parking."

"That's because I surrounded it with white light to protect it."

"What? You can do that?" Zach turned to see her laughing. "Very funny, Keera, very funny."

He fired up the engine, eased into the road and cruised to the next intersection. "Nice car."

"It's good," he acknowledged, his chest lifting at the compliment.

Once they were airborne and leveled out, Zach surprised her by falling into a calm sleep. His energy body was depleted, she realized. And sex the night before wouldn't have helped his condition. The sex. Her sudden physical desire for him had caught her unawares. It couldn't have been the wine, not one glass. And Boggie had died only feet away from where they sat. They were chatting in the middle of a fresh murder scene, for God's sake.

Somehow none of that mattered. And once Zach protested that she was digging into his private life in a way she had no right to. She understood what he was saying: I fix my own problems; I don't need you involved. I respect what you do, but there are limits where you go. This was new.

Her previous relationships had veered between those who wanted guidance every damn minute, and those who froze when the subject of her being psychic came up. That wasn't counting the others who knew she was the only child of wealthy parents and set out to establish themselves as her partners for life. So many like that.

Zach was different. True, he carried a subtle disdain for her wealth and privileged background. Okay, not so subtle. But not with the same undercurrent that others did, the indignant implication that they deserved as much. Zach understood she was born lucky, that's all. He had given his word that he'd help her, and he had. It must have been so overwhelming for him at times, but he never wavered after the first few minutes. He was still with her. And not just because he wanted her body. He knew she wasn't amenable to his clumsy approaches. He knew his looks, his boyish joking, his confidence didn't work on her. Well, only a little.

A shape appeared at her side. She looked up to decline any coffee and found Bardo standing there. Since when did you need to fly domestic to get anywhere? She asked him silently.

We didn't have this kind of transport in my day. It's quite fun, isn't it? Not as fast as traveling by thinking, but there are other advantages.

Even for you?

I'd recommend the cupcakes if they offer you any. They're trying out a new menu.

How do you know they're good? You have no physical taste buds.

I only have to see them, and my soul detects the quality. My spirit stomach soars in delight.

Bardo, have you joined me to point out the tasty options on a flight?

Sorry, I became distracted. Red Leaf knows you're coming. I figured that much. If you get close to the stone, he'll defend it.

If? There's still an 'if'?

Of course. Your mission still has some way to run. Be careful of men with guns.

He was gone. A flight attendant walked along the aisle, offered cupcakes.

"No, thanks," Keera said. "I've lost my appetite." She glanced over at Zach dozing. Unfolded the thin blanket provided and draped it over him.

He woke. "How you doing?" he asked with a sleepy smile. "Anything freaky happen while I was off watch?"

Yes, I decided I liked you. A lot. "It's been quiet. Evil spirits don't like crowded flights."

At Rapid City Regional Airport, they collected a Jeep Wrangler. "We'll need the ground clearance," she told him when he wrinkled his nose at the idea.

They traveled east on Highway 44, heading for the Pine Ridge Reservation. "I've meant to ask," she said. "Do you have your news story figured out?"

Zach rubbed his chin with one hand, steering with the other. "You ever thought of replacing the razor in your bathroom? What I'd write and what would appear in print are two different things. I don't know where to place it yet, either. Let's see how the finale pans out first."

Ever since they had climbed into the car and headed for Pine Ridge, a foreboding had descended on her. Here, in the heart of God's beautiful prairie, killing grounds had been established for centuries. Lakota defending their lives against Crow and

Pawnee, and then all of them defending themselves against the white intruders from the East, while still fighting each other. Now, the two of them had arrived, intent on finding the *Wakan Tunkan.* Red Leaf wouldn't sit back and watch.

They entered the Badlands National Park, paid the entry fee, and drove in silence as the landscape permeated her senses. The grasses bent and waved as they had two hundred years earlier. Scores of eroded buttes and pinnacles reared up out of the grass-lands. Choppy ridges, streaked with brown and ochre layers of sediment, extended to the horizon.

"Why is this called the Badlands?" he asked. "It looks gorgeous to me, in a moonscape kind of way."

"Extreme temperatures, little water," she said. "Beautiful to you and me, not so much if you arrived here in a covered wagon, desperate to find food and water."

They drove south further into the Reservation and passed through small villages. Many of the houses must have been de-signed in a government back room by a clerk at lunchtime. Stocky elongated boxes without charm, their sidings defeated by the weathering of the years. Yards with weeds and rusting cars straddling either side of rutted driveways. In one place, a whole car lay disassembled into its separate parts. A carcass of a gearbox rested in the long grass. Once, the ancestors of these people kept their precious ponies near their tipis; now they kep-t car wrecks.

"This is depressing me," Zach said.

It was doing the same to her. "Welcome to the Rez. The poorest county in the land. The health issues here don't bear thinking about."

One home sported a double mattress propped against a wall; a sagging window frame kept it company. Windblown litter occu-pied ground space.

"That doesn't mean they have to be so damn junky," he said. "You can't tell me people want to live in a junkyard."

"The car isn't junk. It's somebody's bedroom. Probably several persons. The rubbish stays because there's no money for repairs. But don't get me started."

They passed a road sign unrecognizable as to its purpose: several dozen bullets had riddled the metal to mesh. A scattering of Budweiser cans marked the base.

At Wounded Knee, she stopped them. "Let's walk."

She took him to the top of a hill with the graves of Oglala from times past to present, and to view the killing grounds of the massacre across the road.

She pointed to an area near the creek. "One hundred and fifty Lakota slaughtered in the snow by US Army artillery."

She listened for the faint cries of men, women, and children that might still resonate but heard only the wind. No surprise. What spirit would return to the scene of their worst physical moment?

She pointed back at the town. "About fifty years ago, the government came back. Laid a two-and-a-half-month siege after a protest about living conditions. Not so many killed this time—two Lakota, two FBI agents. And the whole protest movement."

Zach stared over the rolling hills. It would have been impossible for him not to be affected by the place.

"How could an army shell a bunch of defenseless people?" He shook his head. "It hardly bears thinking about."

They stopped at the intersection of US 18, and a pickup flew past, straddling the middle of the road. A hand appeared out of the driver's window and jerked upward. A can flew over the roof and bounced twice before settling in the dusty verge.

"There goes the Tidy Town Award for this year," Zach said.

The pickup receded into the distance, the driver alternating between the left side of the road and the right.

"We have a drunk driving problem here?" he asked.

She stared out her window. "The stats are awful. Just don't drive at night, that's all I can say."

He followed the pickup. Stands of yellow pines in the distance came into view, then a water tower. The town of Pine Ridge defined its center with a gas station, and they pulled into it. A twenty-year-old Chevy rumbled past them, wheel arches encrusted with rust, windows rattling with sonic boom.

"There's a diner inside," she said as she opened her door.

"Good, I'm hungry enough to eat a dozen of anything."

"Hot dogs?"

"Please, nothing that reminds me of puppies."

CHAPTER 29

Inside the diner, aisles of snacks filled half the place, tables, and booths the other half. A long counter offered hot food choices. Behind it, a plump girl in her late teens sported a swirly neck tattoo and took orders. Zach dropped into a booth and waited for Keera to emerge from the bathroom.

Several Oglala men at the next table, with the lined, sagging faces of the frequently hungover, discussed something in Lakota. A language in which he'd been proficient a few hours earlier, but now, he realized, he could only recall a handful of words.

Two backpacking girls browsed the food counter. German, or maybe Scandinavian, their blonde hair and creamy white skin contrasting with the rest of the diner's clientele. A lone older man chewed a burger, a coffee beside it. A single feather dangled from the back of his cowboy hat.

Keera returned. "I'll order. What'll you have?"

"A burger will be fine, and water."

She slipped away and waited by the German girls, who eyed her with quick sideways glances. He knew what they were thinking: who's the prettier? Us or her? No contest, girls. Keera outclasses everybody.

She rejoined him at the booth. "The counter girl said to ask at the post office in Oglala if we want horses. The woman that operates it knows a guy."

"Where's that?"

"West of here, not far. We ride about five miles from there to the bend where we cached the Stone."

"And if we don't find it today?"

"If we have a good idea where it is, then we come back with metal detectors that might pick up the knife buried with it."

The counter girl announced that hamburger and salad and fries were ready, and Zach fetched their orders.

"Wanna buy a choker? Traditional Lakota." A young Oglala woman stood next to him. She wore a battered red-and-white high school jacket over jeans and carried a ragged canvas bag. A sizable baby bump told him she was nearing the end of her pregnancy. The same age as Rain Bird back then and scrabbling for a living in the same way. Only now it was easier to sell artifacts than pick berries. A three-row choker with a dangle decorated her slim neck.

"It's real, all right. Real buffalo bone, sort of," the woman said, mistaking his lack of response for disinterest.

Buffalo bones. Images of the camp flooded back. The successful hunt, the joyful feasting on the prairie's bounty. Keera swallowing raw liver.

"You wanna check out the chokers or me?" She was tart, but not enough to blow a sale. "You got a girlfriend with you. Why you checking out a skin?"

"Sorry, sorry." He indicated the spot next to Keera. "You remind me of someone, that's all. Have a seat."

Keera shuffled along the bench, and the woman settled next to her. "There's bear claw necklaces, too," she said. "If you're interested." Her faded blue tee under her jacket wore an illegible statement. Zach forced himself to stop staring.

"What's your name?"

"Susie No Heart." She fished inside her canvas bag and handed a necklace to him. A single bear claw polished to a high sheen was the centerpiece, set off by black, red and silver beading. Much prettier than Red Leaf's and not so aggressive a statement.

He draped it over his fingers. "You make these yourself?"

Susie glanced over to the service counter. "My mother and her friends make them. They got the old designs still in their heads. I add ideas I seen in magazines or movies. We're thinking of building a website to sell direct, maybe blankets too, but money, you know …"

"Does your partner do any of this?"

She gazed out the window, and he noticed the dark circles under her eyes. "There was a guy, but he spent too much time in bars. Hated the Rez and wanted to live in Rapid City. I didn't, but I went. Skins get picked on there. Raymond never backed down, and one day a knife finished him. The guy wasn't charged. Self-defense, the cops said."

"I'm sorry to hear that."

"Bet you're sorry you asked."

"I'm a journalist, I can't help asking questions. I don't mean to pry." She was outwardly contemptuous of him for asking dumb-ass questions like a tourist, pretending to be empathic. She had to stay polite to close a sale, but it'd make a saint prickly.

Susie continued. "I ended with a kid to raise without him and another on the way. My mother helped, and to tell you the truth, I don't know if it was a bad thing he went when he did. He wasn't much for the kids to look up to."

"You mean he was an alcoholic?" Was she playing him with a sob story now?

She laughed, but it sounded like wailing. "Round here, beer is oxygen. They wear beads, braid their hair and try to act the warrior, but all they do is drink, talk and fight each other. Some warriors."

Zach cocked his head at Keera, who returned a blank face. He was on his own here.

"Is this because they have no more hunting?"

"You writing a major league story on us?" "No, no. It's just I thought that, you know ..."

"You know nothing. You're not Lakota, you can't understand what it's like." She leaned over and lifted some fries from his plate.

I was once one of you, he thought, knowing he couldn't, shouldn't even try to explain.

"Everybody says if we got the Black Hills back everything would be great," she said, after chomping the fries. "It's not the Black Hills, and it's not the hunting that's the problem. The Lakota have lost their spirit somewhere, and we can't find it again." She fished a choker out of her bag. Four rows of bones interspaced with turquoise beads. "Thirty-five dollars for this. Forty-five for the first necklace."

Zach put it on the table. "Turquoise is an Oglala thing? I thought it was Navajo."

Susie shrugged. "It is, but white people expect it. Turquoise means any tribe to them."

"Real buffalo bones?"

"Proper imitation sinew and cattle bone beads. No more buffalo left, or haven't you noticed?" Effective sales talk would never be her thing.

"Yeah, but you said—"

"I said what I had to say to make you look. The work will sell itself, it's pretty, and it's real, not made in China or Mexico. Don't your girlfriend like them?"

Zach glanced again at Keera, who seemed content to watch, not talk. "She has plenty already," he assured Susie. "But you got a sale. I'll take both pieces. My mom will love them."

"That's eighty bucks. Pass it under the table, I'm not supposed to sell in here."

He eased out his wallet and plucked out a bunch of twenties, concealing the action with his jacket. "I feel like a kid making his first dope deal. Can't we do this outside somewhere?"

Susie palmed the bills. "Always pick the berries when you find them. What's over the hill only the Great Spirit knows. Old Oglala saying." She gathered up her bag and stood. "Funny thing is, the white men came here, selling us blankets and beads. Now we sell them back. How weird is that?" She navigated past the tables and out of the diner.

Keera said, "You paid way too much."

In the car, she closed her eyes and tried to get a fix on what lay ahead of them. Nothing solid came through. Just the continual whispering undercurrent of hostility. As if the air itself resented their presence.

"You were quiet back there," Zach said.

She sipped from a water bottle. "I start losing control when I hear the drunk stories, the knifing stories, and the lack of ordinary justice for these people. There are other priorities today. I kept my distance."

"Looks like the women still do all the work, huh? What do the men do without hunting and boasting?"

"They drink and boast. Unemployment at eighty percent, average lifespan here is under fifty years. No one's counting coup anymore, just counting cans of Bud."

"Anyone with ideas to fix all this?"

"No. It's almost unfixable. The Lakota nation has to sort itself out, not rely on outsiders. The problem is, if any leaders appear, half the people automatically work against them. It's like a genetic law that they've inherited: thou shalt not follow leaders." She finished her drink. "Let's go."

Zach navigated out of the lot and pointed the car to Oglala. A dam appeared on the left as they drove. "I bet that wasn't there two hundred years ago," he said. "What if the creek we buried the Stone next to is now an enormous lake?"

"This is the only sizable body of water around here. I checked the maps. It doesn't stretch to where we left the Stone." Thank God. Even with a sparse population in the Rez, the years had brought many changes.

A group of houses marking the town of Oglala came into view. They bounced into the empty lot next to the cement post office. Inside, a lone woman sorted mail behind the counter. Apart from the thick plaid shirt she wore, she looked little different from the older women back then. Except she was heavier than her constantly hungry ancestors, and none of the grooves on her face were laughter lines.

"Hi," Keera said. The woman didn't look up.

"You lost or something?"

"Oh no," she said. "We're hoping to rent horses. Do you know who does that?"

"Horses? Sure." The woman stopped sorting and inspected her. "You better see Ikey."

"Ikey?" "Isaac Shy Deer. Drive back along the Eighteen towards Oelrichs. Stop at a blue cabin. He keeps a couple, for God knows what reason." She threw an envelope into a sack hanging off a metal frame. "He's probably there now 'cos my nephew supposed to be there to fix up his pesky heater. It's always breaking." The women resumed her sorting with an embarrassed grunt. Like she'd talked too much.

"Thanks," Keera said.

She plucked Zach's sleeve, and they left. A half hour later Zach pulled the Jeep to a stop outside a blue box of a home. Two horses grazed inside a fenced yard, the grass cropped short.

"Horses make fine lawn mowers," he said. "Cut and fertilize the same day."

A man opened the front door and gazed at them. About sixty years old, though it was hard to be accurate. Around here, visible aging was most likely the result of constant drinking. They walked up to him. Close up, she recognized the flannel shirt over greasy jeans and a cowboy hat with a feather dangling from the back. The solitary diner sitting near them at the gas station.

"Hi," she said. "Are you Ikey? The lady in the post office said you rent horses."

The man dipped his head. "Fifty dollars each for the afternoon if you want to ride bareback like old times. Saddles are extra." He stood still and patient while he waited for a reply.

She glanced at Zach. "How much extra?" she asked.

"Another twenty. Each."

"We'll take them."

Ikey returned inside, swaying with a pronounced limp. He passed a couple of yellow dogs that hadn't moved and reappeared with a saddle and blanket. He placed the saddle on the ground and threw the blanket over one horse. She stroked its nose, and it pushed its face into her hand like an old friend.

"This one's in fine condition," she said, running hands over gleaming, brushed flanks. The horse stomped its foot like it appreciated the compliment.

"My family moved to Sturgis." Ikey hefted the saddle onto the horse's back and tightened the cinch with bent and splayed fingers, the result of arthritis, accidents or both. "These horses are all I got, don't like to see them in a bad way. The horse has been a good friend of the Oglala; we owe them. This one is Moon, the other is Walker."

The saddle, gleaming with fresh polish, was decorated with red, yellow, white and black beading all around its edge. Two feathers hung from the reins either side of the horse's mouth.

"Nice feathers," Zach said.

Ikey glanced over. "White folk want me to paint these horses with Oglala markings, but I tell them those were each warrior's personal medicine. They're not decorations for tourists."

"Of course not." Ikey made another trip into his blue box and came back with the blanket and saddle for the second horse. "These two are trained to stop wherever you let the reins fall."

"That's very thoughtful," Zach said.

Careful Zach, don't mock him.

Ikey gave him a full-frontal gaze, determining whether he was being insulted. Didn't pull out a knife. Must have decided he wasn't.

"Not so good for you city types, though," he said, as he slipped a bit between the horse's teeth. "You fall off, the horse won't come running home to tell me. You might be hurt, especially if you're not used to falling. No good cell reception out there, no emergency service coming to help. Your horse has no medical training, ain't much for sympathy either."

He finished saddling the second horse and handed the reins to Zach. "So, you know what I'm going to do?" Zach shook his head. "You not back an hour before sundown, I'll come looking for you. Know what else that means?" Zach shook his head again. "You better tell me where you're going."

Keera dug out a handful of bills from her jeans and handed them to the man. "We want to ride along Black Tail Deer Creek. Maybe spot old campgrounds."

The old man took her money without counting it. "Old campgrounds? You hopin' to find some forgotten buffalo strips drying on a rack somewheres? You better off buying some jerky at the store."

She smiled at him. She'd met plenty of crusty guys on other reservations and gaining their confidence was impossible. A lifetime's work even to try. "No, nothing like that."

"Leave me the keys to your car," Ikey said.

Zach fished them out of his back pocket.

"The creek is due west of here. But ride up this road, heading north until you find a gap in the fence. Cut through it and then swing west. The owner lives a thousand miles away. No one will bother you."

"Thanks," she said.

"Just one thing, though."

She waited.

"The Black Tail isn't much of a sight this time of year. If it's a romantic ride you want, you're in for a disappointment."

"Disappointment in romance?" She swung into the saddle, caught Zach's eye. "I'm used to it."

CHAPTER 30

Keera followed Ikey's directions, taking them up the track, walking the horses, until they had passed all the dwellings. The gap in the fence was a mile further along the road, and they turned in. They climbed rises and dropped into shallow depressions. A line of trees showed a creek ahead.

"Let's start there," she said, kicking her horse into a slow canter, down a slope of short grass dotted with a waist-high bushes. Zach kept up.

"Reckon I got this horse-riding thing figured out," he laughed as he drew up beside her. "Walker and me are a unit."

"Yeah, right," she said. "You've let go of the conscious and surrendered to the subconscious, that's what you've done. But you'll need more experience before you're proficient. Don't get cocky just yet." She pointed to the stand of trees five hundred yards away. "That should be the creek. By the cottonwoods."

"Race you to it." Zach tapped Walker's flanks with his heels. The horse didn't hesitate, taking the slope like a toboggan, flying towards the trees. She couldn't catch him, pulling up a few seconds behind.

"That was a blast," he said, panting. "Don't know what it is about speed, but when I ride fast, I'm more alive."

"Because you're closer to death, the way you ride." She sucked in air. "Maybe you shouldn't do it again until you're a better horseman. I don't want to lose you so quickly."

They followed the creek's twists and turns for an hour, sometimes guessing the general direction and taking shortcuts due west but never losing it.

"Wasn't it running faster before?" he said.

"That was a different season," Keera said. "And two hundred years changes things."

The ground beneath stayed grassy and undulating. They cantered from time to time, the lengthening afternoon shadows reminding her only a few hours remained in the day.

Zach stood on his stirrups. "That's the campsite." He pointed forward. "I recognize the landscape. The trees are different, but the slope to the creek is the same."

They dismounted. "Around here is where Little Bear guarded the horses." He waved his arms as he paced, retracing his steps as Slow Hand.

She saw the camp as it had been, the horses, the tipis smoking through their tops, the dogs, and the children. Saw Three Dogs puzzling over Slow Hand's words and laughed to herself. Saw Little Bear's mutilated head and her laughter died. That was an image she couldn't shake off anytime soon. She dropped her reins to the ground and walked toward the images.

Zach stared at the other side of the creek. "That must be the stand where we started. The place we became Slow Hand and Rain Bird."

Screams and shouts in the air, horses squealing, and she caught glimpses of feathered warriors running past her, armed and seeking blood. She saw an arrow pierce a throat, and once again Red Leaf buried his tomahawk in a Crow's chest. Strong arms enveloped her. Alarmed, she struggled to break free before realizing Zach was holding her. She clasped him to her.

"You okay?" he asked, searching her face. "Not going crazy on me, are you?"

She took deep breaths, the images gone, the residual trauma taking longer to evaporate.

"You looked frightened, your head twisting this way and that, like bad shit was happening around you."

"I'm fine," she said, still holding onto him. "An unexpected vision, that's all. Proves we're at the right place."

"What did you see?"

"That Crow raid again. Awful."

"You mean like you were there again?"

"Like we were there again." Making no move until he released her.

"Better keep moving," he said.

Another thirty minutes of paralleling the twisting creek and after the creek had taken a wide curve south, she said, "Feels like we're close."

He rose in his saddle, squinting at the landscape ahead. "This has to be the place. I think I remember it."

"Where's the tree with the mark?"

"Can't see it. The trees look younger and shorter. How long do cottonwoods live?"

He was facing her now, and she saw he'd grasped she hadn't done her tree homework properly.

"How long do they live, Keera?"

"Not long enough." She bit her lip, waited for his angry onslaught, but it didn't erupt.

"The ones we saw could have disappeared in a flash flood for all we know," he said, going easy on her.

"We should have marked something else."

"Like we had a choice."

Zach urged his horse along the bank, Keera following him. He wasn't going to press the issue, he remained focused on a successful result.

"Nothing is permanent around here." He looked back along the creek. "I'm pretty sure I measured fifty paces from *that* bend, I turned left and took another hundred and fifty away from the creek. It's here somewhere."

Nothing came to her that he was wrong. They were in the vicinity without a doubt.

He jumped down and ran back to the bend. "If we can narrow it down to a rough area, we'll find it with metal detectors." He paced from the bend and stopped. "This is where I marked a tree; I know it. Then walked up toward this hill." He paced towards her, counting aloud, and stopped.

"Listen," he said. "What's that noise?"

A pickup sped up in the distance.

"Must be a road nearby," she said. "I've counted thirty paces. I hope the stone isn't under tarmac."

He resumed climbing the rise, and she followed, leading the horses. "Not far now," he said.

As they climbed, they expected to see more rolling grassland, somewhere under it, and close by, the Stone.

A red roof came into view.

A sprawling hotel.

A sign in front.

Prairie Winds Casino.

◆ ◆ ◆

They stared at the sign for a long time before Keera broke the silence. "I hope this isn't some cosmic joke," she said. "A casino sitting on top of the *Wakan Tunkan*."

Zach said, "In the middle of nowhere."

"I saw it last time I was here on a field trip, but I didn't realize it was so close to the creek." This was the right spot, without question. They were eighty paces short of the burial site, and that placed the Stone under the casino. Under tons of concrete.

Untouchable.

Unbelievable.

She rested her head against a saddle. "This can't be how it ends."

"Maybe it isn't," he said. "The place doesn't look that old. Why don't we come back, say, twenty years earlier?"

"Because I can't direct us to return to a specific time. Bardo directed the trip to the camp. I couldn't have done all that myself."

"So he knew we would find the casino here."

"Obviously."

"Then he knows we'll figure a way past this."

"Sometimes journeys are more important than the destination."

"What was the point of this journey?"

She lifted her head. "It'll become clear in time."

He caught her eyes and held them. "You think it was about you and me?"

No. The whole thing was too elaborate just for that. It might be part of it, but not all of it. "Why don't we solve the problem in front of us?"

"Pretty big problem, don't you think?"

"They dug up the ground before they laid the foundations. The Stone might be landfill." A slim hope still qualified as a hope.

"So it could be anywhere. Who would know?"

"Somebody does, and we start by asking questions."

He nodded agreement. She'd struck the right note. After all, asking questions was his life.

They led their horses across the road and into the car park, past the pickups, the battered sedans and the RVs with out-of-state plates. One yellow dog slept on a grass divider, didn't move when they passed. Two Oglala, a man, and a woman, sat on a bench outside the front doors with cigarettes. They tied the horses off to a stone trash container near the couple. Zach nodded a hello, but couldn't tell if they acknowledged it.

Inside, slot machines crashed and jingled—the sound of people losing money. Country music from the 1970s played over the speakers. Two tipis decorated one wall, huge timber beams, an unlikely Lakota architectural style, crossed the ceilings.

Most of the players should have been home cuddling grandchildren. Local Oglala sporting longer, darker hair mixed with the silver-haired out-of-towners. Casino staff in white shirts, black suits, and bow ties moved among them.

They walked through the lines of machines and their captives. Keera searched for a display of ancient relics found during construction, but discovered only paintings of hunting scenes and tribal gatherings. A photo display of staff members graced a wall near a Subway outlet.

"No sign of any discoveries," she said.

"Can I help you?" asked a voice behind them. A slim security staffer stood waiting. His tag identified him as Ralph. An Oglala, he wore the polite but hard look of a man used to finding trouble everywhere. "Are you trying to choose a slot? Some people have their lucky favorites, but all of them pay out the same."

"We didn't come here to play slots," she said.

Ralph waited, his face blank.

"We were wondering if they found any artifacts during the casino construction works."

"You're archeologist people?"

"Anthropologists. Oglala hunted around here for many years, and we're interested in any ancient metal objects discovered. The excavations must have been substantial."

Ralph drew himself up. "If this is an official request, then you need to speak to the manager."

Zach said, "It's not official, we're visiting the area on vacation and saw the Casino and figured it was worth asking. Do you know if they found any relics?"

"Not to my knowledge, sir."

"No weapons, knives, old medicine bundles?"

"Like I said, I didn't hear of anything."

A nearby slot player, long braids hanging to his chest, had stopped playing and watched them. Their voices must have carried. Keera tried an appeal to Ralph's basic instincts.

"If they found if anything, it could be worth a lot. Major finds are very valuable."

"Sorry, miss, nothing was found. I would have heard about it." Ralph glanced at the slot player. "Why don't you try the slots by the wall? A guy from Denver won two thousand the other night. Might be your lucky day."

He strolled away. The player returned to his machine. Keera held Zach's hand as she led him out.

"What do you think?" she asked him.

"He was lying, trying too hard to get rid of us."

That the Stone was so close and still out of reach was maddening, making her twitchy with frustration. They could walk over it right now and not know it.

A young boy, a teenager, was stroking Walker. He backed away as they approached.

"You like horses?" Keera asked him.

"I know this one," he said. "Ikey's. Walker. I've ridden her a lot."

"You work here?" The boy smiled. "Nah, I'm under age for casinos. My dad works here. I'm here to pick him up when his shift stops. Saw Ikey's horses and came to say hi."

"We're having a day exploring around here. I was just asking inside if they found any interesting stuff when they constructed the casino."

The boy smiled wider. "Yeah, they did. A cool knife and a healing stone."

"Really?" She kept the next question casual. "They put them in a museum somewhere round here?"

"Lol. My Uncle Calvin, Dad's older brother, he found 'em. Still got 'em. Real hard to get stuff off Uncle Calvin."

She smiled along with him. "What's your name?"

"Danny Yellow Horse."

"We spoke with a Ralph inside. Is that your Dad?"

"Yeah."

"Well, Danny," she said, unhitching her horse, "it's been a pleasure to meet you. I hope we meet again someday."

They crossed the road and prepared to mount up. She turned to Zach. "That Calvin, we have to find him."

"We do? Sounds like our mission just finished."

What? They hadn't located the Stone yet, and he wanted out? What fresh argument did he have now?

"The plan was to locate it and make sure it was with the Oglala. Well, it's here somewhere, and we know an Oglala guy has it. Game over. Home time for you and me."

"We don't have the Stone."

"We don't actually need to hold it in our hands, do we? It's here, in the hands of a local Oglala, and it's safe for future generations. As far I can see, the mission is done. Don't know about you, but I think it's a tricky business to tell the Oglala what to do with a *Wakan Tunkan.* They must be pretty sick of white people giving them advice."

Zach was half right; the Stone was where it belonged. And from now on, they'd have to step delicately through a minefield of cultural attitudes and unforgettable wrongs. "But it's not in the hands of the people. One man has it. What if he's another Red Leaf, regarding the Stone as his personal magic? We have to find it and evaluate the situation, make sure everybody knows it's here. We can't leave and hope news of its existence leaks out."

"I'll write something up for the local paper, the Lakota Country Times, isn't it? They can chase the story."

"Write what? That a teenager told us of a healing stone found here, and we have it on good authority that it's special?"

"Aw, come on, I'll do better than that."

She slapped his shoulder. "No, you will not write a crappy little story. We find Calvin because we have a duty to take the Stone out of the hands of the few and spread its power to the many. Got it?"

Zach rubbed his face like he hated to agree with her. He was relinquishing his argument, and she poked at his pride to help him along.

"His name is Calvin Yellow Horse, brother of Ralph Yellow Horse," she said, and added with delight, "You notice how I discovered the name with a few casual questions? Shall I be the investigative reporter around here, and you can just be the pretty face?"

"Fine. Take some advice from a pretty face and go back to Danny and ask for Uncle Calvin's address."

"I can't do that. Danny will pass the news on and we'll have a reception committee waiting for us at Ikey's. They won't be handing out tourist brochures."

The sun edged lower, throwing shapes and patches on the ground as they traveled east in single file on Highway 18, sticking to the verges. Zach silent, engrossed in thought. He twisted in the saddle, looking back.

"Tell me," he said. "Why did we risk our hides and my sanity on a time-travel trip for the Stone that was sitting around here all this time?"

"It was only here because we removed it from Red Leaf's body two hundred years ago."

"This is seriously messing with my mind. Are you saying it wasn't here a few days ago when you tricked me into the astral thingy, and now it is? Because if that's the case, I want to take depositions from this Calvin guy and hear him swear that the damn thing didn't exist last week."

"Of course it's been here, thanks to our efforts."

"Then why ... why did we go back two hundred years? Why didn't we just come here?"

"We had to go back before we came here. You'll never grasp it, Zach. I don't get it myself and believe me, I've thought about it more than you."

His questions were legitimate. The whole thing was out of whack. Contradictions piled on other contradictions. Time stood still while people zoomed back and forth. Not in his world. Maybe a Stephen Hawking could figure it out. An ordinary person couldn't.

Zach didn't drop the subject. "I have a problem grasping that what happened to me really happened to me, and wasn't a weird twist of my subconscious."

"I was there, remember? I saw the same things. You think Red Leaf trying to kill us yesterday was a figment of your imagination?"

He had no further questions.

She wasn't surprised.

Good luck figuring all that out, Zach.

CHAPTER 31

When they reached Ikey's, the sun was kissing the horizon, the stars taking their time to show up and show off. With a black sky backdrop that God intended; before towns with outdoor lighting wrecked the view. Zach led Keera up the drive, and Ikey ambled outside as they dismounted.

"Find what you came for?" he asked as he removed the saddles and ran his hands over the horses' backs.

"We found a casino," Zach said. "Got talking to this kid who told us the construction workers there discovered a couple of interesting artifacts."

Ikey's face hardened like instant cement. "A kid? What would he know?"

"Said his Uncle Calvin has them."

"This was Danny?"

"Yeah. He knew your horses, said he rides them now and then."

"Oh yeah, that Danny. Nice kid. A bit fanciful, know what I mean?" He slipped the bridle off Moon and replaced it with a simple rope, let it dangle to the ground.

"He seemed fine to me."

"He took a few heavy falls when he was young. Knocked his head hard. You wouldn't know it to look at him, but he comes out with crazy stuff now and then."

Zach glanced back at Keera, but she was letting him run this conversation on his own again. Probably watching and collecting vibes.

Ikey dug the car keys out of a pocket. "Guess you guys are leaving the Rez tonight."

"You know where to find this Calvin Yellow Horse?"

"The thing about artifacts," Ikey said, "is they bring more trouble than you expect, know what I mean?"

"In what way?"

"There's hidden meanings in 'em. Only to be unlocked by those who know what they're doing."

"Interesting. Maybe Calvin can explain their meanings."

"Calvin's place is way off the road. And he don't like strangers turning up at night. He don't like *wasichu* anytime."

Ikey led his horses to the tree and tied them off before disappearing inside his dwelling. Keera took Zach's arm and pulled him away. "He's not talking anymore."

"But he knows, doesn't he?"

"He's part of the welcome party, but he was trying to warn us off."

"How did they know we were coming?"

"Red Leaf. These are his people."

The Jeep was parked ten yards closer to the gate than he'd left it. He touched the hood. Warm. "Looks like somebody took a joy-ride in the rental."

"What do you expect? He doesn't have a car, and we had his horses. Must have had an errand to run. People around here help each other without asking. Looks like you took part in some helping. It could be the reason Ikey's trying to warn us."

He checked the interior. Nothing seemed out of place, nothing new added. Keera appeared unconcerned about any of it. She climbed in and made herself comfortable.

"Let's find a motel," she said. "Hot Springs is closest. We'll come back in the morning."

She didn't stir after she buckled her seatbelt. Closed her eyes and zonked out. He hoped she was gathering fresh info from her guide. Making the whole thing a lot easier.

An hour later, he pulled into the driveway of a motel and killed the engine outside the reception door. A short, spongy woman greeted them; dark eyes friendly behind large glasses.

"Just the one night?" she asked.

Zach nodded. Fatigue had seeped into his marrow. He wanted a bed and Keera's warm body next to his. He signed the guest form, slid his credit card across the counter.

"Room Four." The woman handed him the key. "That's the quietest one."

Outside number four, Zach saw it was going to be a quiet night as promised: there were no cars within forty yards. Their room contained two queen beds, both draped in quilts of violent colors and patterns that would trouble an epileptic. He needed a shower, but Keera darted ahead of him to the bathroom and closed the door. Nobody sensible counted a woman's bathroom time in minutes. He stretched out on a bed to wait.

Keera checked her face in the mirror and wasn't surprised to find it sagging with exhaustion. How much longer did she have to pursue this task?

You edge closer. Don't be disheartened.

Bardo, just tell me where to go and get it. Please.

Events have to play out to reach the results required.

It's all about the journey, right?

Not exactly. The result is important, too. Your actions will affect many people.

Will Zach hang in there to the end?

Notice how he can't comprehend what's happened to him but he stays by your side.

There's a stickability to him, yes.

He'll pursue intriguing events to see how they pan out.

I think he's lost interest in the Stone, he's more interested in me.

He won't let you down, although he's bewildered by your changeable feelings.

So am I.

When Zach opened his eyes again, the light was out, Keera lay asleep in the other bed, and the soft rumble of a V8 throbbed outside their window. He rolled out of the bed and chinked the curtain open a fraction. A red Ford pickup sat behind the Jeep, its exhaust curling up and disappearing into the night air. The slight knocking from the engine suggested an oil change was way overdue.

A match flamed as it touched a cigarette and Zach made out two figures in the cabin; one of them with braids dangling to his chest. As he watched, the Ford's engine throbbed louder, and the pickup rolled away, its brake lights flashing once before it found the highway and accelerated out of sight.

He unlatched the door and peered out as the engine sound faded to nothing. He knelt and checked under their car, but since he didn't know what to look for, he didn't search for long. A walk around it told him nothing more, and the doors tested locked when he pulled on them. Zach returned inside, stripped, showered and checked the window once more before crawling into bed with Keera. She jerked awake when his cold hand slid under her tee and over her breast, and she curled his arm around her. He knew what that meant. Sleep time. He put it down to tiredness.

Hoped it wasn't the other thing.

◆ ◆ ◆

He woke to the sound of the bathroom door opening. Keera stood at the foot of the bed. A towel covered her from chest to thigh; another wrapped her head, and she was using a third one to dry her arms because women maximize towel use. She looked as fresh as a newly opened pasqueflower.

"Do you want breakfast," he asked, "or shall we grab a coffee and hit the road?"

"No leisurely breakfast. I want to see the Stone as soon as I can." He eased out of bed. "Any towels left?"

"There's one," she said, "but have this if you want more."

She tossed him the towel she was holding and pulled the head towel off. The sight of her wet, dark hair tumbling onto her shoulders stirred him. He kissed her bare shoulder but didn't linger. There was that face again, and it wasn't the soft, dreamy one, it was the battle-ready one. He didn't mention the red Ford. She already knew they were being tracked.

Highway 18 hummed beneath the tires as they headed to the Rez. Keera dozed, the weak morning sun lighting her face with the glow of a Botticelli Venus. After twenty minutes she opened her eyes. "How are we going to find Calvin?"

"The post office. The woman will know where everybody lives, and she's quite talkative.

The woman recognized them, and she didn't seem happy about it. "You lost again?"

"No," Zach replied. "Ikey is supposed to take us to Calvin Yellow Horse and show us artifacts that were dug up around here. The thing is, Ikey isn't home right now, and we can't wait too long. We have a flight to catch."

"Well, I don't know where he is."

"Should we try the Pine Ridge gas station again?"

"Nah. He only eats there when the government check comes in."

"Can you direct us to Calvin's place? It'd save us a lot of time."

The woman weighed up the question like it was the trickiest one ever. "Calvin don't fancy strangers," she answered finally. "Especially white ones."

"This is just a friendly visit."

"Not for him. If you hear gunfire, it won't be Calvin shootin' targets. He'll be shootin' at you."

The woman's face gave nothing away. A joke? A warning? The door opened, and a sun-battered couple shuffled in, stopped and inspected the two whites. The woman beckoned the them over, handed them bulky envelopes, and they left.

He tried again. "Look, we're anthropologists on vacation, and we've heard of an interesting find. We'd love to verify the objects as authentic. If so, it might bring more tourists here, more money into the Reservation."

The woman practically guffawed. "Send white tourists to Calvin's place? They better arrive in an armoured car."

He glanced at Keera, who leaned against the counter as if Calvin's address didn't matter one bit. "Guess what happens if we give up on this?" he asked the woman.

"You go home, I have a peaceful life."

"Wrong. I'll tell my colleagues about an interesting relic discovery. They'll be here day after day, asking the same questions I'm asking. For years."

The woman shrugged. "The hell with it. You wanna live dangerous, you can. Head north on 41, past the Loneman School," she said. "Look for a gate with a tin can hanging off it. That's the letterbox."

"Useful to know, but I wasn't thinking of leaving a note."

"I haven't finished. This letterbox has no name, no number. Go through the gate and follow the track to the top of a crest and you'll see Calvin's cabin. If there's a red pickup and a bunch of dogs around, he's home."

A red pickup? "I appreciate the help you've given." He motioned to Keera that they leave.

"I'm still not finished," the woman said. "You're a cocky fella, but you deserve a chance to survive. Don't drive up to his door, don't sneak up to his cabin, either. Sound your horn when you arrive, then walk up, easy like."

"Thanks," he said, and they moved to the door.

"Maybe you should wait for Ikey," the woman added. "I don't want dead *wasichu* on my conscience."

"We appreciate the thought."

"Nice interviewing technique," Keera said as they reached the car.

"My guileless and open demeanor is a blessing."

"Not this time. The information came too easily."

"No way, I worked for it."

"Notice how uncomfortable she was about revealing Calvin's address? She was warning us off."

"Why?"

"She's been told to send us to him."

"Oh."

"And she's not happy about it."

CHAPTER 32

Zach drove them away from the post office. "That woman was warning us off, like Ikey?" he asked her. "How do you know?"

"I just do," Keera said. Don't ask. These things are hard to explain.

"I know something, too. Last night a red pickup found us at the motel. Hung around our door a while."

"And did what?" She locked her eyes front. "And when were you going to tell me this?"

"I wasn't sure what to make of it, but when the post office woman mentioned the red pickup again, I figured it might be significant."

No apology for keeping this important information to himself. Only breezy acceptance that it was fine to mention it whenever.

"Sounds like Calvin's vehicle," he added.

"No kidding."

"Hey, I forgot, that's all. We rushed out this morning, you remember. I didn't have a clue who it could be until you come up with this idea that half the Lakota Nation is waiting to ambush us."

He was lying, but it didn't matter. He was right to protest. She was overreacting. What she could see ahead, even in its amorphous form, was eating at her, and she was taking it out on him. "Not half the Nation, a few men. That's what I'm sensing. From what you've told me, they sound organized. If they traced us to Hot Springs, they might have a contact there."

"Hadn't thought of that," he said. Sounded more mollified.

"I don't know what they hope to do. They have the Stone, they're aware we're looking for it, so what next? Not knowing leaves me edgy."

"Welcome to the world the rest of us live in, Keera." He grinned at her, softening the remark.

The track to Calvin's ran rough and bouncy hard, but the Jeep's clearance kept them moving through the ruts and potholes. The gate with the tin can letterbox was open, and they turned in. Grasses bent in the breeze on either side of them. Ten slow minutes of bouncing and they crested a rise to find a weathered cabin two hundred yards below. Zach stopped.

Calvin's red pickup sat next to a wheel-less Chevy resting in long grass. Someone had hitched a saddled horse to the porch rail. A pair of lying dogs raised their heads in query but weren't interested enough to even bark. Smoke curled out of a narrow chimney pipe.

"That's Ikey's horse," she said. "The one I rode yesterday."

"They must have heard us. What are they doing?"

"Watching. I can feel them."

"How many?"

She slid out. "I don't have x-ray vision, Zach. Let's find out."

He gave a short blast on the horn and climbed out. "Shouldn't we work out a plan?"

"Of course. First, we make sure that the Stone is here. Second, we leave without dying."

"What does your guide say?"

"He's busy elsewhere."

"Terrific."

She glanced his way. A figure was rising out of the grass behind him. Long gray braids, the face resembling Ralph from the casino. An automatic pistol in his hand, the hammer drawn back, ready to fire. Had to be Calvin. Another man appeared next to him. Ralph himself. No weapon. Behind her, a rustling as somebody approached and Zach's face confirmed her fears. Strong hands gripped her upper arms, and she didn't resist. Kept her eyes on Calvin.

Two teenaged Oglala darted past her and made to grab Zach from behind. He didn't follow her cue, didn't know what passive resistance meant. He swiveled, threw a violent elbow back. Blood spattered on one kid's face, and he faltered and fell backward. The other one was Danny, now fierce, and angry. Zach grabbed two handfuls of ears and hair and readied his target for a slamming head butt.

"No," she cried. "Leave him." If he hurt Danny, the men were likely to pistol whip him into submission.

Zach thrust the boy to the ground. Calvin stepped up and lifted his gun to Zach's face. "You wanna deal with a grownup?" he said.

"I'm sensitive to unwanted physical contact, is all," Zach said. "I stay with her. You won't need muscle."

Calvin gave him the stare for a long second, then lowered the gun, eased the hammer down.

Her hidden captor said nothing to reveal himself, but he didn't have to. "Hello, Ikey," she said. His grip tightened a fraction.

"Hello, Calvin and Ralph," she said to the others. The boys she ignored.

Calvin waved the gun at his cabin. "Walk."

As they approached, the dogs trotted over for an inspecting sniff. "*Wahampi*," she growled at them, and they cowered and skittered away.

246

"Hey, the old language still works," Zach said.

Calvin and Ralph exchanged looks. The front door opened, and another young Oglala stood aside for them. They entered the main room of the cabin and were thrust into chairs. No binds, no blindfolds. Yet.

Ikey arranged himself against the window, looking the same as yesterday: hat, feather, no gun. He said nothing. On a chair next to him, a roll of duct tape and a pile of cords. No guessing who those were for. The three young ones stayed at the back, one of them holding a shirt sleeve to his nose. Calvin and Ralph faced her, both grim as a hanging judge.

She scanned the room. A table with four chairs near a wood stove burning low against a wall. In one corner, a small drum. A chest of drawers draped with a Lakota blanket, a couple of objects laying on a rough square of buckskin over the blanket.

The Stone and a rusty knife.

Keera took a step towards them, but Calvin raised his gun, and she sat. She was close enough to see the blue strata and orange dashes glowing under the overhead light.

She asked Calvin, "Are we your prisoners? Why?"

Calvin, older than Ralph, appeared to be younger. His eyes regarded her with obsidian bleakness, but his face carried little evidence of alcohol consumption, unlike many of his generation. No puffy and red-veined skin, no bloodshot eyes.

"Why do you come here?" he asked.

"You know why." She pointed her chin at the stone and knife. "To view the artifacts."

"You knew about the *Wakan Tunkan*," Ralph said, "and you tricked a young boy into revealing its existence. You're here for the same reason all *wasichu* come here," he said. "To steal from the Oglala."

"We're anthropologists, not land grabbers, not oil people."

Calvin's lips curled. "Whites steal. It's in their blood. The *wasichu* take everything and leave us with empty promises. Then they return and remove those promises as well." He pointed out the window. "Look at Pine Ridge and observe the spirit of those walking the streets—that is the result of believing whites."

"Is that why you point guns at us? But we're only interested in the artifacts."

"They don't exist."

She nodded at the Stone and knife. "Looks like they do."

"They don't exist for you. Forget 'em. You stayed in Hot Springs last night and left information about yourselves with a friend. We can find you anytime." He let the threat sink in. "These things, you rode out looking for them and found their burial spot right away. In all the Rez, you came to the place where they once lay. How was that?"

How much of their story would he accept? As much as he could handle. "I dreamt of the Stone for many nights. I saw two Oglala taking it out of the camp, with one warrior following them. They buried the Stone and a knife. They escaped from the warrior, and made plans to return, but they never did."

"Why did they bury the Stone?"

"It possessed powerful medicine, and it belonged to another." She didn't offer more. Give him time to consider what he'd heard. Calvin swapped looks with Ralph and Ikey.

"What was the owner's name?" Calvin asked. "Red Leaf."

A shocked stillness froze the room. Her words blasted apart the order of things, and Calvin had to know it. The Oglala were no longer dealing with despised *wasichu*, they were dealing with someone who knew their secret, who knew Red Leaf. Thoughts and forms and ideas flowed into her, a fresh flood of understanding. Red Leaf had made Calvin his acolyte, and Calvin had recruited the others.

"I was once one of you, many years ago," she said. "When I sat with Red Leaf in his lodge, I angered him with talk. When I asked him to release the *Wakan Tunkan's* power to help all Lakota, he refused." She pointed to the Stone. "He refuses still, and he employs you to guard it."

Calvin's Adam's apple ducked and dived and told her everything. Ikey watched him, waited for his response.

"Red Leaf told you we were coming, didn't he?" she said.

Calvin refused to reply.

"Of course he did. He comes and instructs, helps you out of your body at night, takes you to other worlds. Infects you with his attention, so you keep the Stone hidden in your home. He makes you hold it until he reclaims it."

"How can he reclaim it? He's a spirit."

"Red Leaf is the most powerful person I've ever met, dead or alive. He's no friend of yours."

"You've met him in his death state?" Calvin asked, astonished.

"Two days ago, he appeared in my home and killed a man. Just for revenge, for something that happened two hundred years earlier. It was the wrong man, but he didn't care. He doesn't hesitate to kill—it's his first and second nature. You're but a child to him." She looked around the room and caught each eye. "All of you are helpless before him. You cannot keep the Stone."

The young Oglala shot anxious glances at Ikey and Calvin, but received no visible reassurances. A movement in the corner of her eye made her think Zach was making for the altar, but he hadn't moved. More clues, more certainties poured in. Calvin's skin wore the healthy sheen of a younger man, unlike his brother and Ikey. Calvin had made good use of the Stone's healing power.

"He's promised you eternal life, hasn't he? Promised perpetual health too." She addressed Ralph and Ikey. "Has Calvin changed in the years he's held the Stone? Has he aged like you? I doubt it."

The young aren't concerned about growing old, nor by dreams of perpetual youth. They think they already have it. Ralph ignored this accusation, but Ikey didn't shift his gaze off Calvin. There would be some explaining to do later, but she needed divided loyalties now.

Again, movement caught her eye. In front of the altar. She turned her head to catch a better glimpse. Calvin, too, stared at the same place.

The movement became a solid, a shape. Zach jumped to his feet, chair skidding on the floor.

The image sharpened.

Buckskin pants, bear claw necklace.

Red Leaf.

CHAPTER 33

Red Leaf.

Solid from hair feathers to moccasins, from granite face to burning heart. Only a faint, shimmering outline making him different from the humans in the cabin. Keera wasn't the only one to see him. The boys behind her scrambled back. As far as possible.

Calvin breathed loud and fast, his face colorless. For all his nightly visions of his master, this manifestation had to be a shock, a tectonic shift in his experience. Ralph flicked panicky eyes from Calvin to Red Leaf. Ikey stayed passive, unafraid and waiting.

Red Leaf carried his tomahawk, to her as potent as a real one. The image of it rising and slashing in battle would never leave her. He didn't speak at first, as if glaring at them like a crazed warrior was enough. It took considerable energy to manifest to many people simultaneously. He hadn't been idle on the other side.

"At least he's not holding a real weapon," Zach said, his voice steady. He knew what could happen, and sounded confident of defeating Red Leaf if he attacked them again. She wasn't convinced. This time the healer had help: physical help, six recruits.

Red Leaf stayed near the Stone. His eyes rested on it before boring into hers. "You," he said in guttural English. "You cause me more problems than a spiky thicket."

"And you," she replied, "try to escape the laws of the universe. Accept your fate and leave us be."

"I would have lived for many more years, if not for you."

"You do not call the time of your death."

"The *Waken Tunkun* gives life as long as I want it."

That wasn't true, and he knew it. What he craved was the power the Stone brought to the holder. In his current world he controlled nobody, he was only one of countless questing souls.

"It makes you strong in health, that's all," she said. "Your physical life can be extended, but never made eternal. You should know this by now. It's wrong to ensnare Calvin and his family in your plans."

"My descendants safeguard it for my return."

Return? What was he thinking? A planned reincarnation?

"There were ample opportunities to come back in the past two hundred years, but you didn't take them. Why is this?"

He didn't reply, and she knew why. Once back in a physical body, Red Leaf would be a baby again. With no control over his immediate future until his early teens at least. Nor with any memories or whispers of his previous life until events triggered them. He was waiting for the perfect moment, the perfect parents, and so far, he hadn't spotted his chance.

"You seek the power you once had," she said, "but people don't follow leaders in that way anymore. Those times are gone."

"Nothing has changed," Red Leaf said. "Power is power." He raised the tomahawk. "This gives me power." He pointed to the Stone. "The *Wakan Tunkan* gives me much more power."

Calvin had recovered his composure and was listening. Red Leaf was revealing a new world, a slice of his past life, the reason for his hostility to her. But he still wasn't likely to side with her, he'd follow Red Leaf's orders.

Ralph would take his cues from Calvin, no question. Ikey, she was unsure of. He seemed to be his own man and had exuded a calm self-assurance from the first time they'd met. Violence and anger weren't part of his nature. His aura stayed the steady white glow of peace.

Red Leaf started to speak again, but his words became garbled as his image flickered and sparkled, fading momentarily before coming back into view. Only the top half of his body on display. His manifesting power was waning, and he'd disappear soon. It didn't matter; he'd startled the common sense out of the Oglala, and any one of them could channel him the next few moments.

"Go to where you belong, and let the Oglala make their choices," she said.

Red Leaf bristled, his outline sparking. "It's not your mission to tell me what to do. You have interfered too often. Today is your last day." He switched to Zach. "And yours. Have your death song ready."

Slow Hand's knife worried her: a weapon Red Leaf could grab if he channeled into somebody. The bone handle would hold together, the blade rusty, blunt-edged, but still able to rupture skin and spill blood.

He read her mind. "I've no need for a weapon. I have warriors at hand."

"Too many of them, I think. Any killing here would become common knowledge."

He didn't reply, and it flashed on her—he planned to kill most of them. She spoke to Calvin. "He'll kill all of us to get his way. You know that, don't you?"

"Red Leaf has been my friend for a long time." Calvin calmer after hearing the healer speak. He was Red Leaf's now, and forever, but his gun wavered in his hand.

"Put that away. Red Leaf can enter your body faster than you can stop him. Don't give him a weapon so easily. He'll make you kill everybody in here and leave you with the explanations."

Ikey wore the placid gaze of an older man who'd seen everything in life, and nothing surprised him. But a slight uplift of eyebrows showed that he, too, was facing something new. He tapped Calvin on the arm. Calvin holstered his gun with reluctance and suspicion.

Zach said, looking around at the Oglala, "All of you understand this: when Calvin raises his gun, the killing starts. It will end when everybody here is dead, and Calvin's the only one left alive. Believe us, we've seen Red Leaf at work. This is how he operates. Calvin will survive as Red Leaf's man. The rest of us will be memories."

Red Leaf, fading now but enraged, pointed to Zach. "Him first," he shouted as he vanished.

Calvin drew his gun in a fluid motion, the barrel clearing the leather holster in milliseconds before Ikey jammed his thumb in front of the hammer to prevent it striking the cartridge, and wrenched the gun free.

Zach was already moving as Ralph drew a revolver from somewhere. Zach rammed a fist into his throat. The gun fell clear, Ralph choking and retching. Keera grabbed it and swung it around to face the youths.

"Stand back," she said. "I won't kill, but you won't walk again after I shoot." She held the gun in both hands, like in the movies. All three kids obeyed, but remained twitchy-eyed and nervy.

"Calvin," Ikey said. "You better take a seat and relax." He sat on a chair, chest heaving. Zach stood next to him.

"Ralph," Ikey said. "You sit, too."

Keera wanted to put Ralph's revolver down. She hated the steel of it, but Ikey now gripped Calvin's. And he wasn't letting it go. She lowered hers and waited.

The atmosphere in the cabin altered. The hate, the anger, the violence, all reduced with Red Leaf's departure.

Ikey said to Calvin. "You'd kill them, just like that?'"

"You agreed earlier," Calvin said.

"I agreed that we should shoot at them if they tried to grab the *Wakan Tunkan* and run. Hell, any Oglala would do that much. But not murder."

"He can't be trusted," Keera said to Ikey. "He's been under Red Leaf's spell for a long time."

"You're wrong about Calvin. He's used the *Wakan Tunkan* for healing, not just for himself."

Ralph caressed his throat. "He's done right by me," he croaked. "Shit, I'm gonna need a lot more healing after today."

"Calvin heals?" she said. "Really? Nobody spoke of this."

"What happens here stays in the family. It's better that way."

"Then you agree the Stone should be available to more."

"Maybe, but it will not go with you," Ikey said. "You leave, don't come back." He placed Calvin's gun on the table.

Zach took her arm, she resisted. "It's time," he said. She turned to look at the shrine again. He gave her a few seconds, then tugged her arm. She shrugged his hand off.

She said to Ikey, "Those kids will talk. What they saw here was the most amazing thing ever. You've no hope of keeping this quiet."

"We deal with this, In our way, not yours."

"Like the Lakota have always dealt with things: with violence and war. It won't work anymore."

Calvin stabbed a finger at her. "War, at least, brought honor. Negotiations cost us everything."

"The Lakota were weak back then, this is different. The *Wakan Tunkan* was discovered here, on the Rez. It belongs to the Oglala. Legally and morally."

"I found it," Calvin said, his anger growing again. "It's mine."

Ikey didn't contradict him, but a tiny eye flicker meant he had issues with Calvin. But he wouldn't say much in front of two *wasichu*. The problem lay in making them understand that allowing Red Leaf unlimited access to Calvin wasn't helping anybody. Not as long as Calvin held the Stone.

"If you found it on casino land," she said, "then whoever controls the casino owns the title to the Stone. I'm assuming it's the Oglala Sioux Tribe. It's everybody's, not yours."

"Red Leaf meant me to find it," Calvin said. "That's why it belongs to me." He fidgeted on the chair. "It's time you both left and never came back."

Cavin was shifting attitude. He'd been intent on killing them earlier, and now he wanted them gone. As she rolled the thoughts around her head, the obvious answer surfaced with blinding clarity. Calvin intended to hide the Stone again. Somewhere safe from those who wanted to take it away from him. Somewhere only he could access whenever he needed to.

"Why do I have a feeling, Calvin," she said. "That if we leave, we'll never find it again."

"You got that right."

"Nobody will ever see it again, except you."

Calvin sat simmering.

"Why don't we," she said, "all take the *Wakan Tunkan* to the tribal leaders together? Then everybody can go home in peace."

"The hell with you," Calvin barked. He snatched up his gun, swung the barrel around at her and fired.

She didn't raise her gun. Didn't even think of it. Zach threw himself at Calvin, and they both sprawled on the floor in a tangle of chairs. Zach ripped the gun free. Knelt on Calvin's chest. "You move and I'll fucking club you to death."

Ikey placed a hand on Ralph, keeping him seated. Zach glanced back in her direction, eyes widening. He leaped up and streaked to the back of the room. He dropped to his knees.

A body sprawled on the floor.

Hers.

CHAPTER 34

Zach knelt over her body and lifted her top away from her bloody abdomen. Her spirit floated five feet above him, brushing the ceiling and partially pushing through it.

She'd left her body at the moment of impact. Zach wouldn't, couldn't know this. He cradled her head and murmured words, pleading, begging her to stay with him. Her heart pulsed blood onto the floor, her life leaking away. She felt no pain, but while the body still functioned, she could re-enter. If it stayed alive. *Stop the bleeding.*

"An ambulance, fast." Zach's whole being implored Ikey to make the call.

Ikey pulled out a phone and punched the emergency number. "Gunshot wound, lots of blood lost," he said and gave directions.

"The bleeding." Zach looked around. "Jesus, bandages? Anything we can use?"

He's heard me. Not physically, but the best way—soul to soul.

"Old tees in the bottom." Calvin, still sitting on the floor, gestured at a wooden drawer set. Ikey yanked one open and handed a bunch of rags to Zach. He didn't take them. She saw why—the bleeding had stopped. Her heart wasn't pulsing.

Oh God. I'm not dead yet. Keep trying.

But he stayed kneeling, a frozen statue.

Ikey turned to Calvin. "It's time for the *Wakan Tunkan*."

"It's not for *wasichu*."

"You heard her speak; she isn't one."

Calvin stayed on the floor, sullen and intransigent. Ikey stepped over him and lifted the stone off the altar. He brought it back to her body. Calvin didn't stop him.

Zach placed a cushion under her head and straightened her legs, his face rigid and gray as slate. She read his anguish like he was wailing it to the universe. Ikey settled the Stone on her chest. He knelt and sang, calling on the Great Spirit to help her live.

Hey-a-a-hey! Hey-a-a-hey! Hey-a-a-hey! Ate o ma key yo!

Ralph stepped over to the kitchen tap and poured water into his hand. He moved to the drum and sprinkled water over the skin. He took a pouch of tobacco from his back pocket and added-flakes to the water. Sitting close to Ikey, he began a soft beat, a heartbeat, accentuating the power of the chanting.

Danny also knelt, joining in the healing song, repeating the lines after Ikey. Keera willed her heart to restart, but it remained still and lifeless. She prayed, hope layering over hope, for the tug that always drew her back to a living body.

Instead, dark energy clawed at her, sharp and spiky, making her own energy contract in defense. It was as if she couldn't breathe, which was impossible here. The new energy enveloped her in an icy grip, and she twisted and turned to escape it, and to find its source. She saw him. Red Leaf. He stood a few paces away. No angry, but showing a steely resolve that worried her more.

"It took longer than I expected," he said, "but now you join me in my domain,"

Waves of hatred flowed from him, joined with bitterness and revenge. No one, no entity, could conceal their emotions on this plane, and she should have been prepared for this. There was no barricade against it, no sage sticks, no creating of white light to surround her. It was his willpower against hers. On his home territory.

Keera steeled herself for what was to come, even if she couldn't foresee it. "You can't destroy me. We're equal here."

"Not so, spirit child. I have access to your consciousness, your emotional parts, where the worst pain lives. I can bind you to the physical plane, so you are half in and half out of it."

"How?"

"You cannot leave your friend because of the bonds you have. You will stay close, but unable to rejoin him. Neither will he stop thinking of you, not for the rest of his life."

"This happens to all of us who lose somebody."

"But worse for you. I will trap you forever, witnessing the horrors I deliver to your loved one. And helpless to stop them."

"I don't believe you have the power." *Bardo, I need you, where are you?*

"I will take special care to load your friend with so much despair and longing that he can never function again as a normal human." Red Leaf outlined his plans with the clinical air of a surgeon specializing in pain. "An unrecoverable shell of a man, and you will watch, helpless to change anything."

He'd figured out a method of extracting the most exquisite revenge from both of them in equal measure. And he was right; she couldn't escape it. *Bardo, I need you now, please, please.* His lack of response terrified her as much as Red Leaf's words. *I can't do this alone!*

Red Leaf acknowledged her pleading thoughts with a slight shake of the head. You have no hope, he was saying. He had to be wrong. Had to be.

"I will transform him," he said, "into one who has to be restrained, who cannot comprehend what has happened to him. You will feel his pain, every second of it, more than him because you can understand it but he can't."

Red Leaf's sheer vindictiveness was astonishing. How did this person ever become a healer?

"You refuse to believe me—look at him now."

Zach knelt near her body; Ikey still chanted, Ralph and Danny, repeating the chants. Zach's aura was black, with muddy red highlights. Fear rolled through him, transforming by the second into an uncontrolled, rage-driven depression. His anger thrusting into life, its target Calvin. If she didn't recover.

"He will soon decide that he is to blame for your death," Red Leaf said. "When his physical strength wanes, and he contemplates taking his life to end his misery, I will feed him fresh energy. He will live out his full years. Every moment of those decades unbearable. Because of you."

Revenge superbly constructed. "Why do you stay on this plane? You have enough awareness to pass on. This level is for the newly dead, the confused, not for you."

"Because I have unfinished tasks," he shouted.

"Maybe they were meant to be unfinished."

"No! I was removed from the earth before my time. You know this. You manufactured it. Now you pay." "

But I still have the link with my body. The Stone is maintaining it."

"It cannot keep your body and soul conjoined forever. Your physical healers are approaching. I can slow them until it's too late. Watch."

A new scene opened in front of her. An ambulance was turning into Calvin's track. Lights flashing, but no sound. The vehicle rolled forward, taking the holes and bumps with deliberation.

"I can remove the electrical energy that powers it," Red Leaf said.

"Energy that defeated you before," she said.

"I was unaware of its nature the first time I faced it. Now I understand. Watch."

As she stared at the ambulance, its lights stopped flashing, and it rolled to a stop.

"I can keep it still for as long as I want."

She focused on the vision and willed the ambulance to start. Nothing happened. It couldn't be a matter of just willing it, nothing as obvious as that. Red Leaf had figured out how to manipulate electrical energy after he had returned to this plane—she didn't have the time. He blanked out her vision of the scene.

"No," she cried. "You cannot cut my link. I need him."

Her vehemence surprised her. Her link to Zach was there for a reason, and now it came to her. His half-assed jokes, his cynicism, all this was to test her. To test if her perception was sufficiently acute to see past the mortal man and glimpse the eternal bond they had. Past this life, past any of their previous ones.

She'd been a separate soul that had found her matching half without recognizing him. The awakening released something in her. It raised her to new heights of understanding, and it fortified her. Together, she and Zach could accomplish anything; separated, they each remained incomplete. And now Red Leaf would cut them apart?

No. Not now. Not ever.

Bardo hadn't answered her; he wasn't coming. She was on her own, with no one to turn to. Except for one man. Her husband.

Crazy Elk.

She screamed his name. A new pinpoint of light appeared alongside Red Leaf. Tiny, but brilliant, and growing. Red Leaf took a single backward step to steady himself. His shape morphed into an aggressive stance. Legs planted, his chin thrust forward. His familiar body language had remained a part of him.

"You have no place here," he barked at the pinpoint."

The light grew stronger, and a figure formed. Feathers and buckskin. Crazy Elk.

Thank God.

Red Leaf stabbed a finger at him. "Return to your domain."

Crazy Elk as she'd last seen him. Calm, implacable, and certain of victory.

Keera wasn't so confident. He wouldn't have any extra powers over Red Leaf, and she was sure he didn't possess the same level of anger and revenge.

"You cannot keep her here," Crazy Elk said. "Her earth time is not up, she has to return."

"Her body is lifeless, she has already crossed over. She is mine."

"There is enough time. She can return."

"I will not allow it." Red Leaf stiffened in defiance.

"You are locking yourself in this first plane because of your hatred," Crazy Elk said.

"This is wrong."

"I am the only one who decides what is right or wrong for Red Leaf."

A new light blazed next to Crazy Elk, and it enlarged to show a shorter male figure. Slow Hand. He was different, a confident air previously missing. Like the others, he wore the same clothes from his physical life, but he carried himself more proudly and didn't flinch from eye contact.

He acknowledged Keera with a half-smile and said to Red Leaf. "You never used the *Wakan Tunkan* on me. You let me remain imprisoned in my mind."

Red Leaf retorted, "It was best you withered and died. I didn't expect you to last so long. Even if you had learned to speak plainly, you had no skills to offer."

"As you know," Slow Hand said, "all of us are born to achieve the best we can. You didn't help me reach my best. You don't deserve to be the keeper of the *Wakan Tunkan*."

Red Leaf remained cold and impassive; his attitude from camp hadn't altered with a spell in the spiritual. Slow Hand was still a waste of space.

Another light appeared, then another after that. More lights grew brighter around them. Red Leaf peered at the closest one, and his face hardened.

Three Dogs glared back at him.

The healer scowled, and Keera saw his tomahawk appear in his hand.

How was this going to work? Metal destroys flesh, not spirit.

More lights arrived, and now she heard it. A low murmuring—a thousand tongues speaking at once. They crowded into Calvin's cabin, some of them manifested only partly. She glimpsed more feathers. Oglala.

Red Leaf swung his weapon slowly at his side, inviting attack, and unafraid to meet it. His energy field enlarged, sparking outward.

She glanced at Crazy Elk.

He waited.

But the incoming Oglala didn't.

The heaving, humming mass swarmed around Red Leaf, swamping him with blazing light and white cloud. He lashed out them with his ax, but they kept coming until they enveloped him. He became one light among many, and impossible to identify any longer.

All sounds died. The lights faded, grew smaller and the white cloud dissipated into strands, and then not even that. Where there had been a seething mass of emotions lay nothing. Empty space. Only Crazy Elk beside her.

"What just happened?" she asked him.

"Red Leaf is being taken to a higher campground," he replied. "The place where the plans of the Great Spirit are revealed."

Then she got it. The Oglala had drawn his spirit into theirs, merging with it, so Red Leaf could grasp what they felt, what they understood, what they knew. He would leave his earthly instincts behind and submit to the greater soul learning of the group.

Crazy Elk addressed her. "I made a vow to your father Three Dogs that I would always protect you. Red Leaf will not harm you anymore."

"I thank you," Keera said.

"You were Rain Bird for only a short while, but much of your spirit remained in her afterward. She was a good wife, although she said unusual things from time to time. I understood everything when I passed over."

"Who were those lights?"

"Red Leaf's ancestors and descendants. He has avoided them ever since he arrived here. I have also communicated with other Lakota, who have an interest in what you are doing, and I asked them to ignore his cries to be left alone. Red Leaf was my mentor, and I owe it to him to protect him from himself. He has been too attached to that *Wakan Tunkan* and can no longer think correctly. He needs help to build his new life. Our people will guide him to it."

"I cannot thank you enough."

"We have been watching you trying to bring the *Wakan Tunkan* back to the heart of the Oglala, and we approve. It has not been an easy task, and it remains difficult yet."

As he spoke, a wave of love covered her, astonishing her with its warmth, depth, and strength. The love was not only from Crazy Elk, but it also poured out of the darkness, and it renewed her.

An entire nation, long passed over, was watching, supporting and lifting her to fresh levels of determination. She bathed in the feeling, reveling in the highest emotion known to man. Beyond exhilaration, beyond bliss. This was what death was like, they were telling her. If you accomplish the right goals in your life.

And she was so close to one of those goals.

Crazy Elk said, "You have to go back now. Remember that we were once part of you, and that will never change." He reached and touched her cheek. "Call me whenever you need me. My promise holds forever."

A tug. The tug returning her to the physical world.

Her world.

And Zach's.

CHAPTER 35

Zach saw it first. A twitch of her eyelids. Nerves reacting to a dying brain impulse. A stray signal, not the heartbeat Keera needed to live. Another twitch and the Stone moved, her chest now rising, falling. New breath. New life.

A siren's wail sounded from a distance. Ikey, Ralph, and Danny didn't stop the chanting until the ambulance arrived outside, the siren fading to a growl. Zach leaped up and held the door open.

Ikey stopped the chant. He removed the *Wakan Tunkan* from Keera's chest and, with the others, stood and waited for the medics to take over. Ralph grabbed his gun from the floor and slipped it into his pocket.

The medics bustled in, waving the crowd away from the body. The lead guy blinked at the blood pool. "How many victims?"

"Just the one," Zach said.

The medic rummaged in his bag. "There's a couple of pints of blood on the floor. Nobody else bleeding? You sure?"

Zach nodded. The medic injected a clear solution into Keera. Two others set up a gurney and brought it inside.

"Lucky we're here," the medic said as he worked. "We stopped, just like that, when we drove up the track. Nothing happened when I tried the ignition. All the electrics dead. Thought we'd been hit by lightning out of a clear blue sky. Then, for no reason, we started up again."

"Thank God you did," Zach said.

"What's the patient's name?"

"Keera Miles."

"Well, I have to say, she's a tough nut. Her pulse is much stronger than I would expect after seeing all that blood."

"She had no pulse for twenty minutes."

"No way, your watch is broke. In the hospital, they give the patient five to come around."

Ikey took the Stone back to Slow Hand's knife, bundled them both up in the buckskin, and left them there. He beckoned the three teenagers to join him and spoke to them quietly. Calvin sat in a chair, face blanked as events overwhelmed him.

Keera opened her eyes as the medics drew a blanket over her. Focused on Zach, tried to pull him closer but was too weak to grip his sleeve. "Red Leaf's gone," she whispered. "Take the stone now."

He flicked a glance at the bundle and Ikey standing guard. No problem, I'll just ask him nicely. "I'll deal with it. You concentrate on recovering your strength."

"I nearly didn't return," she said. "Sure you did. Once you remembered the wonderful time we've had together since we met, you zipped right back into my arms." She smiled and closed her eyes again.

The medic tapped him on the shoulder. "We're taking her to the hospital in Pine Ridge. You coming?"

"I'm following." He watched them wheel Keera through the door and maneuver the gurney to the ambulance.

He pulled Calvin's gun from his pocket, held it against his leg, and said to Ikey, "I think the Stone goes with her in case she needs more help. You come too."

Ikey thought on it for a couple of seconds, then scooped the bundle up, removed the knife and replaced it on top of the chest of drawers. He turned to the teens and spoke rapid Lakota to them. Zach didn't catch any of it. The kids did. They nodded furiously.

Ikey pushed past Calvin, who put out a hand and stopped him.

"You taking the Stone?" Calvin said.

"For the girl, in case she needs it again. It brought her back from the dead." Ikey didn't give Calvin a chance to renew his objections about *wasichu*. He jerked his head at the door, and when Zach stepped outside, Ikey followed.

"The cops not here yet?" Zach said.

"They stretched around these parts. They'll come to the hospital once the medics tell 'em it's not a homicide."

"Do we have our stories straight?"

"Only one story. You arrived uninvited, aggravated Calvin with talk of artifacts and shit. He waved his gun around; he's known for that. It went off. Hit your girlfriend. It'll look like an accident. Which it was." He didn't take his eyes off him, daring him to contradict the story.

"The kids. They gonna say the same thing?"

"Already explained it to them. All good."

"All good, unless Keera doesn't make it. Then Calvin's going to pay for this. Big time."

Ikey pointed to the revolver in Zach's hand. "You know how to use that thing? Because if we don't agree on what happens after this, you might have to."

They drove away from the cabin in the Jeep, Zach pushing it down the rugged track as fast as he dared.

"Tell me something," Ikey said, as they reached Highway 18 and swung east towards the hospital. "When did your girlfriend live with us?"

"Long time ago. About two hundred years."

Ikey shifted the bundle on his lap while he thought about this.

Didn't react, didn't seem to consider it so remarkable.

"The knife," Zach said, "belong—"

"You ain't getting it."

"I don't want it. Just letting you know it belonged to a brave man called Slow Hand. He helped defeat a Crow attack on his village close to here. A long time ago."

"Pesky Crow. We always whip their asses."

"He also helped save the *Wankan Tunkan* for the rest of you."

"Saved it from who?"

"Whom. Red Leaf. The old healer who wants it back."

The old healer. What a warm, cuddly description of a cold and implacable killer.

Ikey said, "Gun or no gun, sonny, you don't correct my words in my country."

"Sorry." So touchy, these Oglala. "Thank you for being helpful back there. Calvin's not a man to listen to reason, is he?"

"He's got his reasons. You heard some of them."

"But you weren't scared of him, like the others."

"We go back a ways."

As if that explained everything. Zach said, "If Keera dies, Calvin pays. We didn't come with bad intentions, only to talk. There was no need for gun play."

"She won't die. The Stone brought her back so she could live on. A real Oglala would know that."

"He's not walking away from this. He'll face murder, or attempted murder, charges."

Ikey thought on this for a couple of miles. "What did you come here for, anyway?"

"We came to make sure the Stone was in the right hands. That's all. Jesus. I'll tell you something else, Calvin's not the right hands. If he gets it back, he'll hide it."

"He found it; it's his to use."

"It's his to use on all the people, not just him and a couple of family members."

"You sticking your beak into Oglala affairs like you have a right to." Ikey glared at him. "You just a do-gooder. We have plenty of them already. They come, they go, everything stays the same hopeless mess it was to begin with. The way the government wants it."

The old guy had a point. If Keera agreed, they should pack up and leave. They'd done enough. If she agreed. If she lived.

Ikey said, "How did you hear about the *Wankan Tunkan*?"

How much to tell him? Nothing. Too much to explain, too much for Ikey to believe. Keera could explain if she wanted to, not him.

"Us white people have our ways and means of knowing things. Keera had a dream."

Ikey shifted in his seat. "Been having dreams myself. Dreamed I pitched my tipi with my band near here. Many years ago. I was old, with a bad leg, worse than now. My name was Three Dogs, but I only owned two critters. Once I owned three, but my favorite died, and I never replaced her. Because I wanted to remember her every time somebody used my name. Funny thing, I only got two dogs now, 'cos three seems wrong to me."

This was getting seriously weird. Used to be past and present were well separated. But here, on the Rez, the Oglala lived in both at the same time.

Ikey continued. "Had a daughter then. Your girlfriend reminds me of her. Don't know why; they don't look alike. The healer in my band wanted to kill her. Said she was infected by a walk-in spirit. I didn't let him." Ikey turned to him. "Know what I'm saying?"

"Yeah, you tried to protect Keera because she reminded you of your dream daughter. Thanks. I understand dreams. I was once Oglala, too."

"That a fact? Well, if you were Oglala before, you weren't much of one, I'm sure of it. Correcting your elders like that."

Such a cantankerous soul to share a ride with. You couldn't even thank him without a problem.

"Reason I tell you," Ikey said, "is when Red Leaf appeared, I recognized him from the dream. The same healer. I knew he wanted to harm your girl."

"I cannot thank you enough for using the *Wakan Tunkan*—you brought Keera back. I'm sure Calvin would never have done it."

"Calvin thinks in a straight line. He ain't for turning corners too fast."

The road ahead was clear of cars and ambulances. Maybe Keera had already been delivered into the hands of surgeons. Sacred healing stones were remarkable, but they didn't stitch up wounds or replace blood. That wasn't their power: they only brought people back from the dead.

"How good is this hospital at dealing with gunshot injuries?" he asked.

"You reckon you can take the *Wakan Tunkan* off me with a gun?"

"For God's sake, I'm thinking of Keera, not you."

"The hospital? They used to it. They probably the best at gunshot stuff the world over. Your girlfriend be fine. Won't feel like eating for a while, though."

"Stomach wounds are serious, aren't they?"

"They leave a long mental history. People who are gut shot get real nervous around guns after that. I hear it's a painful way to go."

Jesus. He should have insisted on them leaving after they discovered that Calvin had the Stone.

"So," Ikey said. "Where d'ya think the *Wakan Tunkan* should be after today?"

"It stays on the Rez."

Ikey's face relaxed a fraction. "That saves me the trouble of making sure of it. I feel I can trust you even though you speak white words. But I'll stay close until you're both gone, and the Stone is left behind. Somewhere safe. We need it. Stop people dying so fast."

"People here would live longer if they drank less."

"If you lived here, white boy, you'd drink more than you thought possible."

CHAPTER 36

Zach found the hospital on the other side of Pine Ridge. He removed Calvin's gun from Keera's bag and slid it under his seat. Ikey watched him without expression. He led them into the reception with the familiarity of someone who'd been there a hundred times and pointed to Zach.

"His girlfriend's here with a gunshot wound." He said it like Zach couldn't speak English. "He wants to know how she's doing."

"The surgeon's still operating," the receptionist said. "It could take a while. You can wait down the hall."

"How was she when she arrived?" Zach asked.

"She was responding, that's all I can tell you. The surgeon will fill you in later."

Fill me in? He's going to empty the heart right out of me if he brings bad news.

They found a small waiting area. It held an Oglala mother and a ten-year-old boy holding his wrist like it was a wounded bird. They sat opposite them.

"What happen to you?" Ikey asked the kid.

"Fell off a horse," he replied. "Oglala don't fall off horses unless they got Crow blood in them from somewheres. Remember that next time."

The mother glared at Ikey, but said nothing. Zach placed Keera's bag on the floor, but Ikey clutched the Stone wrapped in its skin on his lap. A nurse stepped in and nodded to the mother and boy. They left without saying goodbye.

"You always that friendly to your neighbors?" Zach asked.

"I'm gettin' old. See little point in saying the same old shit."

"At least you have more social skills than Calvin."

"Calvin reminds me of my dogs. They don't know how to talk, so they bark."

"Must make conversation with him difficult."

Ikey leaned back in his chair and crossed his legs at the ankles. "Calvin and me known each other a long time. I know what he's thinking most times. Right now, he's talking to the tribal cops. He's saying that your girlfriend was holding Ralph's gun. She was getting heated. A white girl, a white girl telling him what to do with a healing stone. He was worried for his life, so he picked up his weapon, and it went off accidentally. I forgot to check the safety after I took it off him."

He let that information sink in long enough for Zach to understand Keera could be in trouble. She had the gun out first, not hers, not registered to her. Calvin had a plausible self-defense claim. Ikey carried on like a crusty old git, but inside he was sharp as a battle lance.

The surgeon walked in. Tall and still gowned and capped, face mask dangling from her neck. She removed the cap, and blonde hair tumbled to her shoulders.

"I'm Stephanie Bronski, Keera's surgeon. One of you is her friend, I believe?"

Zach stood, his eyes searching hers.

"Keera's okay," she said. "The bullet didn't penetrate the abdominal cavity."

"That's good, right?"

"It didn't strike any vital parts, and it didn't rupture the stomach and spill the acid contents over tissues not designed to cope with it."

Zach exhaled.

"Although the bullet missed major organs, it passed through an artery resulting in excessive blood loss. No serious bone damage apart from a graze to the hip bone. Keera will stay here until we're sure the blood vessels aren't leaking at the sutures, and there is no infection. I expect her to recover. You can see her in about thirty minutes when she comes round."

"Thank you for all you've done."

"There'll be lasting mental trauma issues of course, and physical scars. But rehab and counseling should help her back to normal."

She shrugged away years of sweat and tears. You've done well, surgeon lady, but the Stone did all the hard work before you.

"Keera stopped breathing for twenty minutes, then she started again."

Bronski gazed at him like he was a lunatic. "Highly unlikely. The time frame is impossible."

"I was there, too," Ikey said. "I saw it."

The surgeon tilted her head in disbelief.

"Calvin Yellow Horse was there, too. And his brother Ralph. And others. We all saw it."

"Just by herself? The patient was unconscious, not breathing, and she came back with no outside assistance? I find this hard to accept."

"She had help." Ikey lifted the bundle and unwrapped it to show the Stone. "This is a *Wakan Tunkan*, a sacred healing crystal. We placed it on her and sang healing songs until she came back."

"Interesting." Bronski glanced at the Stone and over at Zach. "You're not local, you're not even an Oglala. How are you involved in this?"

"I was with Keera, who is an assistant anthropology professor at the University of Chicago. We were here on a private visit when we heard about the *Wakan Tunkan*. The accidental shooting took place as we were viewing it."

She pursed her lips. "How accidental was this shooting?"

"Very accidental," Ikey said.

"I only took up this position a month ago, and I am amazed how many accidents I have to stitch up each Saturday night." She turned to leave.

"Wait," Ikey said. It wasn't a tone of voice to ignore.

"What?"

"You keep this Stone here. Use it for our most desperate cases."

Zach stared at Ikey. His face set like he expected stiff opposition and determined to overcome it. What was he trying to do?

"You're kidding me." Bronski grew irritated. "You want me to allow this stone into my operating theater? With a couple of healers in their ceremonial hide outfits, feathers in their hair, shaking their instruments, which are all crawling with bacteria? And they'll bring in their smoky herbal sticks as well, I suppose."

Ikey lifted the Stone up, like an ancient priest presenting a sacred object to his people. "There's a time for modern medicine, and time for ancient ones. After the operation, when our people need more help than you can give, when they hang between life and death. That's the time for it."

"I've been here for only a couple of months, and I'm acutely aware of local sensitivities, and trying to accomodate everyone. But I will not sing healing songs to my patients. I'd be dismissed for professional idiocy."

"You won't. The healers sing the songs. We got plenty on the Rez. You keep the *Wakan Tunkan* safe and allow them access to it."

"This is a hospital, not a ceremonial ground."

The hospital was the perfect place for the Stone right now. Away from Calvin's unhinged attitude and made accessible to others.

Ikey had seen this. And more. Ikey shot him a look that seemed to say: you get what I'm doing here? He sure did. The signal was bright as airplane lights: I'll give you a haven for the *Wakan Tunkan*, you leave Calvin alone.

Zach said to Bronski, "Here's the future you're choosing. I'm a reporter, and I intend to write a story in the local media how a miracle Sacred Stone, this *Wakan Tunkan*, saved Keera's life. There were seven witnesses. And you have refused to allow the Stone to be used on other patients. Have I got the details right so far?"

She reddened from the implied threat. Zach continued. "I'm guessing a whole bunch of people will ask unpleasant questions. You want to face them?"

She didn't walk away. The thought of angry Oglala making their views known was enough to keep anyone thinking.

"Of course, the television news will love this. It's a great story, full of human interest: a miracle Stone being suppressed by bureaucracy. You'll need security people to usher you through the hordes of reporters shoving microphones in your face. Telling their audience that Pine Ridge is new Lourdes."

Bronski flashed an impatient side eye. "You don't know what you're asking."

Ikey said, "We're not asking."

She waited for the rest of it.

"The Stone belongs here," he said. "Where it works with your medical skills. How it does this, where it stays permanently, we can work out later. Right now, it needs a safe place. We're standing in it."

She surrendered, almost. "Okay. I promise to let the administration make this decision."

"They'll make the right one if a coupla hundred Oglala come to talk to them," Ikey said.

She held out her hand for the Stone. He didn't move. "Where will you keep it?"

"We have secure storage for the drugs we require. It'll be in there. Safe. Okay?"

"Let me see it."

"That would be against the rules."

"I don't care."

Bronski took this in and walked out of the room. Ikey followed her.

Zach sat down to wait. It wasn't possible for the young Oglala to stay quiet about what they'd seen at Calvin's. Not just the Red Leaf apparition, either. Once the word got out that a *Wankan Tunkan* was performing miracles, an endless stream of the sick and dying would arrive at the hospital. Not only locals. Everybody in the world grabbed at the chance of a magical healing once they heard of it. He didn't need to write any story—it would write itself.

The hospital administration would have to set up a structure to cope, which would involve the Oglala leaders. The Stone no longer Calvin's alone. Sounded like the mission was completed. Ikey returned. Without the bundle.

"I hope you won't talk the surgeon into handing the Stone over to you when I'm gone," Zach said.

"For now, at least, it stays here. If I get my way, it'll stay here forever."

"What happened to the cops?" Zach asked.

"When they finish with Calvin, they'll be here. They know the victim ain't going nowhere." He jerked his thumb at the door. "Calvin's gun. Why don't you give it to me and I'll take it to the lawmen. Tell 'em what happened, tell 'em you're both here and real keen to set the story straight about the accidental shooting."

"You think they'll accept what we say?"

"No one died. If your girlfriend don't complain, the cops won't push it."

Doesn't complain? Damn sure Keera won't let this rest.

A nurse entered. "Miss Miles is awake," she said. "And she's asking for a Zach."

"Be right back," Zach said.

He took Ikey to the Jeep, pulled out Calvin's gun, and handed it to him. He held out his hand. Ikey shook it like they'd just settled a minor bet, and walked away without another word.

CHAPTER 37

Keera looked as lively as pizza dough. With wires and tubes stuck in it. Still lovely. Blue eyes, cloudy with pain-killers, examined his for clues.

"How do you feel?" Zach asked.

"Ngunnh." He kissed her forehead.

"Shall I explain what's happened?"

"Ngunnh."

"The word is, you'll be fine. Coupla minor marks on your perfect body. Nobody will notice, certainly not me."

Silence. Maybe he shouldn't have started with the beauty issues.

"Ikey has organized the Stone to stay in the hospital. Away from Calvin, where it can be used for healing when required."

She blinked in confusion.

"It's all good, they kind of agreed," he added quickly.

"Calvin," she croaked. "He tried to kill me."

"Listen. The cops will come soon. Asking questions. Ikey and me think it's best if we play down the whole shooting thing as an accident."

"Tried to kill me."

Her strength returning at his news, her croaking now a harsh whisper.

"If you don't press charges against Calvin, the Stone stays in a safe place. If you go ahead, Calvin will claim self-defense. You were holding a gun already. All the Oglala in the cabin will back him up. He'll get off. And possibly retrieve the Stone."

"Ikey arranged this with you?"

She was growing stronger by the minute. Soon, he'd be defending himself in vigorous discussion. Hell, he already was.

"Not as such. Once he started on the surgeon, brow-beating her to allow the Stone to help other patients, I realized what it would cost. And I helped him."

"How?" He repeated the conversation with Bronski, tiptoeing through the tricky parts about media pressure.

"You're such a bastard at this," she said.

"We all work with what we have, Keera. If she used her administrative power to hide issues, I'd use my position to expose them."

She stayed quiet for a couple of minutes. Sighed deeply.

"It's in the right hands," he said. "That was our aim, correct?" No response. The dropping of attempted murder charges required more than a few seconds consideration.

"You weren't in the ambulance." Her words slow, like just being awake wore her out.

"I followed behind, with Ikey, and the *Wakan Tunkan* if you needed it again. What happened to you while you were gone from us? You said something about Red Leaf."

"He came, he went. Crazy Elk saved me."

"Crazy Elk, huh? What was he doing up there? Boasting, as usual? Did you give him my best regards?"

"It wasn't a good time."

"About the story, we have to get it straight, we have to make it simple: you can't remember a thing. The shock of the bullet's impact erased your memory of everything that happened immediately before. You recall coming to see the Stone, then nothing."

Her face contained her entire response—stinging disdain.

"Keera, there's no other way if we want to close this. The Stone's in safe hands, no lasting injuries for you. Mission accomplished. Applause and medals all round."

She was looking past him. Zach swung around to find a monk smiling at him. Not some flimsy, wavering apparition. This guy was solid enough to walk into.

"Jesus," Zach said.

"Sorry, I'm not him," the monk said, amused. "You can call me Bardo."

The spirit guide. In person. How the hell do you greet a spirit? The one who started this whole thing. "Um ... pleased to meet you."

"Ditto."

Ditto? Weren't spirit guides meant to be more formal?

"It's not necessary," Bardo said. "I find it relaxes people more if I stay within their colloquial comfort zone."

He's reading my mind! "I won't access your inner thoughts if you don't want me to."

"Please don't. How long have you been in here?"

"Not sure. Time slips away from me on the physical plane. We don't have it elsewhere."

"Bardo," Keera said, "you never warned me I'd end up in a hospital."

"You know me better than that. You've handled everything well. As Crazy Elk said, your time was not yet up."

"But I have a serious gunshot wound."

"You're pulling through just fine. The operation scars? They're nothing. Like all Oglala, you carry wounds for life."

Keera appeared displeased at his reply. It didn't seem to bother

her to argue with a ghost, a spirit guide no less.

"And the police will accept this story of an accident?"

"They have more pressing matters than an apparent accidental shooting. They know Calvin, they tolerate him. Until he kills somebody. He's deluded and angry, not evil."

"And the Stone? It's saved now?"

"Its future is more solid than before. You've played your part, and now others will play theirs."

Bardo, Zach noticed, preferred to avoid direct answers. Bet that drove Keera mad.

"The *Wakan Tunkan*," she persisted. "Is it in safe hands?"

"Now? Of course."

"Anything else I should know?" she asked Bardo, obviously skeptical of his guarded responses.

"There is no permanency in the physical world. Change is its only constant. Go home and rest. It's been a long two hundred years for you." Bardo shimmered, smiled his goodbyes and faded from view.

Zach stared at the empty space the monk had occupied. "Why did he have food stains down his front? He looked like he'd just left a boisterous refectory."

"It reminds him of his former life as a gluttonous monk." She closed her eyes. Opened them again. "It's not over. That's what he said. It's not over."

"You think that? I heard him distinctly say that it was over for us. Go home, he said. Get some rest he said."

"He wants us to rest before the next stage."

"Seriously? After all we've been through? It must be somebody else's turn by now."

"Who else knows what to do?"

"Do what?" Keera wasn't making sense.

"Calvin," she said.

Zach said, "I've explained about Calvin. It's all good."

"Calvin won't let the Stone go. He'll approach the hospital and claim ownership. From what you said, they were reluctant to take it. Then he'll hide it." She closed her eyes, visibly exhausted by her short explanation.

"If he tries that caper, the deal's off. You can accuse him of attempted murder." Even as he spoke, he knew this wasn't realistic. A courtroom was the worst possible place for them. The wrong story would emerge; Keera's career destroyed, his as well. He'd always be remembered as that wacky reporter who pretended to time travel to get a story. Surely she would come to see it this way. Only Ikey stood between Calvin and the Stone. And he wanted Calvin protected from any charges. He'd explain this simple equation to her again when the drugs wore off.

Keera was watching him. Probably reading his mind. Probably intending to make it up for him. She said, "Am I leaving today? I need my own space."

"You can't even walk across this room. Anyway, the surgeon says you're here until she says you can go."

"No!" She tried to throw aside the bedcovers and jump out of bed, but the drugs had worked their deadening magic. She could hardly raise her arms.

"See."

She slumped back, regarded him with palpable resentment.

"I'm not responsible for your enforced confinement," he said.

"You're not helping me leave either."

"That's the meds talking. I'll take no notice."

She drifted away again. When minutes passed without her waking, Zach pulled a chair up to the bed and sat. And waited.

◆ ◆ ◆

Keera woke. Zach was slumped in his seat. Her bag lay on a small white cabinet, too far to reach. Nor did she want to test her stitches by stretching. Whatever they had given her rolled through her veins like a railway train. It felt foreign, pervasive and dangerous. At home she could access her herbs, meditations, and spiritual strength techniques to heal herself more naturally. So, she had to leave the hospital, a place where people came to die.

There was the other thing. She was startled to find she didn't want to lose him, or even stop staring at him. Did he feel the same? He seemed to, Bardo had suggested it was so, but she needed to be more certain. She wriggled cautiously to the edge of the bed until she was inches away from him. Leaving one hand on her heart, she rested the other one on his chest. Both hearts beat in sync. A historic first.

Zach lifted his head. "What are you doing?" he mumbled.

She snatched back her hand. "Making sure you were for real."

"I'm real all right. How are you feeling?"

I'm not ready to tell you yet. Not all of it anyway. "I'm in a chemically altered state, and I'd like to be home where I belong."

Surprisingly, he didn't argue.

"I'd like to be there with you. Hospitals are unsettling to me, God knows what they do for the sick." He yawned and stretched. "I need a thousand years sleep. And not on a chair, either."

"So, you'll help me get home as soon as possible? We need a lot of time together, and the sooner we start, the better."

He sat up. "A lot of time together?"

"Yes. For convalescing and replenishing our spiritual reserves."

"Oh."

"Also, a debriefing would be useful."

"A what?"

"The *camp*," she said. "You may have seen things I didn't."

Watched him repeating her lines in his head, reading between them.

"Oh sure," he said, brightening. "I saw lots and lots of things. It'll take ages to describe them all."

"But we were only there such a short time."

"My mind is a sponge. I soaked up everything."

He was getting the picture. Best to make sure, though. "How thorough were you?"

"Very thorough, perceptive and methodical. Your reputation will soar when you publish your next paper on the Oglala. You won't have to give me any credit, I'm happy to be a background guy."

"I'll definitely make sure you get your due reward."

"We'll share experiences, that sort of thing," Zach said, becoming more animated as he grasped the possibilities ahead. "Weeks of debriefing lie ahead of us. Maybe longer. We'll put our heads together, two minds working as one, both hearts beating as one."

"It might take forever," she said.

"I'll be there to the end. Hungry for anything you can throw at me."

"So, we need to be home sooner rather than later, don't we?"

"I'm on it. I'll see the doc right away, explain how things are."

Keera closed her eyes, smiling. She heard him rise from the chair. His lips touched hers. She responded tentatively at first, then with a growing appetite for the moment. Her arms lifted clear of the bedcovers and pulled him closer.

THE END

ACKNOWLEDGEMENTS

As always in the process of fiction creation there are others who labor to make the author appear better than he thought he was. My thanks go to the members of the Internet Writers Workshop for their perceptive comments and suggestions.

In particular, I'd like to acknowledge Robin Cain, Karen Maric, Bill Bartlett, Lynne Hinkey and Tim Sharp who stayed with this work from the first chapter to the final one. Dave King offered perceptive suggestions on plot and character that improved the work enormously. So did beta reader Anna Albo. Thanks to Anita Saunders for the final proofing.

THE PARKER RIMES COLLECTION

The Backward Time Traveler

A psychic receives an impossible task: to travel back 200 years and rescue a Sacred Stone from a Sioux tribe. She's persuaded take along a pesky reporter, but he's more interested in her body than her so-called mission. Great.

Inserted secretly into a band of Indians, they struggle to adapt their city ways to a more brutal lifestyle. Their situation abruptly worsens after a bloodthirsty Crow attack. Even more alarming, the door to the past isn't easily closed once it's forced open.

The Upside of Death

Psychics don't get kidnapped: they're supposed to be smarter than that. Keera Miles blames herself for not staying psychically awake and dodging this disaster. Now, she's forced to watch and wait as her captors' plans to extract money from her wealthy father grow more violent. When her reporter boyfriend Zach unexpectedly locates her and attempts a desperate rescue, he's easily thwarted by these ex-military Russians.

But she knows Zach will never give up. And the afterlife is her second home—a crucial advantage. If the disintegrating Russians don't kill her first.

The Art of Dash

When Chicago journalist Zach Bones incriminates a major drug dealer Jason Virgil, he discovers he's been set up. Virgil is killed in jail on the orders of his rival Frankie Ritchie, and Zach's now a conspiracy suspect. Worse, the dead and wrathful Virgil begins to extract revenge on everybody involved. Including Zach.

His psychic girlfriend Keera can save him, she thinks. But after Virgil murders his killer by psychic attack, she realizes that no human can stop him.

Never Show Them Money

When too much money is not nearly enough. Zach Bones, a reporter on the *Chicago Post*, has liberated three million dollars from a Russian kidnappers' bank account. Now he's offering the money to a rival syndicate in grateful payment for them eliminating his psychic girlfriend's kidnappers.

Trouble is, these Russians believe if he took money out of one bank account, he could do it again. For them. And forever. Even worse, the hot-headed Olga arrives in town determined to avenge her father's past death at the hands of these Russians.

While Zach searches for a solution, his girlfriend Keera enlists the aid of her spirit guide Bardo, whose enigmatic advice is hardly better than no advice at all.

The Darker You Get

Reporter Zach Bones is still in possession of Russian mob money. He'd like to keep it; his psychic girlfriend Keera says give it away —it's dirty. A hitman Lev wants it also, and uses a sniper rifle to make his point. The cops can't understand why a hitman would target an ordinary reporter, and grow suspicious of Zach's lack of explanation.

He can't find a solution that leaves him with a life worth living. And Keera's abilities can only do so much to protect both of them. Especially when Lev is steadily losing his grip on reality.

Eye of the Beholder, a novella

Zia checks out a dating website. It lets her view her prospective soulmate's world through his eyes. She sees blue skies. Leafy trees. A car interior. And a pair of feet—chained together.

Disturbed, Zia searches for the truth in the glossy world of people-matching, and uncovers disturbing surgical procedures. Worse, her bestie is involved...

Catch Your Death, a novella

There's weird, and there's seriously weird. One of them can really wreck a girl's evening. And every evening after that. Reporter Ruby Moskewitz is interviewing a famous Professor of Biology when he vanishes during a meal break. Just like that.

Has this got something to do with his new drug that turbo boosts brain activity? When she contacts his university, she's told the professor has a contagious condition and had to be isolated urgently. This is a lie, she knows it, and she sets out to find him. Ruby has one advantage— she holds the drug that bestows normal people with abnormal powers.

About The Author

Parker Rimes has spent his life in Europe, Australia, the UK and the US. When not writing, he likes to read four or five books a week. Some of them he completes.

In the course of his journalist life, he interviewed over a thousand people who claimed paranormal experiences occurred in their homes. Many of these stories seemed truthful, and inspired his career as a fiction author.

His favorite pastime is discovering new verbs, and wishing he'd thought of them first. He likes animals but prefers that most of them stay in their own home. His favorite wines are those sold close to wherever he lives.

Diligent research for his novels led him to enroll in a school for mediums, where he failed nearly every psychic test. But he can now predict where to find a good parking space slightly better than the average person.

His home page is www.parkerrimes.com

www.ingramcontent.com/pod-product-compliance
Lightning Source LLC
Chambersburg PA
CBHW011439170626
46807CB00008B/3230

* 9 780645 096408 *